THE MAZAROFF MYSTERY

J.S. Fletcher

Spitfire Publishers

CONTENTS

ABOUT 'THE MAZAROFF MYSTERY'

Whilst touring the North of England in a chauffeur-driven Rolls-Royce, Salim Mazaroff and Mervyn Holt depart from the Great North Road at Marrasdale Moor and reach a solitary inn. Mazaroff mysteriously disappears while walking the moors alone. His dead body is discovered in Reiver's Den.

Was it an accident, or was it murder? Where is the victim's money, rings and tie-pin? Who killed Salim Mazaroff?

About the Author

Joseph Smith Fletcher was a highly successful English novelist of the early twentieth-century and Yorkshire's most prolific author. An almost exact contemporary of Arthur Conan Doyle, he went on to become one of the leading exponents of crime-writing's 'Golden Age'. Among the characters he created were the clerical detective Reverend Francis Leggatt, vicar of Meddersly, the young newspaperman detective Frank Spargo and most famously of all, Ronald Camberwell, private investigator, who stared in an eleven book series. He rose top prominence for his crime novel *The Middle Temple Murder* ('One of the most enjoyable crime novels of its period... skilfully constructed' *Martin Edwards*) and due to President Woodrow Wilson's publicly-proclaimed admiration for his work. A native Yorkshireman, he also wrote extensively on the history and landscape of the northern England county, work for which he was made Fellow of the Royal Historical Society. His regional writing led him to being called 'the Yorkshire Hardy'. He died in 1935.

Praise for J.S. Fletcher

'No living story-teller handles a mysterious crime more cleverly than J.S. Fletcher'
The Times

'My favourite mystery writer'
President Woodrow Wilson

'J.S. Fletcher is one of the cleverest spinners of a detective yarn'
The Scotsman

'J. S. Fletcher's unravelling of a murder plot keeps the reader guessing all the time'
Evening Standard

CHAPTER 1 MR MAZAROFF

It was Dick Harker who first put me in touch with the man whose mysterious murder, while in my company, formed the basis of what came to be famous in three continents as the Mazaroff Affair. Harker and I were old schoolfellows; we entered the Army together as subalterns; we were in the same battalion throughout the Great War; we were wounded on the same day, and in the same scrap—a fortnight before the Armistice; we were sent to the same home hospital, and were eventually discharged from it at the same time, each unfit for any further military service, but fortunately in possession of our full complement of limbs. And the first thing that struck us, then, was that the world upon which we emerged was a vastly different world from that which existed when we went out with the First Hundred Thousand; and the second, a sure conviction that nothing was ever again going to be what it had been before. We were on the threshold of the utterly unknown, and it was excusable in each of us that for a while we loafed, mightily, about London, watching and wondering. Harker walked into my rooms in Jermyn Street one morning while I was still at breakfast, and flung down a copy of *The Times*, indicating a blue-pencilled advertisement in the Personal Column.

"That's your job, Mervyn," he said in his usual direct fashion. "Get busy!"

I took up the paper and read the advertisement before making

3

any remark.

The Advertiser, who has recently returned to England after a prolonged absence, and is desirous of making an extensive tour through the Northern Shires, in his private automobile, desires the company of a bright, sociable, well-educated, and well-informed young gentleman, preferably an ex-officer, invalided out of the service, whom he would entertain most hospitably and remunerate generously. Applications, with full and precise details and references, to be addressed, Box M. 5343, *The Times*, E.C.4.

I laid the paper aside and went on with my breakfast.

"There'll be about ten thousand applications," I remarked. "More or less—more, if anything."

"Somebody will emerge," asserted Harker. "Why not you!"

"Or—you?" I suggested.

"No!" he answered peremptorily. "It's your job. I've another notion in hand for myself. Odd advertisement, though, isn't it? —some millionaire chap, I should think. Makes one a bit inquisitive to know who he is."

I think it was more out of curiosity than anything that I replied to that advertisement, setting forth my qualifications and detailing my references. The references were unexceptionable: the qualifications as boldly stated as modesty permitted. Yet I never expected any reply: I knew well enough that there were hundreds of men whose qualifications and references would be just as good as my own—why should I be singled out? It was therefore with a good deal of surprise that, about a fortnight later, I received and read the following letter:-

HOTEL CECIL,
8th September, 1919

My dear Sir,—I am much obliged to you for your letter of the 23rd August. I think you and I would get on together very pleasantly, and I shall be further obliged to you if you will call on me at this hotel tomorrow morning about half-past twelve o'clock so that we may have a little talk.

    I remain, my dear Sir, truly yours,
    SALIM MAZAROFF

I was puzzled by the signature. Somehow, the phrasing of the advertisement had given me the idea that the advertiser was an Englishman who had been away from his native land for a long time, returned to it, and was anxious to revisit the scenes of his youth. But there was nothing English about the name of my correspondent, nor could I tell what nationality it represented. Nor could Dick Harker.

"But what's that got to do with it?" said he. "No doubt the old chap'll give you a jolly good time, and a fat cheque at the end of it. Don't let the opportunity slip. Be punctual!"

I walked into the Hotel Cecil next morning at precisely twelve-thirty. Evidently Mr Mazaroff had already given certain instructions about me, for as soon as I enquired for him, I, in my turn, was asked if I was Mr Mervyn Holt, and on my assenting, was handed over to an attendant who whisked me off to a private—and palatial—suite of rooms. He installed me in an ante-chamber, tapped at an inner door, murmured my name to somebody within, closed the door, informed me that Mr Mazaroff wouldn't keep me one minute, and went away. And I discovered at once that Mr Mazaroff was really a man of his word, for before a minute had gone the door opened again, and he stood there with outstretched hand.

I took a good look at him as I went forward. He was certainly a man worth looking at, a notable man, who would have been singled out of a crowd of other men. I judged him to be just about six feet in height; his breadth corresponded; altogether he gave one the impression of bigness and solidity. His age it was difficult to estimate: his brown hair and beard were grizzled, and between his eyes and his moustache there was a good deal of seam and wrinkle; he looked like a man who has weathered storms, and been under fierce suns and drying winds. There was a distinctive air of good nature, good humour, even of benevolence, about him, but it was somewhat discounted by a long, sharp nose and close-set, small eyes, and further by a cast in the left eye. But his smile was pleasant enough; so was the twinkle of his eyes, and there was nothing cold nor formal about his handshake.

"Glad to see you," he said, almost brusquely.

"I——" He stopped there, as if at a loss for further words, and leading me into the sitting-room from which he had just emerged, offered me a cigarette from a box that lay on the table. "Glass of sherry?" he went on, pointing to a decanter and glasses. "Join me—just going to have one myself—before lunch."

I was certain by that time that wherever or however Mr Mazaroff had come by his un-English name, he himself was a Scotsman: there was no mistaking his accent. I felt more at home with him after making this discovery, and accepting his offer of hospitality I sat down in the easy chair he drew forward. We looked at each other.

"I hope you're feeling quite well again after your wounds?" he asked.

"Quite fit, thank you," I answered. "Fit for light work, anyway."

"Aye well," he said, nodding, "as I said in my letter, I think you and I'll get on very pleasantly, if you care to come with an old fellow like me. I'd—I forget exactly how many applications —two or three hundred anyway. I picked out half a dozen, and went thoroughly into their references—and you were the result. I heard about you just what I wanted to hear—so there we are. What do you say, now?"

"I shall be pleased to go with you," I answered. "I hope I shall be able to do all you want. You think I shall?"

He twirled his glass in his fingers and laughed.

"It's little I want but company," he replied. "I'm a lone man— neither kith, kin, nor friends. I've been out of this country many years, and now I'm back I just want to dander round a bit, seeing places. An idle time, eh?"

"You've no fixed plan?" I enquired.

"No more than that we'll just get into my car and go north," he answered. "Stopping where we like and when we like. I'll tell you I've a fancy for old towns, anything old and grey and cool. I've been twenty years in hot climates, and the thought of an old English town makes my mouth water. Cathedral cities, and the like—ruins—grey walls—green trees, eh? You take me?"

"The Great North Road, then, will be a good route to follow," I said. "There are places along that——"

"And that's just what I was thinking!" he broke in, almost with boyish eagerness, reaching for a folding map that lay on a side-table, and spreading it out between us. "I've been studying this chart. Places like Huntingdon, Stamford, Grantham, Newark, York, Durham——"

"And lots of others, a bit off the road, one side or the other," I put in. "I know that road and its surroundings—well!"

"That's it!" he exclaimed joyfully. "We'll do very well—just progressing northward. I've no particular object—except that when we get far North there's a place I want to turn aside to —Marrasdale Moor—just to renew acquaintance. But that's in the future—there'll be a lot of country to cover before we get that far." He folded up his map, tossed it aside, and gave me a queerly shy sort of glance. "What about terms, now?" he asked diffidently.

"I think I ought to leave that to you, Mr Mazaroff," I answered. "I'd prefer to."

He gave a sigh of what, it was plain, was sheer relief.

"That's just what I'd like you to do," he said simply. "That's a thing that gentlemen shouldn't bargain about. Leave it to me— you'll not regret it. I'm a very rich man, laddie, and rich men are entitled to have their little games and fancies, eh? Very well, now—and when can you be ready to start?"

"Any time, with a couple of hours' notice," I replied.

He rubbed his hands at that—I never saw a schoolboy more eager about his holidays than he was about this jaunt.

"Good—good!" he exclaimed. "Then I'll just tell you what we'll do, Holt. Bring your kit along here this afternoon, and we'll start about five o'clock, and run gently along as far as we like before dinner time—there'll be some old town where we can spend a peaceful evening and a quiet night in an old-fashioned hotel. I've a fine Rolls-Royce car in the garage, and a thoroughly dependable chauffeur, Webster, a trusty, good, sensible fellow, and we'll be as right as rain. Come by five o'clock. That'll suit you? Good!—and now we'll just go down and take a bit of lunch together."

Mr Mazaroff and I spent a couple of hours over that lunch and our cigars and coffee. He proved himself a knowing and generous host, and a great talker. His talk was worth listening to. I soon discovered that he had seen many strange places and peoples—without giving me any definite information about himself or his pursuits he let me know that he had travelled extensively in various out-of-the-way parts of Asia and Africa. Arabia, Persia, India, Burmah, Somaliland, Uganda, Rhodesia, the Transvaal, the Cape—all these cropped up in his desultory talk. And the more he talked, the more I was convinced that he was a native of somewhere north of the Tweed—so much so that I felt bold enough at last to plump him with it.

"You've seen a tremendous lot of the world," I said. "But—I should say you're a Scotsman?"

He laughed, as if the suggestion pleased him.

"Aye, well, and that's a natural impression you'd get, Holt," he answered. "I'm not, though. I'm a Border man. I was born on the English side of the Tweed, amongst the Cheviots. But I spent the first fifteen years of my life on my grandfather's farm in Selkirk—and that accounts for what you're thinking. We'll perhaps take a look at the old place in our march—but they're all gone, my folk."

He sighed, a little sadly, at this reflection, but in the next instant recovered his spirits and began to talk gaily of our journey. Presently I left him and went away to make ready for it: at five o'clock I was back at the hotel with my luggage, and by a quarter past we were off, in the most luxurious car it had ever been my fortune to ride in, or ever to set eyes on.

There is no need to chronicle in detail the doings of the earlier stages of our tour. We followed out Mazaroff's line of going as far as we liked, and stopping where and when we chose. It was difficult to get him away from towns like Stamford and Grantham—at York, after a preliminary inspection of the old city, he announced his intention of staying a week; we stopped ten days. It was during this pause in our peregrinations that I got my first instance of his Oriental-like generosity. Coming down to breakfast one morning, he found me busy with many letters and small parcels; asking the reason of my unusually large mail, he learnt that this was my birthday. He made no remark on that except a joking one to the effect that he'd completely forgotten that he had one. But when I sat down to dinner that night and unfolded my napkin I found concealed there a crisp, new Bank of England note for five hundred pounds, and when, after gazing at it, I looked at him across the table, he blushed like a boy detected in playing off a practical joke.

"Mr Mazaroff!" said I. "You are too princely in your generosity!"

He looked round fearfully, as if afraid that the waiters should hear.

"Hoots—toots, laddie!" he muttered. "No such thing! Put it in your pouch, and say no more about it—I'm sure you merit a lot more than that wee bit of a matter!"

I knew what he meant. All the way North, he was never tired of drawing me out about the war, and my own doings in it. It was of no use to profess that one had forgotten; he would have the whole tale. He used to get immensely excited about it; his eyes blazed, his arms worked; he was marvellously uplifted at an episode of victory and correspondingly cast-down at one of defeat; sometimes he would whoop loudly at a particularly stirring passage. And for all the youngsters who had done their bit he professed an admiration which was akin to veritable hero-worship.

"Great fellows, grand fellows!" he would mutter. "Oh, if I'd been but thirty years younger!"

We got on together splendidly—he was an excellent, a fatherly-and-brotherly companion. At the end of a month he and I were inseparables. We had then run into the crisp October weather of the North, and were on the Southern edge of Northumberland. There, after consulting his map, he gave his chauffeur orders to cut across country. North by West, making by way of Hexham and Wark for the wild lands beyond, and for a particular place marked on the chart as the Woodcock Inn on Marrasdale Moor.

CHAPTER 2 THE WOODCOCK INN

For about an hour before we came to this, our immediate destination, we had traversed a peculiarly wild and lonely stretch of country, by roads which, it was very evident, were not at all to the taste, from a professional point of view, of our chauffeur, Webster. High roads we had said goodbye to at Hexham: thereafter we had travelled first over rough surfaced lanes and eventually over moorland tracks. One such led us to the Woodcock Inn, marked in Mr Mazaroff's map as a wayside house, standing in the midst of apparently houseless country. But when, rounding a heather-clad bluff that sloped sharply down to our track, we came in sight of it, I was amazed to think that a hostelry of any sort should be found in such a desert. It stood, a gaunt grey mass of stone, on the edge of a great moor ringed about by high hills—as veritable a solitude as one could set eyes on. Beyond it there was not a sign of human life or habitation.

"What an extraordinary place for an inn!" I exclaimed as we moved nearer. "What custom can they get there?"

But Mazaroff waved his hand in a circular fashion towards his surroundings as if to signify that he held their geography well within grasp.

"I know this country," he said. "Used to come here when I was a youngster. And though it's true there isn't a sign of life about us except what's signified by the old inn yonder, it's not such a desert as it looks at first sight. There's nothing on the moor

—Marrasdale Moor—but you'll observe that there's valleys cutting in between the hills that run down to its edge? Well, there's villages in those valleys, and farmsteads, too, and more than one sizeable country house. Just beyond the Woodcock yonder there's a village that the moor takes its name from—Marrasdale —a sizeable place. And there's another in yon valley to the right —Birnside—and far up that opening that you see between the hills in the distance there's a little market-town, Gilhester— aye, I mind them all well enough, laddie, though it's more years than I care to estimate since I set eyes on them! And the names of the farmsteads, too, I remember—Willieshope, and Blackhaugh, and Halstoneflatts, and many another!"

"There'll be people you remember," I suggested, "and who'll remember you?"

"Not after all these years!" he answered quickly. "And between you and me and the post, Holt I've no wish to remember people, nor—more particularly—to be remembered by anybody. We're just strangers—tourists—dandering round, sightseeing, and with a fancy to bide a while in these solitudes. That's the line, eh?"

"Exactly!" said I, taking his cue. "I understand."

He pointed at the chauffeur significantly.

"He's no idea that I've ever been in these parts before," he murmured. "I've said nothing to him. Those chaps have a trick of talking about their masters in inn kitchens, you know—I don't want it to be known that I'm other than a complete stranger to the place."

I was wondering why he should be so mysterious about this when we drew up at the door of the inn. Seen at close quarters it was a big, rambling structure of grey stone and plain, unornamented architecture, with extensive stabling adjoining it—the sort of place that suggested the old coaching days. And now that we were in the heart of the moor, I saw that at a little distance beyond the inn, the wide heather-carpeted expanse which I had thought unbroken was intersected by a broad high-road, shining white in the light of the afternoon sun, and running from

West to East until it disappeared behind the far-off hills.

"That's the road from Scotland," remarked Mr Mazaroff. "Many's the thousand—aye, and ten thousand!—men and cattle that's trodden that road, laddie, since it was first made. They used to bring great droves of oxen along it—that's the reason of a big wayside inn like this being set here. Well, here we are—and who keeps the old place now, I wonder? What's that name on the sign?"

There was a plain board-sign over the wide, open door of the house, undecorated save for a faded painting of a woodcock flying across a moorland scene. Beneath it, in tarnished gilt letters appeared the words *The Woodcock Inn by James Musgrave.*

"It was Haneshaws that had it when I was last here," murmured my companion. "Dead and gone, no doubt, all of them! And this man no doubt'll be Musgrave."

A man had appeared at the open door, and was coming across the road to us. He was a middle-aged, good-looking fellow, dressed in sporting clothes, and whether it was that we had aroused him from an afternoon nap, or that he was of a naturally slow and backward temperament, he seemed to be half-asleep of eye and equally slow of movement. But behind him came a woman, a sharp-featured, alert, quickly-observing woman, neat and precise in her attire, and eminently business-like, who slipped past the man and gained the side of our car first. It was she who did the talking.

"Good day, ma'am," said Mr Mazaroff. "You'll be the landlady, no doubt?—and this'll be your husband? Aye, well now, we're thinking of breaking our journey here for a day or two, perhaps for two or three, just to look round this grand country of yours. You'll have accommodation?"

"Oh yes, indeed, sir!" answered the woman, taking in the car and its occupants with appraising eyes. "We've excellent accommodation, sir—we often have tourists travelling in their own cars."

"Well-aired beds, now?" questioned Mr Mazaroff. "No damp sheets?"

"Our beds are always well aired, sir, in the travelling season, and our rooms are very good ones," she answered. "Since this motoring became fashionable we've a lot of custom, and we're prepared for it. If you'll step within, sir——"

"Aye, but now what about your table?" asked Mr Mazaroff. "This Northern air makes one sharpset, you know, and you seem to be a long way from markets. What can you give us to eat?"

The landlady quickly satisfied him on that score: it was very evident from the glib fashion in which she rattled off the resources of her larder that we should do very well, and that the cellar was as handsomely provided as the larder was filled.

"That'll do very nicely, ma'am," said Mr Mazaroff, "and so we'll just get down, and maybe your master will show my man where he can house the car and then we'll have the luggage brought in—a grand view you have here, and fine air," he continued, as he stepped down and moved towards the door, "and a good old-fashioned house, no doubt."

"I think you'll find it comfortable, sir," said the landlady as she led the way inside. "We've had customers here that said they were sorry to leave it. There's a sitting-room here, sir, that you can have all to yourselves."

She showed us into an old-fashioned parlour, snugly furnished with solid old stuff, and lighted by tall, narrow windows that looked out on the moor and the hills: Mr Mazaroff at the mere sight of it gave a grunt of pleased satisfaction.

"Aye, aye!" he said. "This'll do grandly—keep this room for me, ma'am, as long as we stop. Holt!" he exclaimed, when he had conferred with the landlady about dinner that evening and she had left us to ourselves. "This is the sort of thing I like—man, you never get the same comfort in those great overgrown modem hotels that you get in an old-fashioned English inn! This is the sort of place I've dreamed of, many and many a time when I've been in places where there wasn't the shade of a wall nor the leaf of a tree to creep under—a cool, grey, sleepy place where time seems to stand still. I like this. Holt—and we'll just take a whisky-and-soda together and have a look round before our dinner."

We had the whisky-and-soda, and we went out to look round. It needed small powers of observation on my part to show me that Mr Mazaroff was as well acquainted with this old wayside inn as its landlord and landlady were. Although he said nothing whenever Musgrave or any of his people were about, I could see that he knew every stone of the ancient buildings and every yard of their surroundings; now and then he muttered some reminiscence to me or whispered that something had been added there or was missing from here. There was a walled garden at the side of the house: he wandered about it with the familiarity of a man who has known a place intimately. As we were coming out of it, we saw Musgrave at its gate, a basket of apples in his hand; Mr Mazaroff went up to him and pointed to a square depression in the middle of the lawn.

"Looks to me, landlord," he remarked, "as if there'd been a cock-pit there in the old days."

Musgrave nodded, and his usually sleepy eyes showed some spark of interest.

"You're right, sir!" he answered. "There was! Long before my time, of course. I've heard of it from old fellows that live hereabouts. That sort of square, in the middle of the grass-plot, was it. They used to hold what they called cocking-matches here of a Sunday afternoon, sir—gentlemen used to come from far and wide, bringing their birds with them, and there the birds fought, while their owners sat round, on these raised banks, and watched and betted. I've known just one or two old men that could remember those days, but they're gone now."

"Good old times!" murmured Mr Mazaroff. "Or—bad old times!"

"More bad than good, I should think, sir, by all accounts," replied the landlord. "I understand there were some fine old goings-on here in those days."

"Quiet enough now, at any rate," observed Mr Mazaroff. "Isn't it!"

"We're pretty busy now and then, sir," answered Musgrave.

"This morning's brought a lot of custom. And that high-road yonder is still used a great deal by drovers—it'll be thronged enough tomorrow, for it's Cloughthwaite Fair next day, and there'll be a deal of traffic passing here."

We had come up to the gate of the garden as Mr Mazaroff and the landlord talked, and now, as Musgrave was about to open it, two ladies came in view from behind the high wall, walking along the half-grass track by which we had motored during the last three or four miles of our journey. Musgrave lifted his hand as they glanced in our direction; each gave him a nod and a smile as they passed on before the front of the inn. At one of them I merely looked; to the other I gave more attention. She was a girl of possibly twenty one or two years, brown-haired, light coloured, slim and graceful in her country coat and skirt, distractingly pretty, as I could see in that brief glance; the other was a tall, handsome woman of middle age, somewhat stern and cold in manner, despite the gracious response which she made to the landlord's civil greeting. From their dress and appearance these were evidently folk of consequence; at their heels, or frisking around them, ran half a dozen dogs of various breeds, all of them patricians in their own particular line.

I glanced at Mr Mazaroff as the ladies disappeared. He, too, was gazing after them; it seemed to me with unusual attention —perhaps because until then I had never seen him manifest the least interest of any sort in women.

"Neighbours of yours?" he asked suddenly, turning to Musgrave.

"That's Mrs Elphinstone, sir, of Marrasdale Tower," replied the landlord. "That's the big old house across the moor—you can just see the chimneys over that covert of young pine on the ridge yonder. Used to belong to Sir Richard Cotgreave, did Marrasdale Tower—been in that family hundreds of years, by all accounts. When Sir Richard died, a few years since, this Mr Elphinstone bought the place and came to live here: most of the land hereabouts is his."

"Mrs Elphinstone, eh?" said Mr Mazaroff. "And the young lady?

—Miss Elphinstone, of course."

"No, sir," replied Musgrave. "The young lady is Miss Merchison —Miss Sheila, as we all call her. Mrs Elphinstone's daughter by a previous marriage, sir—I believe Mr and Mrs Elphinstone hadn't been married very long, themselves, when they came here."

I fancied I detected renewed interest in the expression of Mr Mazaroff's face during this explanation. But he was a good hand at concealing his thoughts, and he turned and waved his hand towards the wide prospect before us.

"So Mr Elphinstone of Marrasdale Tower owns most of what we see?" he suggested.

"Well, not what you might call most, sir," replied Musgrave. He set down his basket of apples and began to point out distant landmarks. "Mr Elphinstone's estate, sir, runs from here up to the village, and then across by the foot of the fells to a point near that blue hill in the far distance, and from that right back here, taking in the whole of Marrasdale Moor. But those Moors to the South and East, sir, High Cap Moors, they belong to a London gentleman, Mr Verner Courthope, a banker. He's got a shooting-box right in the middle of 'em—High Cap Lodge they call it— and he's there now, with a small shooting party."

"Good sport hereabouts?" asked Mr Mazaroff, half indifferently.

"There's a fine lot of grouse this year, sir," replied Musgrave. "Mr Elphinstone and Mr Courthope, they've both had rare good bags."

With occasional bits of gossip of this sort, our first evening at the Woodcock went off very pleasantly. I wondered what we were going to do with ourselves next day in so solitary a place. But Mr Mazaroff, it seemed, had notions of his own, which he promptly explained on coming down to breakfast.

"Holt, laddie," he said, with a confidential nod, "you'll understand me, I'm sure—I want to have this day to myself, looking round old spots, you know, alone. And also, there's a man I want to see on a bit of business. So—you'll amuse yourself till evening, when I'll be back in good time for dinner?"

"Of course!" I agreed. "I'll be all right. Don't bother about me."

He thanked me, almost as if I had been the first person to consider. Presently, carrying a stout stick, he went out—and I noticed that just before leaving our sitting-room he put on a pair of blue spectacles, with some remark about the glare of the sun. He went off in the direction of the village, and I saw no more of him until he turned up again just as dinner was ready at seven o'clock. He was very quiet and thoughtful during dinner, and it was not until he was half-way through his after-dinner cigar that he suddenly motioned me to draw my chair close alongside his own.

"Holt!" he said, "I've something to tell you. And, man!—it's the strangest tale you ever heard in your life!"

CHAPTER 3 LOST

I suppose I gave Mr Mazaroff a wondering and perhaps a half-uneasy stare, for he nodded reassuringly as he drew his chair still closer to mine.

"Nothing to be frightened about, Holt, my lad," he said. "Just a—a coil, as you might put it. But—a bad one! And, as I said just now—as strange a tale as ever you heard. Anyway, one of 'em."

"Yes?" I said. "About—yourself?"

"Self and other folk," be replied, with a grim smile. "Other folk!—aye, there's the devil of it! If it were only myself, now!—but there's more than one affected. And yet, now I come to think it over, it's only what might have been expected—just that!"

He turned to the window and for a moment or two sat staring fixedly and in silence across the moor, stretching away in the rapidly-gathering twilight. But I saw that it was not at the moor, nor at the darkening mass of the hills beyond, that he looked, but at something far off in his memory. Curiosity got the better of me, and I broke in on his thoughts.

"I'm all in the dark, Mr Mazaroff," I said. "Am I to listen?"

He started—then gave me an emphatic nod.

"Aye!" he answered. "You're to listen, Holt, for I've nobody else to tell it to, and I'm wanting counsel on it, and you're a sensible youngster. It's just this—you saw the two ladies that passed us by yesterday afternoon when we were talking to the landlord at his garden gate?"

I nodded an affirmative—I might have added that—in my mind's eye—I had been seeing the younger of the two ever since, and had spent the whole of that day thinking about her. But I kept that bit of news to myself.

"Aye, well!" he continued. "They don't know it, and nobody knows it, only me. But it's just this, Holt, my lad—that's my wife and daughter!"

I was smoking one of Mr Mazaroff's prime cigars at the moment, and when he said this I started so violently that it jumped from between my teeth and fell to the floor. It seemed to me that a whole age—an aeon, if you like—elapsed in the mere act of stooping and recovering it. And I wondered at the calmness and banality of my reply when I sat upright again, looking at him.

"Musgrave," I said, quite steadily, "Musgrave called the elder lady Mrs Elphinstone, and the younger Miss Merchison—Miss Sheila Merchison."

He gave an impatient laugh.

"Musgrave here, Musgrave there!" he retorted. "He knows no better, and no more. But I'm telling you that that's my wife, laddie, and the lassie's my daughter, and unless I see some way out of the complications there's the devil and all to pay!"

There was a pause between us then. He sat twiddling his big thumbs, and, as he had discarded the blue spectacles, the cast in his eye looked, somehow, more sinister than usual. I began to sense the mysterious in him, and to realise that his was, to me, an unexplored personality.

"I don't understand," I said at last.

"I'm going to make you understand, Holt," he answered. "This is the way of it—yon good-looking lassie's name is Merchison, sure enough. And—Elphinstone though she may call herself, and no doubt think she's a right to call herself—so is her mother's. And—so's mine. Merchison!"

"Not Mazaroff, then?" I exclaimed.

"I've a right to that, too," he said. "Legal right—all correct and proper. It's been my legal name for many years, and it'll remain so. But I was born Merchison—and not so far from here, too—and I was married Merchison. And yon's Mrs Merchison, for all she's married to Elphinstone."

"And I don't understand any more now!" said I.

"Well, Holt," he answered, "I'll make it as plain as I can, and maybe it's not such a tangle as it seems when you get hold of one end of the thread and pull steadily at it. You see, I was born hereabouts—my father was a well-to-do estate agent in these parts, and I was an only son—only child, in fact. My father and mother died when I was a mere youngster, and after that I lived with my grandfather on his farm near Selkirk, across the border yonder. Then he died, when I was just about two-and-twenty, and he left me all he had, a tidy lot of money, and that, put to what my parents had left me, made me a pretty rich man. And I was headstrong and impetuous, and always for having my own way, and there was nobody to keep me from having it, nor from indulging myself in any whims that came into my head. And I came across a high-mettled girl that was pretty much like myself in that respect—a parson's daughter that was just mad to get away from her folks and her home and the dullness of it all—and we got wed in more than the usual haste, and began to repent as soon as we'd done it!"

"Why?" I asked.

"Man!" he answered. "We hadn't a taste in common! We'd nothing in common, except obstinacy and self-will! And we found we were the worst pair to pull together that ever was harnessed. I was all for adventure, and travelling to see the world; she was all for setting up a grand establishment and playing the big lady amongst the folk that had previously bored her to death. I saw in less than a year that things would never do—so I just took matters into my own hands."

"In what way?" I enquired.

"I'll not deny that it was a high-handed, cavalier, maybe selfish and egotistical way," he answered reflectively. "It wasn't the way I'd take now, with a soberer mind and more knowledge of the world. But what I did was this—I went to a lawyer and pledged him to secrecy. Then I realised all that I had—a nice lot! —and divided it into two equal shares, and made one fast to her for life—she'll have had it always; never less, Holt, than fifteen hundred a year of her own. And that done, and all secure for her, I just took my share and cleared out."

"Without telling her?" I exclaimed.

"Aye—she knew nothing about it," he answered. "What was the use? I just went. Right away. Nobody—not even the lawyer body—knew where. To be sure, I left word for her that i was going travelling for a few years—but I didn't let on where."

"So—you ran away from her?" I suggested.

"If you put it that way, I did," he assented candidly. "It was the only thing to do. There'd have been unpleasantness, otherwise. A silent and quiet departure—the only thing for it, in my judgment."

"And—the child?—the girl we saw yesterday afternoon?" I asked, after a pause. "Was she born then?"

"No!" he answered with emphasis. "She wasn't! If she had been, maybe I'd never have gone—indeed, I'm sure now I wouldn't have gone. But she was neither born, nor did I know she was likely to be born. She came eight months after I'd left."

"You heard of it, then?" I suggested.

"Never knew of it till today!" he exclaimed. "I've been making some enquiries, without revealing my own identity. These country folk, Holt, are rare hands at knowing family histories and secrets, and they're equally good at retailing what they know."

"Of course, Mrs Elphinstone—as she's known here—believes you to be dead?" I said. "That goes without saying."

"Oh, to be sure!" he answered. "She married this Elphinstone a few years back, just before he bought this Marrasdale Tower estate. Aye, she believes me dead as Adam—and here I'm alive!"

"What are you going to do?" I asked.

"What would you do, yourself, Holt?" he replied anxiously. "Tell me your plain opinion, man!—I'll not be offended at anything you say. As I've remarked before, I've a great opinion of your common sense. Say, now!"

"I think I should just go away, saying nothing," said I. "After all, you left her. And—if you reveal yourself, it'll mean breaking up what's probably a satisfactory settlement. Mr Elphinstone and the——"

"Oh, by all accounts, they suit each other as well as we suited each other ill!" he broke in. "Aye, this settlement's all right. But —the girl's my daughter."

"She's never known you, Mr Mazaroff," I remarked.

His bronzed cheeks reddened at that, and he shook his head.

"You're right, Holt, you're right!" he said, almost humbly. "And it's my own fault. Well—up to now, nothing's happened. Nobody knows but yourself."

"You've told no one?" I asked.

"Not a soul!" he asserted. "I've just picked things up—information. Nobody knows—nobody has the least idea—those folk at Marrasdale Tower least of all."

"After all these years it would be something of a startling revelation," I observed. "It needs some reflection. And——" But then a new idea struck me, and I regarded him doubtfully. "I suppose, if it came to it, you'd have to prove that——"

"That Salim Mazaroff is Andrew Merchison," he interrupted. "Oh, that can be done. There's the cast in my eye, and a birthmark on my right arm, and there's papers and people—not just at hand, to be sure, but findable—that can substantiate all that."

"How came you to take such an unusual name?" I ventured to ask him. He laughed softly, as if the reminiscence pleased him.

"I'll tell you," he answered. "When I first went off, it was to India. I knocked about there a good deal, and in the Persian Gulf, and in adjacent parts. Then I went further South—to Durban and thence into the interior—the diamond districts. And in Durban I foregathered with an old man of like tastes to mine—in fact he and I lived together and traded together. His name was Mazaroff, and he left me all his money—no little—on condition I took it. So I did—why not? At that time, I'd no intention of ever coming back to England again."

"Mr Mazaroff," said I. "Did it never strike you that your wife, believing you dead—as I suppose she did—would marry again?"

"I can't say that it did," he replied. "I'm a bit slow, perhaps. I ought to have thought. But I didn't. And now—there's the situation!"

"What are you going to do about it?" I asked.

"I don't know," he answered frankly. "Nothing in a hurry. And as I say, nobody knows but you and me. There's no fear of my being recognised. I've talked to a dozen people today who knew me in the old days, and in my blue spectacles they hadn't the least idea as to who I really was."

He got up then, and went out, to stroll about the front of the inn, alone. That night he said no more on the subject of his revelations, nor did he mention the matter in the morning. We spent most of that day in motoring to some ruins twenty miles away: when we returned in the evening there was a good deal of business being done at the inn—men were returning in numbers from the fair of which Musgrave had spoken, and every room in the house was crowded except our own private parlour. And there were groups of men and horses in the road when, after dinner, Mr Mazaroff, remarking to me that he wanted to have a good think all by himself, crossed over to the open moor and strolled away across the heather. I never saw him again—alive.

It was about half-past seven when he went out and vanished into the undulations of the moor. I went out myself soon afterwards, and was out, wandering aimlessly about amongst the sheep-tracks, until past nine o'clock, when I returned to the inn. He had not come back. Nor had he come at ten—and when eleven struck from the old grandfather clock in the stone-walled hall I sought out Musgrave and his wife, seated at their supper-table after the toils of an unusually busy evening. Webster, Mr Mazaroff's chauffeur, was supping with them.

The landlord and landlady were not inclined to any uneasiness or alarm. During our forty-eight hours' stay they had discovered that Mr Mazaroff was, as they put it, an affable and friendly gentleman, inclined to sociability—their present opinion was that he had dropped in at one of the moorland houses, and was still there, comfortably chatting. But when twelve o'clock sounded, and he was still absent, Musgrave's face lengthened, and he began to talk about the foolishness of going out in the dusk and dark in strange places.

"Are there any places on the moor where he could come to harm?" I asked.

"That depends," replied Musgrave. "There's places he could fall over in the dusk, and there's others—bog-land—that he could sink into before he knew where he was, dark or light. Them that doesn't know these moors shouldn't wander about 'em, after dark."

It was on the tip of my tongue to remark that Mr Mazaroff knew those moors well enough, or had known them, but I checked myself, and instead of saying anything went out on to the road before the inn. It was black night then, and the silence was intense. There was scarcely a star to be seen, and on the hard-surfaced roads that led from the village and across the moor itself not a footfall sounded.

I went back, resolute that something must be done. Musgrave got lanterns for Webster, me and himself: we went out on the moor, leaving instructions with Mrs Musgrave to keep a strong light burning in the front windows of the inn, and to make an arranged signal to us if Mr Mazaroff returned in our absence. We dispersed in different directions, listening always for any cry of distress.

We were out in that way until a faint grey light began to show beyond the Eastern hills: at that we went back to the inn. None of us had heard or seen anything. And now Musgrave and his wife set up a different theory. Mr Mazaroff had wandered too far, called in at some house, and been pressed to stay the night: he would turn up at breakfast time.

I had no belief in that. Webster and I got some food and hot coffee, and went out again—he one way, I the other. Mine took me towards the dawn. And the sun had just risen in all his autumn glory, and the fells were shimmering in the morning mists, when suddenly rounding a sharp bluff in the rise and fall of the moorland, I came face to face with the girl of whom I had been thinking for two days—Sheila.

CHAPTER 4 YOUTH'S FREEMASONRY

Sheila was sitting by one of the reed-fringed pools that lay amongst the heather and the moss. Unconscious of any presence save that of a solemn-eyed spaniel who sat at her side, she had drawn off her shoes and stockings and was dabbling her feet and ankles in the dark waters. A sudden start of realisation came over me at the sight of her. All unaware as she was of it, there was I, anxiously searching for a man, who, if his story was true, was this girl's father!

The spaniel caught sight of me and barked. His mistress looked hastily in my direction, saw me, seemed to realise that she had seen me before, and though she blushed at being caught in a somewhat mystifying situation, accepted it calmly. She gave me a friendly nod—and at the same time began to put on her foot-gear.

I purposely remained in the rear until she jumped to her feet, faced me, and laughed, pointing to the pool.

"There's a superstition about that well," she said, without preface or hesitation. "They say that if you dip your feet in it six times, within an hour of sunrise, any time between Michaelmas and Martinmas, you'll live happy ever after. So—I was trying it."

I went nearer, encouraged by her frank smile and manner.

"I hope it'll come true," I said. "As for myself, I'm not at all happy just now."

A look of concern came into her eyes.

"No?" she responded. "Not? Why?"

"I believe you saw me, yesterday—no, the day before—near the Woodcock, with an elderly gentleman?" I said. "You went by. Well, he's missing—lost!"

She came a little nearer to me; as if unconsciously, her eyes swept the moorland.

"Do you mean—here?" she asked. "On the moor?"

"That's just it," I assented. "He went out from the inn, last night, after dinner, alone, and he's never returned. You know these parts? Are there places——"

"There are many dangerous places," she interrupted hastily. "Have you searched?"

"Several of us, all night," I answered. "We've seen nothing, heard nothing of him."

"Your father?" she asked, eyeing me half sympathetically.

"No—a friend, with whom I'm travelling," I replied. "I'm awfully anxious about him. It was unusually dark last evening, and I'm afraid he's come to harm—fallen over something or into something. Yet—we've been a great deal over the ground."

"Who searched?" she demanded.

"I have been out all the time," I said, "and our chauffeur, and Musgrave. In almost every direction, too."

"Musgrave doesn't know the moor," she remarked. "At least, only superficially. I wonder if our people—gamekeepers, you know—have heard anything? If you'd walk with me to the house——" She pointed across the moor to where the gables and chimneys of Marrasdale Tower showed above the surrounding trees. "We might hear something there," she continued. "My stepfather, Mr Elphinstone, will be out and about now, and he may have heard something from the men. We can go there in a few minutes."

She led me across the heather by a winding track that took us through a part of the moorland which I had not previously traversed. We talked—I told her something of our adventures up to that point: I also told her Mr Mazaroff's name, and my own. Of his secret history or of the fact that he already knew the district

I carefully abstained from saying anything.

"And you say there are really dangerous places?" I asked when we had come to some understanding of the situation. "You, of course, know the country?"

"There are several dangerous places," she assented. "Places where the moorland paths run along what are virtually precipices, and other places where, in the dark, you can quite easily walk into a bottomless bog! Only those who really know the moors well ought to venture on them after dark. Of course, if you know the tracks——"

We came before long to Marrasdale Tower—an ancient, irregularly-built place that looked like an old Border fortress. There in the courtyard, talking to a man in velveteens, we met Mr Elphinstone, a tall, thin, grey-haired, studious-looking man, who glanced at me wonderingly over the top of an unusually large pair of spectacles. His stepdaughter led me up to him without ceremony: I had already discovered that she wasted no time on formalities.

"This is Mr Holt—Mr Mervyn Holt," she said. "He and a friend of his, Mr Mazaroff, an elderly gentleman, have motored from London, and are staying a few days at the Woodcock. Last night Mr Mazaroff went out alone on the moors, and he's never returned. Mr Holt wants to find him: he's anxious."

Mr Elphinstone, who looked to me to be one of those men who take in things very leisurely, nodded, and glanced at the man in velveteens.

"A gentleman lost on the moor, eh?" he said. 'Um! Parker—go and enquire amongst the men in the stables and in the gardens. Some of them cross the moors from one point or another, don't they? Yes—just ask. Um! Lost all night, eh? Dear me! Er—won't you come in, Mr—er——"

"My name is Holt, sir," I said, prompting his absent-mindedness.

"Holt, eh?" he answered, with a sudden gleam of interest. "Um! I was at Merton with a man of that name—in fact, we were at Rugby together, before our Oxford days. He and I were great

28

rowing men. He's vicar of some country parish in Buckingham-shire now, I believe—long time since we foregathered."

"I think you are speaking of my father, Mr Elphinstone," I remarked. "He was at Rugby and Merton, and he's now Vicar of Chellingham, near Aylesbury. I remember now that he has in his study some old photograph groups of Merton crews—I think I've seen your name underneath one or two of them."

He turned and gave me his hand, shaking mine, in evident high delight.

"Bless me!" he exclaimed. "Now just imagine it! This is a great pleasure. I thought much of Holt—he was a fine, handsome fellow—now I come to look more closely at you, you're the very image of what he was in those days! Come in—come in!—this is excellent!"

He pushed me before him into a room where Mrs Elphinstone was evidently waiting breakfast for her husband and daughter. She did not see me at first, being concerned with tea-making, but she evidently recognised Mr Elphinstone's step.

"Are you and Sheila never coming to breakfast, Malcolm?" she demanded. "The tea——" Then she turned and saw me, and I saw that she recognised me as the young man whom she had passed two days before. Her finely-marked eyebrows went up in wonder at my presence in her breakfast room. Mr Elphinstone pushed me forward.

"Marion!" he exclaimed. "A truly most wonderful and fortunate thing! This young gentleman is the son—and the very image—of my old friend Tom Holt! Isn't it extraordinary that he should drop on me from the clouds like this? He came—let's see, how did he come?—oh, I remember now, Sheila brought him, to be sure."

"Yes," said Sheila, "and you've already forgotten why I brought him! Mother," she went on rapidly, "Mr Holt is staying at the Woodcock with that old gentleman we saw him with the other day—they're motoring. And the old gentleman is lost, and Mr Holt has been out all night searching the moors for him."

Mrs Elphinstone gave me a politely welcoming, if somewhat

frigid handshake, and pointed me to a chair near her tea-tray.

"Then I'm quite sure Mr Holt will do with some breakfast," she said, in practical fashion. "Attend to him, Sheila—your father will let everything go cold—Mr Elphinstone," she continued, turning to me, "is so very—absent-minded, we'll say, that—there you see, he's off now—gone, of course, to find some memorial of the days in which he knew your father—just like him! Tea or coffee?"

"This is very kind of you," I said, as I watched Mr Elphinstone meander away into other rooms, evidently on the search for something, "but I really ought to be looking for my missing friend. His absence is getting serious, and——"

Sheila interrupted me to tell her mother all about it; as she finished the man in velveteens came hovering near the open window.

"Well, Parker?" called Sheila. "Anybody heard anything?"

But Parker had no news to give. He had questioned all the men in the stables and the gardens; none had seen or heard of the missing gentleman. By this time Mr Elphinstone had returned with an armful of books and old photographs: he wanted to monopolise me, but his wife impatiently waved him away.

"Really, Malcolm!" she exclaimed. "Mr Holt can't look at pictures of you and his father when he's so anxious about this unfortunate old gentleman of his! The poor man may be lying in some out-of-the-way place on the moors with a broken leg! Can't you make some sensible suggestion?"

Mr Elphinstone, thus adjured, laid aside his collection of memorials, took off his spectacles, sat down, helped himself to some fish, and after a few reflective sips at a cup of tea, leaned across the table towards his step-daughter.

"How would it be to enquire at High Cap Lodge?" he suggested. "Verner's people might have heard something, or know something. I believe he has watchers out, at night—we haven't, now."

"Good!" said Sheila. "I'll take Mr Holt across there presently. That," she continued, turning to me, "is my cousin Verner

30

Courthope's place—High Cap Lodge. Your friend may have wandered on to his ground, you know—Verner has all the moor on the South-east and East—a wild district. We'll go see him."

We each made a hurried breakfast and set out, Mrs Elphinstone dropping one or two practical hints, and Mr Elphinstone very earnest that as soon as I'd found Mr Mazaroff (whose disappearance didn't seem to trouble him greatly) I should return to Marrasdale Tower and look at his books and papers. Our way led towards the hills, and became rugged and lonely.

"My cousin has a small shooting party at his Lodge," announced Sheila, as we came in sight of our destination, a long, low-roofed building set amidst pine-trees in a defile of the moors. "There's himself, and his manager (Courthopes are bankers, you know, in the City), a man named Armintrade, whom I loathe, and another man, a London doctor, Eccleshare, whom I detest! They shoot all day, and I believe they sit up playing cards or billiards all night, and I suppose we shall find them at breakfast."

She was evidently well acquainted with High Cap Lodge and its arrangements, for without any ceremony or delay she led me in by the front hall, down a passage and thrust open the door of a room that looked out on a fine stretch of moor. Three men, lounging around a well-spread breakfast table, turned in astonishment at our entrance, examining me closely.

I, in my turn, took a good, close look at them, individually and collectively, as they pushed back their chairs and rose to their feet. For I had a sudden notion, and one that closely bordered on suspicion. I remembered that when Mazaroff had intimated to me that he wanted to spend that first day at the Woodcock alone, he had also said that there was a man in the neighbourhood whom he wanted to see on business. And for the moment it flashed upon me that as all these three men were from London, the man to whom he referred might be one of them: two, at any rate, were connected with banking and financial matters; so, also, as I knew well enough by that time, was Mazaroff.

31

But I got no help from my inevitably superficial examination of the three. One, obviously the host, was a youngish man of a somewhat heavy and sullen cast of countenance, good-looking in a rather animal fashion, but with too much jowl, and over much sign of temper about his eyes; I saw at once that he was by no means pleased to see me, a stranger, in Sheila Merchison's company. The second was a sleek and sly-looking middle-aged man, with a carefully trimmed beard and a somewhat supercilious air—this I presently discovered to be Armintrade, the bank manager. And the third was a great, fleshy man, a sort of man-mountain, clean shaven, heavy of feature, especially of nose and lip, whose ferrety eyes fastened at once on my companion in a fashion that made me restive, stranger though I was to everybody there.

Sheila paid no more attention to the two guests than was represented by a curt nod: she went straight up to Courthope.

"Verner," she said, "this gentleman is Mr Holt, whose father is an old friend of Mr Elphinstone. Mr Holt is staying for a day or two at the Woodcock, where he came with a friend, Mr Mazaroff, in Mr Mazaroff's car. Last night Mr Mazaroff, who is an elderly man, went out on the moor, and he's never returned. Have you or your people heard or seen anything of him?"

I'll do Verner Courthope the justice to say that he showed some polite concern in the matter. Neither he nor his two guests could tell me anything, but Courthope went out with Sheila and myself to a shed at the rear of the lodge, where two gamekeepers and some other men were waiting, and of them he made enquiries. That resulted in nothing, but he promised that in the course of the day's shooting he and his party would keep their eyes and ears open as they went about the moors. Only once did he address a remark directly to me.

"You were only here for a day or two, then?" he asked, with a curiosity which he could not conceal. "Not stopping?"

"Our stay would have been very short," I replied. "Now, of course, I've got to find my companion." He nodded, and Sheila and I presently went away in the direction of Marrasdale Tower.

We had walked some little distance in silence when she suddenly turned on me with a look which showed me that she felt instinctively certain that I, out of sheer youthful sympathy, would understand what she was going to say.

"If a man's known by the company he keeps," she said, almost bitterly, "what about my cousin Verner? Did you ever see two more utterly detestable men than Armintrade and Eccleshare! I loathe the sight of them! And—and yet my mother wants me to marry Verner Courthope; insists on it! Well—I just won't— won't!"

CHAPTER 5 SOLE DEPOSITARY

I was so much taken aback by this sudden outburst of intimate confidence that I lost my tongue, and could only stand looking at my companion—I dare say like a great, shy gaby. She reddened a little under my gaze, but her attitude became still more confidential and appealing.

"I dare say you think I'm an awful ass for saying things like that?" she said hurriedly. "But—you're young, and there's nobody about here who is. You wouldn't like to be forced into doing what you don't want to do, would you?"

I gave her what was meant to be a very critical inspection, under which she reddened still more, though she faced me frankly enough.

"From what I've seen of you," I said, "I should say that nobody could make you do what you don't want to do!"

"I wish my own mother would see that," she responded quickly. "She's been trying to force Verner Courthope on me for the last twelve months! and—I won't!"

"You don't like him?" I suggested.

"Not that way, anyway," she answered. "He's all right to talk dogs and horses to, and he has his good points, but as for anything else—no!"

"Why is Mrs Elphinstone so keen about it?" I enquired.

"Oh, I don't know!" she said, half-impatiently. "She and his mother—my aunt, you know—sort of settled it between them.

Verner, now that his father's dead, is nominal head of the bank, and he's piles of money. And I'm afraid my mother is fond of anybody and anything that's mixed up with money."

"And Mr Elphinstone?" I suggested.

"Mr Elphinstone is about as useful to appeal to as one of the folios in his library," she answered. "He lives in dreams all day— as you might see. Outside his books and his papers and his collections, he just does and approves all that his wife ordains."

"What are you going to do, then?" I asked.

She gave me an arch glance—and, for the first time, though I had looked at her closely enough before, I saw something that gave me a start. There was the slightest, the very slightest suspicion of a cast in her left eye, just as there was—but far more defined and noticeable—in Mazaroff's. And I remembered then what I was in danger of forgetting—that I was talking, if we got to strict fact, to Mazaroff's daughter. Indeed, beyond this faint resemblance, I thought I saw other, stronger ones. But the arch glance was followed by a laugh, half-shy, half-malicious.

"Do?" she said. "What, to checkmate my mother and Verner? Why—I'll marry somebody else!"

We exchanged very candid glances at that.

"Is—is there anybody else?" I asked.

She looked at me from under her eyelashes.

"No!" she answered.

I don't know what I was going to say then. I have a vague notion that I was very near a blunt declaration that I had fallen in love with her at first sight. But at that moment we turned the corner of a plantation and came across Mr Elphinstone, who was mooning along with a sort of alpenstock in his hand, and obviously lost in the clouds or mists of his own reflections. He came to earth with a start on seeing us.

"Oh, ah, to be sure!" he exclaimed. "I believe I was coming to meet you. Holt—you must come and lunch with us. I want to show you a lot of things that would interest your father. He and I——"

I interrupted him, peremptorily: it was the only thing to do.

"It's awfully kind of you, sir," I said, "but I can't do anything until I've found or heard of Mr Mazaroff. I must use every endeavour to find him."

His mouth and eyes opened widely, and he nodded his head several times.

"Oh, ah, the missing man!" he exclaimed. "True, true!—I'd forgotten him for the moment. Deplorable! And you've heard nothing yet?"

"Nothing, sir," I replied. "And so I must go and do something."

"What'll you do, now?" enquired Sheila.

"Get hold of the police and have a thorough search of the district made," I answered. "And there's no time to be lost, so you'll excuse me if I hurry away."

I went off without more ado—I knew very well that I should see her again before the day was out and in other days to come. She let me go with an understanding nod, but before I had made a hundred yards of the heather, Elphinstone bawled after me.

"If not to lunch, come to dinner!" he shouted. "Bring your friend!—glad to see him."

I waved my hand in response, and went on across the moor to the Woodcock. Webster was standing on the road before the open door.

"Heard anything?" I demanded as I got near him.

"Not a word, sir," he replied. "Nothing!" Then as I left the heather he stepped towards me. "There's two men waiting for you inside, Mr Holt—want some information. One's a police-sergeant; the other's a newspaper reporter."

"Then it's got out, Webster," I said. "That makes it all the stranger."

"Oh, it's all round the district by now, Mr Holt," he answered. "Everybody knows. I've talked to lots of people this morning who saw Mr Mazaroff about, the first two days we were here, and to one or two who talked to him the second day, and they all know he's missing. But I've neither seen nor heard of anybody who saw him last night—it would seem as if he clean disappeared when he walked out of that door."

"There's no doubt of that, Webster," I said. Truth to tell, I was already wondering if Mazaroff had made a clean disappearance on purpose. He knew the district; he would know where to go in order to get a train; there were great trunk lines on either side of us, at a few miles distance; by this time he might be in London, vanished for the second time in his life, and for practically the same cause. But that was all surmise: I turned to the inn.

"Well," I said, "come in, Webster, and let's hear what these fellows want."

The two men were waiting for me in the private sitting-room which Mrs Musgrave had turned over to Mazaroff and myself on our arrival, and it was easy to see that each, in his own way, was professionally eager for news. The policeman introduced himself as Sergeant Manners of the County Constabulary, stationed at Marrasdale; the reporter as Mr Bownas, district representative of the leading county newspaper and of one of the London press agencies. Manners was a big, military-looking man; Bownas a little, ratty chap, content to scribble in his book while the sergeant did the questioning. That quickly turned to a point which, it was very plain to see, the police-mind considered all important.

"This gentleman now, sir," asked the sergeant, when I had given him the main facts of the case, "he'd be a wealthy gentleman, no doubt? That car of his, that I've just seen in the garage outside—he wouldn't buy that for five shillings, as you might put it, what?"

"You may take it that Mr Mazaroff is a wealthy man," I answered, with an eye on the reporter's pencil.

"And in that case likely to have wealth on him when he walked out of this house, no doubt?" continued the sergeant. "Valuables, of course. Now, it would be useful to me if I'd some idea of exactly what the gentleman did have on him!"

"He would have a good deal," I admitted.

"Money, now—cash?" suggested the sergeant.

"He carried a lot of ready money," I said.

"Watch and chain, likely?" he asked, with a knowing look.

"An exceedingly valuable watch and chain—gold," I replied. "And, if you want to know, he had a very fine diamond in his neck-tie, and another in a ring on his left hand. He'd also a solid gold cigar-case and a solid gold match-box."

The sergeant gave me an emphatic nod.

"Then I'll tell you what it is!" he exclaimed. "And no mistake either! This is a case of murder and robbery! What!—here's a gentleman with all that on him walks out on a lonely moor in full view of all those drover chaps that was about here last night and comes from Lord knows where—why, of course, some of 'em followed him, and did him in for what they could get! Murder, sir—that's what it is, and followed by robbery—never heard of a clearer case!"

"If it be so," I asked, "how is it that his body hasn't been found? For the moors have been well searched—hereabouts, at any rate."

"Ah!" he answered, giving me a significant look. "You don't know these parts, sir. They're wilder nor what you'd think. There's places here where you could drop a body, quiet like, and nobody'd ever find it—ain't there, Mr Bownas?"

Mr Bownas also favoured me with a glance of deep significance.

"Fissures in the rocks," he said darkly. "Bog-holes. Lots of places. I should say that, if you meant to do it, you could hide the vestiges of a crime for ever on Marrasdale Moor."

"What are you going to do?" I asked, turning to the sergeant.

"Well," he replied reflectively, "it'll have to be reported to head-quarters. There'll be a proper search made, and enquiries. Of course, in my opinion, it's as I say—some o' them drovers has done him in and rifled his pockets. We must circulate the news far and wide—Mr Bownas here'll put pieces in the papers."

Mr Bownas waved his note-book.

"It'll be in every principal newspaper in England, London and provincial, tomorrow morning," he announced. "Capital headlines it'll make, too. You haven't got a photo of the missing gentleman?"

"No!" I replied. "And I'm not at all sure that the missing gentleman will like so much publicity. If he turns up——"

The sergeant laughed—there was more of superior knowledge than of scorn in the sound; clearly, he considered me very innocent.

"Turn up!" he exclaimed. "Lord bless you!—he'll never turn up, not if he went out with all that valuable property on him. Murder and robbery!—that's what it is. You ain't a relation, I think?" he went on, eyeing me narrowly. "Musgrave, he said he thought as how the two of you were just travelling together—friends?"

"Precisely," I assented. "Friends."

"And your name?" he continued, pulling out a pocket-book and a stub of pencil. "I'd best do things in order. And address—when you're at home."

"Mervyn Holt, late Captain, the King's Own Oakshire Light Infantry," I answered. "559a Jermyn Street, London, and Chellingham Vicarage, Aylesbury—either address."

"And this young man?" he continued, imperturbably, pointing to Webster. "Driver, isn't he? I'll have his name and address, too—you see," he continued, scribbling down the chauffeur's information, "you can't get too many particulars in these cases, Captain, as no doubt you're well aware. Now, for all that we know, one o' you two might be the guilty party in this matter, and then where should I be if I hadn't got particulars about you?"

"Where, indeed?" I responded. "Pray don't fail to ask for more if you want them. You'll find Webster and me here at any moment."

Neither he nor the reporter smiled at the obvious sarcasm: their faces remained as grave as an undertaker's, and with a final remark from the sergeant to the effect that this was a bad job, and he expected it to work out as he had predicted, they went away.

What the local police did I don't know, but when darkness fell that night I was still without news of Mazaroff. Nor did we get any during the next day, and when the third night after his disappearance came, I began to feel certain that that disappearance was premeditated and intentional, and that he had just cleared out in order to avoid the revelations of which he had spoken to me. Taking him altogether, I thought he was the sort of man to do this. And yet, there was no need for it—he could have gone away with me, and the car, and Webster. As it was, Webster, the car, and I were left behind.

It was just coming grey dawn on the third morning, and I was awake, wondering what to do, when a knock came at my door. I sprang out of bed, opened it, and found Musgrave and Webster, half-dressed, in the passage. The landlord gave me a look.

"They've found him!" he whispered. "Least-ways, they've found——"

He seemed to choke at that, and I turned eagerly to the chauffeur. He, too, showed signs of unwillingness. But he got some words out.

"They've found a body, Mr Holt," he said. "Some place on the Moors——"

"Reiver's Den," interrupted Musgrave. "Foot of the rocks there."

"And brought it here," continued Webster. "It—the fact is, sir, the—the head's—the features, you know—gone! But the clothes, sir—they're his!"

I dressed hastily and went down with them to the outhouse wherein its finders, a local policeman and a game-watcher, had laid the body. I am not going into details about it here—but, as somebody muttered, there were stoats and weasels and similar carnivorous animals in hundreds on those moors. Still, those were Mazaroff's clothes, and there was the birth-mark he had told me of.

"At the foot of the rocks, in Reiver's Den it was, amongst a mass of bracken," whispered the local policeman. "It struck us to take a look and—and we found it. Like—that!"

The news had already spread, and Manners, the sergeant who had questioned me, came hurrying along. He examined the clothing. There was not as much as a penny-piece left in the pockets; watch, chain, rings, pocket-book, papers, were all gone. He turned on me with a look that was as triumphant as it was significant.

"What did I tell you. Captain?" he murmured. "Didn't I say murder and robbery? And wasn't I right? What could be plainer?"

I made no answer. I was thinking of other things. However he had come by his death, the fact remained that Mazaroff was dead. And there was I, as far as I knew, the only person in the world who knew his secret—a secret which meant that I should presently have to carry this strangest of stories to Marrasdale Tower.

CHAPTER 6 MR CROLE
OF BEDFORD ROW

I'll give Manners, the local police-sergeant, this credit—although he was a pig-headed, one-idea'd fellow, clinging obstinately to his original theory that Mazaroff had been followed on the moor by some of the riff-raff who had been about the Woodcock that night, and murdered by them for what he had on him, he did his best to save me trouble. I was utterly at a loss what to do, and the necessary immediate proceedings were matters of perplexity. But Manners knew everything, and took everything in hand.

"What's to be done. Captain?" he said, repeating my question. "This is to be done. He'll have to be laid out here—there's no mortuary in this wilderness. Then I notify the coroner. He'll hold his inquest here, at the Woodcock, likely some time tomorrow. There'll not be much done then—just elementary particulars and identification, so that he can be interred. The inquest'll be adjourned. And then—we set to work to find the murderers. Plain as a pikestaff."

"You think it is murder?" I questioned. "He may have fallen from those rocks that they speak of, you know?"

Manners curled his moustache with an air of superiority.

"Where's his money, and his diamond ring and pin, and his pocket-book, and what not?" he asked sarcastically. "No, Captain, it's as I've said all along—murder first, robbery afterwards. My notion," he continued impressively, "is this here—he was followed and struck down in some lonely place by these fellows. Then they went through him, and took all he had. Then they carried him to the top of Reiver's Den, and flung him over. That's how I work it out. And I lay I'm not far wrong!"

"I suppose you may trace the murderers through their trying to dispose of the things they took from him?" I suggested. "Valuables like those——"

"You're right. Captain," he agreed. "That's just what we shall do. And what I want you to do now, so that I can show it to our inspector, is to make out a list, as near as you can do it, of what he had on him. For as you say, valuables like those aren't so readily got rid of. Put it down on paper—accurate—Captain."

Before I could begin this task, Eccleshare came to the Woodcock. He had heard of the discovery, he said, and had hurried over from High Cap Lodge to offer his professional services. And just then, up drove the local doctor, on the same errand. The two of them went to the room where the dead man had been laid out. They were there some time. At last Eccleshare came back, alone. His manner was severely professional.

"Mr Holt," he said, as the police-sergeant and I approached him, "your friend has been shot."

He made this announcement with a curious gravity. But Manners and I both let out exclamations of astonishment.

"Shot, doctor?" said the police-sergeant. "Why, I never noticed——"

"Perhaps not," interrupted Eccleshare quietly. "But you noticed that some wild animal or animals had destroyed the features, and it perhaps didn't occur to you to examine the back part of the head. He wore his hair rather long, and it was unusually thick for a man of his age. He was shot through the head, from behind; shot dead. And by an ordinary fowling-piece. Look there!"

He held out a plump, smooth white hand, unclosed it, and showed us, lying in the palm, a couple of pellets.

"Riddled!" he said significantly. "That's number twelve shot. And that's how he came by his death. Shot, from an ordinary fowling-piece, at close quarters."

I saw that Manners was considerably taken aback by this opinion, which was corroborated by the local doctor, who just then came out and joined us. It upset the police-sergeant's theory, for it was not likely that the cattle-drovers whom he suspected would carry a gun.

"Well, gentlemen, if it is so, it is so," he muttered. "But—who'd be likely to be out on those moors with a gun after dark?"

"That's for you to find out," said Eccleshare. "We simply tell you the cause of death. There's no doubt about that."

The two medical men went away, Eccleshare previously turning to me and saying that if there was anything he could do for me, I was to let him know, and Manners, for the first time, betrayed symptoms of uneasiness.

"This is a queer business. Captain!" he said. "Shot! That never came into my reckoning. And as I said just now, who could have been out with a gun at that time? Dark!"

"It wasn't dark when he went out," I remarked. "It was scarcely dusk."

"In that case——" he began, and then paused, as if reflecting.

"There's a fair lot of people who take out gun licences about here," he continued. "Gentlemen, farmers, keepers, such-like. Well!—I must be doing something. But now, about him?—you know where his relations are to be found, of course? They'll have to be communicated with at once. Better telegraph to 'em."

The predicament! There it was—full facing me. But I was not going to tell this somewhat thick-headed policeman that Salim Mazaroff was really Andrew Merchison, and that his wife and daughter were within a mile of us.

"Mr Mazaroff had only just arrived from South Africa when he and I set out on this journey," I replied. "He had not been in England for many years."

"Well, friends, then," he suggested. "There'll be somebody in this country that ought to be told. Lawyers, now—a wealthy man 'ud have lawyers, to be sure."

"I'll look through his papers, upstairs, and see what address I can find," I answered evasively. "There'll be something, of course."

He left me then, saying that he must go and report at the market-town, and as it was now near breakfast time, I made shift to swallow some food. But in truth I was in no mood for eating and drinking. That secret of Mazaroff's weighed on me like lead. Ought I to keep it to myself?—or ought I to go straight to Marrasdale Tower and tell Mrs Elphinstone what I knew? It seemed to me that I ought, for there was this about the situation—if Mazaroff was really Merchison, then his wealth (and I was something more than certain that he was very wealthy) would surely go to his wife and daughter. Yet it was no pleasant task that confronted me. I had taken rather a fancy to old Elphinstone—it would be highly distasteful to walk in on him and tell him that his wife's first husband had been alive all the time—and so on. And there was Sheila, with whom—it was useless to deny it—I was already in love: I loathed the idea of having to tell her that the father she had never known had been foully murdered at her very door! Yet——

Even then the advice I was longing for was coming to me as quickly as an old horse and a ramshackle fly from the station beyond the hills could carry it. Such an equipage drove up to the Woodcock as I left the breakfast table, and from it descended first a keen-looking, sharp-featured, middle-aged man, whom I at once set down as either a solicitor or a barrister, and second, a younger man, smart, alert, well-dressed, who was something of a cross between a military man and a fashionable actor. They hurried into the hall; through the open door of my sitting-room I heard my name spoken. I went forward: the legal-looking man turned and gave me a sharp inspection.

"Mr Holt?" he said. "I am Mr Lincoln Crole, of Crole & Wyatt, Solicitors, Bedford Row. I heard of Mr Mazaroff's strange disappearance from the London papers last night, and I caught the night mail here. Now, has Mr Mazaroff been found—or heard of?"

"Yes," I replied. "He was found this morning. Dead. Murdered."

He gave two successive starts at the last two words—then pointed to the room which I had just left.

"Let us go in there," he said. "This," he went on, as I led them in and closed the door, "is Mr Frank Maythorne, whom you may have heard of as one of the cleverest private enquiry agents living. Now, Mr Holt, let me explain—as I said just now, I read about this matter in the papers—your name, of course, appeared—and as I have acted professionally for Mr Mazaroff since his coming to England, I was much concerned. Finally, I decided to come down here, and to bring Maythorne with me: I knew, you see, that Mazaroff has no friends or relations in this country, if anywhere, and—well, for certain reasons I was anxious about him. Now we know the worst! But we have travelled all night, and as we couldn't get any breakfast at Black Gill Junction, where we left the Scotch mail, we must get some here, and you must post us up while we eat."

I was unfeignedly glad to see Mr Crole and his companion: it was a positive relief to be able to share that awful secret with men accustomed to deal with such matters. I ordered breakfast for them, and while they ate and drank, I sat with them, and Mr Crole and I exchanged preliminaries. He was a good man to deal with—lucid, precise, and explicit in his statements.

"I'll tell you in a few sentences all that I know of Mazaroff, Mr Holt," he said, as he set to work on his eggs and bacon. "He introduced himself to me a few weeks ago at my office in Bedford Row. He told me that he was an Englishman who had been out of England for many years, and during his absence had amassed a large fortune in India and in South Africa, and especially in South Africa. He said that he'd now returned to this country for good, and he wanted to buy a really nice house in London and settle down in it. He had heard of our firm as notable conveyancing solicitors, and had come to see if I could help him. I promised to look out a likely house for him while he took this tour in the North—and that's practically all."

"I don't know much more," I said. "I can tell you how I came to know him——"

He interrupted me with a smile and a wave of the hand.

"Oh, I know all about that, and about you, Mr Holt!" he exclaimed. "When Mazaroff put that advertisement in *The Times*, he brought the applications to me—most of 'em, anyway. We picked out half a dozen of the likeliest, and I went thoroughly into the qualifications and references. It was I who advised him to fix up with you. You got on together?"

"Splendidly!—admirably!" I said. "No one could have been kinder, more considerate than he was—we'd grown to be very close friends."

"Aye!" he replied. "He seemed a likeable and kindly man. But now, as you'd got so friendly, I wonder if you'd observed something about Mazaroff's habits—something, to be plain with you, that caused me alarm, and sent me off, up here, with Maythorne there, as soon as ever I read of his disappearance. Had you?"

"I can't say that I had," I answered.

He bent across the table, eyeing Maythorne and myself significantly.

"I lunched and dined with Mazaroff two or three times," he said in a low voice. "And I learned a bit about him. Aren't you aware, Mr Holt, that he carried diamonds in his pockets—loose! —as if they'd been so many half-pence?"

That gave me a genuine start of astonishment.

"No, indeed!" I exclaimed. "I never saw him produce any diamonds—never!"

Crole laughed—dryly.

"I only hope he left them behind him in London, then," he said. "But I doubt it, even if you didn't see them. He'd made the greater part of his fortune in that sort of thing, and I tell you that he carried, loose on him, stones that looked to me to be worth—no end! I remonstrated with him, but he only laughed. Now—ask Maythorne there what he thinks, professionally."

Maythorne, who had been occupied in devoting himself to one of Mrs Musgrave's very fine cold hams, smiled.

"I think that a man who carries loose diamonds in his pockets, and pulls them out in public places, as you say Mazaroff did, is asking for trouble," he remarked. "And the probability is that he was followed here."

"I never saw any suspicious characters here—or anywhere else during our journey," I observed.

"You wouldn't!" said Maythorne dryly. Then, becoming gravely attentive, he added: "Just give us the plain facts up to now, Mr Holt—briefly."

I told them of all that had happened from the moment of Mazaroff's going out alone on the moor to the bringing of his mutilated body to the Woodcock that morning. And all the time, an undercurrent of something between resolve and hesitation was running in my mind—should I tell the secret to these two? Yet, I knew very well that I should, and suddenly, making sure that nobody would interrupt us, I told them, word for word, of all that had passed between me and Mazaroff on the second evening of our stay at the Woodcock.

They were good listeners—and of the sort that gives absolute attention and makes no comment, until a story is told. But as soon as I had finished, Crole spoke, sharply and decisively.

"I believe all that!" he said. "I felt sure there was a queer mystery about Mazaroff. Well, there it is! And the next thing is—it'll have to be told to Mrs Elphinstone, who is really Mrs Merchison. And at once!"

"The sooner the better," agreed Maythorne. "Because—there are things by which he can be identified, that birth-mark, for instance."

"Yes, at once," declared Crole. "He may have died—probably has died—intestate. He made no mention to me of any will. If he has died intestate, and his identity as Merchison is established, then this lady and her daughter benefit: the daughter mainly, of course. Holt, you and I must go to this place—what is it, Marrasdale Tower?—immediately. A fine revelation!"

"A job I don't like," I remarked.

"No doubt—but there'll be a lot to do that none of us will

48

like before we're through with this," he said, with a grim smile. "Come, you and I will go, and leave Maythorne to his own devices. He'll not be idle."

I presently led Crole across the moor in the direction of Marrasdale Tower, giving him on the way some account of the people he would meet there. We met one of them before we reached the gates—Sheila was just coming out, and I saw at once that she had heard the news.

CHAPTER 7 THE MEMORIAL TABLET

The solicitor—a naturally observant man—jogged my elbow while we were yet some twenty or thirty yards away from Sheila.

"The daughter, eh?" he whispered. "Fine girl!—pretty girl. Knows nothing, of course?"

"Nothing!" I replied. Then, I, too, whispered: "You'll remember that Mazaroff had a decided cast of the left eye? Yes—well, she has, too!—the very slightest; scarcely noticeable, but there."

"Adds piquancy, sometimes," he said knowingly. "Well, the mother; first. Leave it all to me, Holt—I know how to manage these affairs. Professional experience, you know."

I was only too glad to leave everything to him, and I said so. But now we were close to Sheila; she came up to me with genuine sympathy expressed on her pretty face.

"I'm so sorry to hear this bad news," she said quickly. "I suppose it's true?—we've only heard very little."

"True enough," I answered. Then, as she glanced at my companion, I said, "This gentleman is Mr Mazaroff's solicitor—Mr Crole. He's just arrived from London—and he's anxious to see Mrs Elphinstone."

She showed no surprise at this; probably she thought that Crole wanted to ask some questions about the neighbourhood. She turned back to the house, motioning us to follow.

"Mother is somewhere about," she remarked. "Mr Elphinstone

has gone to a magistrates' meeting—he won't be home until afternoon."

She led us through the gardens and into the house; we found Mrs Elphinstone in the morning-room, buried with letters and papers at her bureau. She gave us an unmistakably questioning look as we entered; it seemed, indeed, not too friendly, and I heard Crole make a little sound under his breath as if he realised an inimical atmosphere. But Sheila, after her fashion, relieved us by going straight to the point.

"Mother!" she said. "It's quite true about this unfortunate Mr Mazaroff. He's been found dead on the moor, and this is his solicitor, Mr Crole, from London, and he wants to see you."

Mrs Elphinstone stared at Crole as if she had just heard that he had come to ask for her daughter's hand or some other equally outrageous thing. She was one of those women who can make people uncomfortable by simply staring at them, and had she stared at me as she stared at Crole I should have turned and fled. But Crole remained quite at his ease, and his bow was as frigid as Mrs Elphinstone's manner.

"Merely to be permitted to ask a few pertinent questions arising out of the death of my client," he said. "I may mention, first, a fact of which perhaps neither of you is aware. Mr Mazaroff was murdered!"

This announcement produced different effects on its two hearers. Sheila made a low murmur of horrified astonishment; Mrs Elphinstone gave Crole a quick glance.

"Are you sure of that?" she asked.

"That is the medical opinion, ma'am," replied Crole, with another frigid bow. "I know of no reason to dispute it. My client was shot—dead."

Mrs Elphinstone pointed a finger to chairs near her desk.

"Won't you sit down?" she said, with faint politeness. "You say you want to ask me some questions—pertinent questions? I really can't conceive what they can be! I know nothing whatever about this poor man."

"I think you saw my late client the other day?" suggested

Crole, whom I had fully posted in every particular of our stay at the Woodcock. "He and Mr Holt were standing at the garden gate of the inn when you and your daughter passed by."

"Oh, that!" exclaimed Mrs Elphinstone. "Yes, I suppose I did see him—a tall, bearded man, wasn't he? I just glanced at him."

"You didn't recognise him, ma'am?" asked Crole, with a keen look.

Mrs Elphinstone gave her questioner a particularly freezing stare.

"Recognise him?" she demanded haughtily. "Really!—what do you mean?"

I had been hoping that Crole would gradually approach the revelation which he had come to make—for some reason, vague enough, but still there, I did not want the truth blurting clean out suddenly before Sheila. But Crole had different views, and in the next instant he had expressed them.

"What I mean, ma'am, is this," he answered bluntly. "The man whom you saw, though he has of late years called himself Salim Mazaroff, was the man whom you married some years ago—Andrew Merchison. A fact, ma'am!"

I expected something—say, dramatic—to follow on this. But nothing happened—that is, nothing particular. Sheila's lips opened a little in astonishment, and her eyes turned from Crole to her mother. As for Mrs Elphinstone, sitting bolt upright, very stern and dignified, at her desk, she might have been carved in stone for any change that came over her countenance. She looked at Crole as if she was seriously wondering whether he was an insolent liar or a crazy lunatic. Suddenly, and swiftly, a satirical, contemptuous smile showed itself round the corners of her finely-cut thin lips, and she rose quietly from her chair.

"Follow me, if you please," she said.

We followed her, in silence—Crole first, Sheila and I in the rear. Sheila looked as if she wanted to speak to me: I purposely kept my face averted. Although Mrs Elphinstone was ahead of us, her presence was there, and it was a bit too awe-inspiring for me—I had rather have faced a battalion of Huns: it seemed, somehow, as if she was leading Crole and myself to instant execution, or, at any rate, to incarceration in some adjacent dungeon.

She marched us through two or three rooms, into the hall, out of the house, across the grounds, and to a doorway set in the East wall of the gardens. Opening this, she passed through; we followed, and found ourselves in the village churchyard, amongst ancient yew-trees and tapering cypresses. Straight ahead she went, looking neither to right nor left, and so through the porch of the church, and under its fine old Norman doorway into the shadowy nave. Marching up that to the chancel, she suddenly paused, pointed upward, and giving Crole a frowning look, spoke two words: "Look there!"

We looked. There, on the North wall of the chancel, was a plain, square tablet of Aberdeen granite, whereon were deeply incised and gilded a few words.

In Memory of
ANDREW MERCHISON,
Sometime Resident in this Parish.
Drowned in Mombasa Bay, October 17th, 1899.

I glanced at Crole. His face was inscrutable. He merely looked at the tablet, read the inscription, and turned, with a nod, to Mrs Elphinstone.

"Now come back to the house," she commanded. Once more we fell into line, following her. I was by this time filled with all sorts of doubts and perplexities. Had Mazaroff told me the truth? Was he some man posing as Andrew Merchison? Were there two men who had corresponding marks and blemishes? What did it all mean? And had these things anything to do with the murder?

Mrs Elphinstone marched us back to the house, and up the old oak staircase that led from the big hall. She went along one corridor after another until she came to a door. Selecting a key from a bunch that hung by a silver chain from her waist, she unlocked the door, and ushered us into a small room, wherein there was nothing but an old-fashioned bureau, a chair set before it, a book-case filled with old volumes, and a side-table, whereon lay a much-worn cabin trunk. She went straight to this and laid a hand on it.

"Now," she said, looking at Crole. "I am doing more than anyone has the right to ask me to do! I am only doing it to set at rest, once and for all, the utterly ridiculous idea that you mentioned when you came here—uninvited. You will please listen to me!— It is quite true that I married Andrew Merchison, when he and I were very young and foolish and headstrong. We did not get on. He made full provision for me: shared equally all he had with me, in fact, and left me: I didn't know when he went, nor where he went: he left word that he was going to travel. Eight months later, this girl was born. I and my friends did our best to find him, and make him acquainted with that fact: we failed. I never heard anything of him until the early part of the year 1900, when I got a letter from the Captain of a steamer which traded between Bombay and Durban. You shall read it."

She produced another key, unlocked the cabin trunk, and from a pocket inside it took out an envelope, from which she withdrew a letter written on several sheets of foreign note-paper. She handed it to Crole.

"You and Mr Holt can read that together," she said. "Read it carefully."

I read the letter over Crole's shoulder. It was from one James Sinclair, who introduced himself as Captain of the S.S. *General Clive*, trading as a rule between Bombay and Durban. He said that on his last voyage from Bombay he had taken on board at that port a passenger named Andrew Merchison, whom he described: Mr Merchison was bound for Durban. In the course of the voyage, a stay was made off Mombasa. On the 18th October, the steamer being at anchor in Mombasa Bay, Mr Merchison disappeared. He was last seen, rather late at night, sitting on a rail of the ship, aft, smoking his pipe. No one ever saw him again. The writer's belief was that Mr Merchison had had a sudden attack of faintness or giddiness, lost his balance, and fallen overboard, probably striking his head against the side of the ship as he fell. He added, naively, "the waters of Mombasa Bay are thickly infested by sharks." Nothing being discovered about his passenger, he had examined his effects, found Mrs Merchison's address in a memorandum book, and therefore now wrote to her and at the same time forwarded Mr Merchison's cabin trunk, and all that it contained, with other small matters lying about his cabin: he drew particular attention to the fact that in a pocket in the trunk there was a considerable sum of money in gold, chiefly in English sovereigns.

The solicitor read this letter through in silence, and silently handed it back to Mrs Elphinstone. She replaced it in the trunk.

"This trunk and its contents have remained intact ever since I received them, now many years ago," she said. "Now you come and tell me that this stranger, calling himself Mazaroff, was in reality Andrew Merchison! Absurd!"

"Nothing absurd, ma'am, in my telling you that," retorted Crole, with the least touch of asperity. "As you will see when you hear what our young friend here has to tell. Now, Holt," he went on, turning to me, "you will just tell us precisely what Mazaroff confided to you, the second night of your stay at the Woodcock. Tell the whole story."

I told the whole story, as we all stood there in that little room. I left nothing out: I laid stress on Mazaroff's assertion that he could easily substantiate his identity, and how, and on the utter confidence with which he spoke of the matter. But, though I watched Mrs Elphinstone closely during my narrative, I saw no sign of any wavering on her part; instead, there was incredulity, scepticism, even ridicule in her expression.

"The thing's absurd!" she declared in the end. "Utterly absurd! The man was probably some adventurer who had got hold of certain facts about Merchison's past history, and wanted to make money out of his knowledge!"

I glanced at Crole, and Crole looked at Mrs Elphinstone as if he were sizing her up in a new light.

"Um!" he said quietly. "Now that, ma'am, if you will pardon me for using plain speech to a lady, is indeed an utterly absurd suggestion! Mr Mazaroff, or, as we should call him, Mr Merchison—though he had a perfectly legal right to the other name, according to his own account—so far from being a needy adventurer, was a wealthy man, a very wealthy man! And if you will pardon me still further, I will just put something before you. If this man was, as he asserted himself to be, and as we shall probably prove, Andrew Merchison, who married you twenty-two or three years ago, your second marriage with Mr Elphinstone is no marriage'at all! You are, of course, protected from any consequences of such a marriage by the fact that when it was contracted you had not heard of Merchison for many years, and had the best grounds for believing him to be dead. But as he was not dead, you are still, in law, Mrs Merchison, and——"

"What is all this leading up to?" demanded Mrs Elphinstone. "I ——"

"To this, ma'am," continued Crole, lifting an admonitory finger, "and a very important point, too, as you will quickly see. Although I have had very little dealing with this unfortunate man, I have had some dealing, while he was in London, and it is my distinct impression that he has died intestate. You understand me, of course—that he has left no will."

"Well—and what has that to do with me?" questioned Mrs Elphinstone.

"Merely this," retorted Crole, picking up his hat, which he had laid aside while he read Captain Sinclair's letter. "Merely this, ma'am. If he was Merchison, and you his wife, and this young lady your child, you and she come in, between you, for every penny he's left! And there will be a great many pennies, or I'm a Dutchman! My advice to you, ma'am, is this—before settling on an attitude of incredulity and denial, just step across to the Woodcock, and see if you cannot satisfy yourself that the man lying there, sadly disfigured, but identifiable, was not the man he claimed to be? *Verbum sapienti*, ma'am—I dare say you know enough Latin to know what that means!"

With this Crole made one of his old-fashioned bows and walked out, and I followed him, leaving mother and daughter standing looking at each other. We went through the house and out into the gardens, in silence. As we passed the gates, Crole pulled out a snuff-box and took a hearty pinch.

"That's a damned flint-like woman, Holt!" he said cynically. "Hard—hard—and obstinate!"

CHAPTER 8 THE LANDLORD'S GUN

My own impressions of Mrs Elphinstone were precisely those which Mr Crole expressed so emphatically. But I was just then thinking of other matters.

"If the real Andrew Merchison was drowned in Mombasa Bay," I said, "how could——"

Crole interrupted me with a sharp, sceptical laugh.

"Aye, but was he so drowned—there, or elsewhere, or any-where?" he exclaimed. "My own belief is that he was never drowned at all!"

"But the letter—and his belongings?" I suggested. "What can one make——"

"Oh, I can make a lot!" retorted Crole. "From what bit I saw of him, and from your account of him, Mazaroff, or Merchison, was a queerish chap, all his life. I can quite understand that he just disappeared at Mombasa, for good reasons of his own. What easier? For all that Sinclair, the writer of that letter, knew, Mer-chison had arranged for a boat to come off for him at a certain hour at night—it comes, and he slips off into it and is clean gone. Easy!"

"Leaving his money and things behind him?" I questioned.

"He could have sent money and things—especially money —ahead of him to wherever he was bound, said Crole dryly. "Didn't you tell me he spoke of Durban?"

"Of Durban, yes," I answered. "It was there he took the name of

Mazaroff."

"Aye, well," continued Crole, "no doubt he'd some reason—other than the one he told you of—for leaving his old name behind him. He may have wished folk in both England and India to believe that Andrew Merchison was dead. But letter or no letter, cabin trunk or no cabin trunk, monument or no monument, I believe that Salim Mazaroff was Andrew Merchison, and that he was murdered as Merchison, and not as Mazaroff."

"As—Merchison?" I exclaimed, pausing in sheer surprise. "But —who knew him, here, as Merchison?"

"That's got to be found out, my lad!" he answered, with a knowing look. "Come on—let's see what Maythorne's up to."

We found Maythorne standing at the door of the inn, in company with Musgrave: Maythorne gave Crole a sort of informing smile as we came up to them.

"Mr Musgrave has just made a discovery," he said. "His gun is missing."

Musgrave, to whom we turned instinctively, made a sullen movement of his head; he was evidently vexed.

"Not three months since I gave twenty pounds for it!" he muttered. "Very near brand new it was! Couldn't have believed it could ha' been taken from there, neither. But of course, it's been done that night we'd all that crowd in. Still——"

"And where was it taken from?" asked Crole.

"It was taken from the private sitting-room that Mr Holt there and the dead gentleman had," replied the landlord, with a glance at me. "Hung on the wall, on two hooks it was, just inside the door—you may ha' noticed it, Mr Holt?"

"Yes, I noticed a gun there, certainly," I replied. "But—I hadn't noticed that it had gone."

"Nor me—only I haven't been into that room this last two or three days," said Musgrave. "It was the missis that found it out —she came to me about it just now. Of course, some o' them drover chaps poked their noses in there, and seeing nobody about, helped themselves to it!—easy enough, that would be. Neither you nor your friend were in much that night, I think, Mr

Holt?"

"Mr Mazaroff went out soon after dinner," I answered, "and, as you know, he never returned. I was out myself for some time. So the room would, of course, be empty."

Musgrave growled and shook his head.

"I ought to ha' seen that the door was locked when you gentlemen went out," he remarked ruefully. "Well—I'll have to set the police on to it."

"Was the gun loaded?" asked Maythorne. "I suppose not?"

"Well, it was," admitted Musgrave. "I kept it loaded—you never know what you may want in a lonely place like this. Of course, nobody but me was expected to touch it, and the hooks are a good height up the wall."

"Dangerous, though, to keep a loaded gun about, don't you think?" said Maythorne good-humouredly. "Doesn't take the fraction of a minute to slip a cartridge in. By the bye, what sort of cartridges were there in your gun?"

"Kynoch's number twelves," replied Musgrave Promptly. "Always use those."

"That might help you in tracing the gun," remarked Maythorne. "You should tell the police that." He turned from the landlord towards the moor, motioning Crole and myself to follow him. "I'm going to have a look at this Reiver's Den," he said. "Better come with me. Odd, isn't it, that Musgrave's gun, loaded with number twelves, should disappear on the very night on which Mazaroff is shot dead? Didn't you tell us, Mr Holt, that the doctor showed you some shot which he called number twelves?"

"He did," I assented.

"I suppose this doctor—what's his name—Eccleshare?—knows number twelves from number tens?" he suggested. "There's a difference, eh?"

"He's a shooting man himself," I replied. "Staying at High Cap Lodge with a shooting party."

"Ah, then he'd know what he was talking about," he remarked, and turned from me to Crole. "Well—and Mrs Elphinstone?"

Crole told him all about our doings at Marrasdale Tower as we walked across the moor. He listened and said little—already he struck me as the sort of man who takes everything in and gives next to nothing out. But I noticed that his eyes grew brighter and his whole air more alert when we came to Reiver's Den—a dark, rock-bound cavity, or coombe, in the heart of the moor, lying in a ravine between the hamlet of Birkside and High Cap Lodge; black, gloomy, eerie; just the place tor murderous deeds. There was a local policeman on guard there; he told us that he was to stay there until the inspector and the Chief Constable arrived, and he showed us the place where Mazaroff's body had lain and been discovered. This was amongst a mass of gorse and bramble at the foot of an almost perpendicular rock, some thirty to forty feet in height: the policeman pointed to the top of it.

"My mate, what found him," he said in a confidential whisper, "he says as how when he first come across him, he thought as the gentleman had fallen over them crags in the darkness. But of course he hadn't—and 'cause why? If he'd ha' fallen from there, he'd ha' broken his neck and every bone in his body; big, heavy man like that he was. And there wasn't no bones broken. My impression, gentlemen, is as how he was murdered first, and carried here afterwards. Look how these here shrubs is trampled down!"

Maythorne was closely examining the surroundings: I noticed that he, too, was apparently struck by the evident trampling of the gorse and bramble. Once or twice he stooped, as if to look closer at his objects—once I saw him pick something from the ground and thrust it into his waistcoat pocket. Presently he came back to where Crole and I stood with the policeman. He swung his walking-cane jauntily towards the formidable wall of rock above us.

"If a gun were fired in this ravine, those rocks would give back a fine reverberation," he observed. Then he looked at the policeman. "You didn't hear anything that night?" he asked with a smile. "Though I suppose your beat isn't far off?"

"I heard nothing," agreed the policeman. "Out that night I was, from dusk, all along top side of the moor, and never heard no unusual sound at all. Don't know nobody as did, neither. There's a cottage close by here—just back o' that clump o' beech —the folks there, they didn't hear nothing. Not—nothing whatsoever!"

"Oh, there's a cottage there, is there?" said Maythorne. "And who lives in it?"

"Old shepherd and his missis—Jim Cowie, his name is," replied the policeman. "I was talking to him about this affair just now—they heard nothing. As I said before."

Maythorne turned away, towards the clump of beech. We followed him, along a narrow track that ran at the foot of the rocks, under the lower branches of the trees, and past a high hedge that enclosed a garden and a stone-walled, heavily-roofed cottage. We went up a flagged path to the cottage door; Maythorne knocked; a woman's voice, shrill and cracked, bade us enter.

A pleasant smell of something good greeted our nostrils as Maythorne lifted the latch; inside, it a round table drawn up in front of a turf fire, an old man and an old woman sat eating their dinner. At sight of us, the old woman rose politely, but the old man stuck to his seat, eyeing us with no friendly glance. He got in the first word, too, surlily, and with no good temper, before Maythorne could address, him.

"Don't know nothing about that there affair in. the Den yonder!" he growled. "Tell'd the policeman just now we neither heard nor see'd anything, and don't want no bother about it. We didn't hear no shooting that night—couldn't, 'cause we goes to bed as soon as 'tis dark. And if you be come about the crowner's 'quest, I ain't nothing to tell, and, don't want for to come to it— something else to do!"

My good friend!" said Maythorne soothingly. "We're not from the coroner, nor from anybody else. We only wanted to ask you where this footpath that crosses Reiver's Den, and goes outside your garden, leads to? We're strangers."

"There now, master!" remarked the old woman, glancing reprovingly at the old man. "You see now!—this gentleman's only asking his way. You mustn't mind him, sir," she went on, turning to Maythorne. "He's had two or three asking him about this terrible affair, and of course he knows nothing. The path, sir?—it leads across the moor to High Cap Lodge, sir; Mr Courthope's place."

"Then it makes a short cut to—where, now?" asked Maythorne.

"Well, sir, it's a short cut from Mr Courthope's to Birnside, and to the Woodcock," replied the old woman. "But it's little used, sir—it's little better than a sheep-track."

"And we didn't see nobody along it that night, neither one way nor t'other," growled the old man. "Don't know nothing—ain't got nothing to tell—nothing!"

We backed out, closed the door, and went away. Maythorne smiled—inscrutably.

"All the same, Mazaroff followed this path," he said. "Why? Did he want to go to High Cap Lodge?—Mr Courthope's place? Or—had he been there and was coming away from it? Who knows? However, I want to go up to the top of those rocks."

He turned off the path, and began to make his way to the head of the ravine through the scrub and undergrowth: Crole and I followed. It was stiff work, climbing and scrambling up there; at last we came out on a sort of plateau, overlooking the black depths in which Mazaroff's body had been found. And there, a solitary figure, staring out over the widespread view of moor and fell, stood another old man, older, it seemed, than the crusty and ancient fellow we had just left; greyer, more gnarled and wrinkled, but erect and alert, and evidently quick of hearing as a boy, for at the first sound of our approach he turned sharply upon us, with swift, appraising glances from eyes as clear and bright as a hawk's. But this was no shepherd—we saw at once that he was a man of some standing: a gentleman. His somewhat well-worn clothes, of grey tweed and rather large pattern, of the sort affected by sporting men, were fashionably cut and carefully put on; there was a fine old cameo in his white neckcloth; his shooting boots had been scrupulously cleaned by a servant who knew how to do such things; altogether, he was a well-turned-out old chap, and his healthy colour and snow-white moustache added to his quite distinguished appearance. He stood watching us until we were close to him; then, suddenly, he gave Crole, as the eldest of our party, an understanding smile.

"The place already attracts the curious, sir?" he observed, half-ironically. "Odd!—how quickly this sort of news spreads abroad!"

"We have something more than idle curiosity to bring us here, sir," retorted Crole, almost sharply. "We are the dead gentleman's friends!"

The old man nodded—neither Crole's words nor manner seemed to impress him in any way.

"I suppose he'd have friends—yes!" he muttered, as if to himself. Then he glanced them all over, and his keen inspection settled on me. "Is that the young gentleman who was with him at the inn?" he asked.

"You're quite right in your surmise, sir," replied Crole. "May I in my turn ask—as you seem interested in the matter—if you can tell us anything to help us?"

The old man smiled, and looked from one to the other.

"Can I tell you anything to help you?" he repeated. "Well, I could tell you of something, but whether it will help you or not I don't know. Yet—it might. I heard a gun discharged—hereabouts—on the night this man was missed."

"That's something!" said Crole. "And—you were near, sir?"

The old man turned and pointed down the moor towards Birnside.

"You see the place there?—a mere hamlet—Birnside," he said. "I live there. It is, as you will observe, only two or three hundred yards away. That is my house on this edge of the place—you see the gables?"

"And about what time would that be?" enquired Crole.

"About what is usually my bed-time," replied the old fellow.

"Ten o'clock. That night, however, I was up later than usual."

Crole looked at Maythorne.

"That must have been the shot," he said musingly. "I suppose, sir," he went on, turning to our informant—"I suppose it would be a very unusual thing to hear a gun discharged on this moor at such an hour? Ten o'clock at night!"

But the old gentleman smiled and shook his head.

"Not at all," he answered. "Far from it. I often hear a stray shot in the night. Keepers, you know. Of course, that's more likely to occur on clear or moonlit nights. This, however, was a rather dark night. But——"

What further he was going to say, I don't know. Just then the policeman at the foot of the rocks, whom I had been watching while the talking was going on, and had seen to be pottering about the bushes, looked up, and waved his hand excitedly.

"Come down here!" he shouted. "I've found something. A gun!"

CHAPTER 9 THE CAPE TOWN POSTMARK

This sudden announcement on the part of the policeman occasioned a general start of surprise. But it went further in the case of the old gentleman. He let out an exclamation which seemed to indicate absolute astonishment.

"A gun!" he said. "Impossible!"

I saw Maythorne glance at him—a shrewd, questioning glance, as if he wondered what the old fellow meant. But he said nothing, nor did Crole—we all began to descend the rocks to the dense undergrowth amidst which the policeman stood. He was gingerly handling a sporting gun, and as we drew up to him, he nodded towards a clump of overgrown gorse.

"Shoved in beneath that!" he exclaimed. "That's where it was. There was a glint of the sun on the barrels—that's how I came to clap eyes on it. Bit rusted, here and there—that's along of the dews."

Maythorne silently held out a hand, and the policeman, after a remark about the danger of playing with firearms, passed the gun over to him. He opened the breech—there were two cartridges in the barrels; one, in the choke-bore barrel, had been discharged. Maythorne glanced at Crole.

"Odd!" he said. "Why didn't he use the right-hand barrel?"

The old gentleman, who seemed to be fascinated by the sight of a weapon that had doubtless been used by a murderer, laughed a little.

"If that's the gun that was used to shoot this young gentleman's elderly companion," he remarked, "as I, personally, have no doubt it was, there's a good reason why the murderer used the left-hand barrel. Perhaps," he added, looking slyly at Maythorne, "you're not a shooting man, sir?—if not, I may tell you that the left-hand barrel of a fowling-piece is always narrowed in the bore as it approaches the muzzle: the notion, of course, is that the shot, or discharge, is concentrated rather than diffused. If a man wanted to shoot another man dead, at close quarters, as in this case, he'd naturally use the choke-bore barrel in preference to the other."

"Much obliged to you, sir," replied Maythorne. "What you say inclines me to a definite conclusion—that the murderer was a man who was thoroughly accustomed to the use of guns of this sort, and that the murder was committed in cold blood—shall we say of malice aforethought?"

"I think you might safely say that," answered the old gentleman, with another sly smile. "Yes, yes—of malice aforethought —excellent term! Well—you appear to be accumulating evidence."

Then, with a polite nod, he turned and went off, climbing the rocks and high ground very nimbly for so old a man. Maythorne watched him for a minute or so; then glanced at the policeman.

"Who is that old gentleman?" he asked.

"That's Mr Hassendeane, of Birnside House, sir," replied the policeman. "Though he's generally called Mr Wattie—Christian name's Walter. Old as he is, sir, it's not so many years since his father, old Squire Hassendeane, died, and as he was always known as Mr Wattie while the old man lived it's stuck to him, d'you see, sir?"

"I see," said Maythorne. He was still handling the gun, and presently he drew Crole's attention and mine to a name and address engraved on a plate let into the stock—*J. Musgrave, Woodcock Inn, Marrasdale.* "This is the landlord's missing property, sure enough," he remarked. Again he turned to the policeman. "Didn't you say you were expecting some of your superior officers along here?" he asked.

"Sergeant Manners said as how he was going to bring the Inspector and the Chief Constable along," answered the policeman. "I was to stay here, on guard, till they came. And I wish they'd come, for it's getting to my dinner-time."

"Take care of that till they do come," said Maythorne, handing back the gun. "Show them exactly where you found it, and draw their attention to the fact that one cartridge has been used and that there's a live one still left in the right-hand barrel. Tell them, if you like, that you've already shown it to Mr Holt and his friends—they'll know whom you mean."

We left Reiver's Den then, and went back across the moor. Crole seemed inclined to discuss things, but Maythorne said little, though as soon as we reached the Woodcock he sought out Musgrave and told him of the discovery of his missing gun. He hurried over his lunch, and as soon as I had finished mine, addressed me.

"The police are sure to come along here after the finding of that gun," he remarked. "And I want to be beforehand with them in a matter they don't seem to have thought of, and perhaps won't think of. I want to examine Mazaroff's belongings."

"Just so!" murmured Crole. "That, of course, must be done. Luggage, clothes—and so on. I suppose there's no difficulty about that. Holt?"

"None that I know of," I answered. "But I don't think there's much to examine—he was travelling light."

We went up to the dead man's room—a big, old-fashioned bed-chamber, the windows of which looked out over the moor. Everything there was just as Mazaroff had left it—he was a man of unusually tidy and orderly habits, who hated to see things, thrown here and there, and all his belongings were laid about the room on a system of his own. As I had remarked downstairs, there was comparatively little to look over; a couple of suitcases had contained all that their owner had thought it necessary to bring away from his rooms at the Hotel Cecil. There was really nothing to examine in toilet articles, linen, clothing, and the like, and we found no papers of any description in the suit-cases, nor in a dressing-case on the table. Maythorne did the searching while Crole and I looked on, deeply interested in the way in which he examined the dressing-case for a secret drawer —which he failed to discover, probably because there wasn't one—and the clothes for secret pockets. There was nothing se-cret—but in the waistcoat pockets of a well-worn tweed suit he found a number of loose diamonds, large and small, and in the trousers pocket of the same suit, an old purse.

"What did I tell you?" exclaimed Crole as the diamonds came to light. "He did carry diamonds, loose, on him? He once pulled out a handful when he and I were lunching at the Holborn Res-taurant—there were men, strangers, all round us, and he only laughed when I made some remark about the danger of carrying and openly exposing such valuables. Look at those, now—must be a dozen or so stones there, loose in his pocket! I suppose these diamond men get used to it, and think no more of such mat-ters than a farmer does of carrying samples of wheat and barley. Do you suppose those are worth a lot, Maythorne?—You know more about it than I do."

"Can't say," replied Maythorne indifferently. He had laid the diamonds aside on the dressing table, and was examining the old leather purse, we standing at his side and watching him. He took from it little that was of interest; there were some ordin-ary coins, gold and silver, of the Imperial coinage; some others, in a separate compartment, had been evidently kept as curios-ities, such as a Kruger half-crown, a British West African nickel halfpenny, a Mombasa rupee, a Portuguese silver ounce, and a German East African coin with the effigy of the Kaiser: there was also some Egyptian and Indian gold money. Maythorne paid lit-tle attention to these things; he was more deeply interested in a crumpled scrap of thin paper which he found in an inner pocket of the purse and smoothed out before us.

"Look at this!" he said presently. "Here's something, at any rate."

The scrap of paper was a receipt for a registered letter, despatched from Cape Town, and addressed to the Imperial Banking Corporation of South Africa, 695, Lombard Street, London. Maythorne pointed to the date—January 17th—on the postmark.

"Nine months since," he remarked. "How long had Mazaroff been in England when you met him at the Cecil?"

"A few weeks," I replied. "As far as I know."

"I know," said Crole. "He came to England in July—about the end of the month."

"Then the letter, or packet, or whatever it was, to which this receipt refers, was sent off from Cape Town to the London branch of this bank some months before Mazaroff came here," observed Maythorne. He turned the receipt over. "There's an endorsement on the back—letters and a figure," he continued. "See? Bl.D.1. What's that mean, I wonder? And are these in Mazaroff's handwriting?"

"That's his writing, sure enough," I said. "He'd a rather curious way of making his capitals."

"Probably refers to the contents of the packet," said Maythorne. "Bl.D.1.—I may find out the meaning yet. Well, here's one thing—we know now who his bankers are in London. But perhaps Mr Holt knew that already?"

"No, I didn't," I answered. "It may seem odd, but I didn't know. As I've told you already, he seemed to carry a good deal of ready money on him. I never saw him produce a cheque-book—he always paid our hotel bills in cash-notes."

"And no doubt pulled out a handful of 'em?" suggested Maythorne, with a grim smile. "Eh?"

"He certainly appeared to have a liberal supply in his pocket-book," I admitted. "He was a bit thoughtless in that way—I mean about showing his money, though I'm sure it was done in a quite unconscious fashion."

Maythorne produced his own pocket-book, and carefully put away the receipt.

"We'll just keep the knowledge of that to ourselves, for the present," he said. "If the police come here this afternoon, as they're pretty sure to, after that gun business, and want to examine his effects, let 'em. We'll put these diamonds back in the pocket I took them from—they're welcome to see those, and anything else. But I'll keep this scrap of paper to myself—I want to work things up from it."

The police came to the Woodcock a little later—three of them: the Chief Constable, an Inspector, and Manners. They asked a lot of questions of Musgrave about his gun, and of me and of Webster about our movements on the night of the murder, of Crole, about the dead man's identity and position; of me again about the money and valuables he was likely to have on him. And in the course of their investigations a fact came out of which I, until then, had been unaware. It turned out that after dinner on the night of the murder, while I was busied in writing some private letters, Mazaroff, who was naturally a sociable man, had strolled into the bar-parlour of the Woodcock where a highly-diversified assemblage had gathered—farmers, cattle-dealers, drovers, idlers, all homeward bound from Cloughthwaite Fair. There, according to the evidence of Musgrave's barmaid, he had made himself very agreeable, and had treated the entire company to drinks and cigars, which he paid for with a five-pound note, taken, said the barmaid, from a note-case that seemed to be pretty full, and in open view of anybody and everybody.

This bit of news appeared to give considerable satisfaction and even relief to the police officials, and Manners, who lingered behind when his superiors went away, found it impossible to refrain from communicating to me his belief that they were on the right line of pursuit.

"I know something already. Captain," he said, with a mysterious wink. "It won't do to say exactly what, you know—mum's the word, at present. But I found out a bit myself, this noon, and of course I shall follow it up. Takes time, all this sort o' thing, to be sure—but there's an old saying—slow *and* sure! That's my line. And—not so slow, neither. Now tomorrow morning there'll be the inquest. It'll be a mere formality, to start with.

A bit of evidence—necessary evidence—and then the coroner will adjourn for, say a fortnight. That's to give me a chance. And if I don't put my hand on the right man in a fortnight—well, I shall be surprised!"

I communicated the police-sergeant's optimistic notions to Crole and Maythorne over a cup of tea that afternoon. Maythorne, of whose calling the police had been left in ignorance—they had regarded him as merely some friend of mine or of Mazaroff's—seemed to understand Manners' standpoint.

"Following the most probable line," he remarked. "A sensible one, too. Put it to yourself. Here's an evidently wealthy man, travelling in a luxurious car of his own, puts up at a roadside inn, goes into a public bar-parlour, lets it be seen that he's lots of money on him, and strolls out on a lonely moor after night has fallen. What more likely than that one of the men before whom he's just pulled out his purse should slip after him, murder him and rob him?"

"With Musgrave's gun?" I asked.

"Nothing out of the way about that little detail!" said Maythorne. "Didn't I hear you tell those police chaps that after you'd finished your letters you took them off to the pillar-box up the road at the end of the village, leaving this sitting-room unoccupied? Yes—very well, what was easier than for the murderer to take down the gun from those hooks, and slip out after Mazaroff?"

"That would presuppose a knowledge that the gun was there," remarked Crole.

"Precisely," agreed Maythorne. "But Holt has already told us—or the police, in our presence—that when he went out he left the door open, and there were no doubt local characters about who knew quite well what was in this room, and what hung on that wall. I think Manners has got hold of a good theory—murder for the sake of robbery. But—whether it's the right one or not—um!"

"You doubt it?" I asked.

He gave us a candid, confidential smile.

"If you really want to know," he replied, "I neither doubt it nor agree with it. At present I don't know where we are. I'd like to know a lot of things yet. In particular—who was the man that Mazaroff said he wanted to see, hereabouts? Did he see him? If so, when—and where? If he hadn't seen him, was he on his way to see him at the time of the murder? Again—does this man, whoever he is, know Mazaroff as Mazaroff or as Merchison? Was Mazaroff murdered as Mazaroff, an unknown man here, or as Merchison, a man who had been known here?"

"Ah!" muttered Crole. "My question!"

"In other words," continued Maythorne, "had this murder its origin in the sudden temptation of some chance predatory rascal who saw his opportunity of robbing a rich man, or have we got to go back—and if back, how far back?"

CHAPTER 10 THE YORK SOLICITOR

The inquest, duly opened next morning by the local coroner in the largest room of the Woodcock, promised, at the beginning of the proceedings, to be a brief formality, a cut-and-dried affair, pre-arranged as to detail between the coroner and the police. The twelve jurymen were farmers, shepherds, gamekeepers of the neighbourhood: the few spectators who gathered in the public part of the improvised court out of sheer curiosity were folk of the surrounding moorland. Probably they expected to hear sensational evidence, but—to begin with, at any rate—there was none to hear. Crole, as a solicitor whom he had employed in London, and I, as his travelling companion, identified the dead man as Salim Mazaroff, and told what we knew about him: Eccleshare and the local doctor testified as to the cause of his death: the men who had found the body at Reiver's Den gave evidence as to the circumstances under which they came across it. At this stage the coroner was about to adjourn the enquiry—an interruption came through the entrance of Mr and Mrs Elphinstone and Sheila, with whom appeared an elderly man of professional bearing; Manners, by whom I was sitting, whispered to me that this was Mr Wetherby, Mrs Elphinstone's lawyer. I communicated this to Crole, on my other side; Crole nodded, as if in full appreciation of the development.

"Just what I expected!" he muttered. "She's thought things over. Now then——"

Wetherby lost no time in letting the authorities know why he and his party were there. After a whispered word with the officials he was on his legs.

"I understand, sir, that you were about to adjourn this enquiry," he said, addressing the coroner. "Before you do that, I wish to make an application to you on behalf of my client, Mrs Elphinstone, of Marrasdale Tower. To support it, I shall have—very briefly—to refer to some past history. Mrs Elphinstone, as Miss Jean Linton, was married, some twenty-three or four years ago, to a Mr Andrew Merchison, who formerly had some connection with this neighbourhood. The marriage was not a success, and, to put matters plainly, Merchison, within a comparatively short time and after making due provision for his wife, deserted her, and, it was believed, went off to the East. Eight months after he had gone Mrs Merchison had a daughter—the young lady whom you now see here. Miss Sheila Merchison. The birth of the child was duly advertised in several English and Indian newspapers, in the hope that Merchison's attention might be attracted, but no response came from him. Merchison, indeed, was never heard of again until some years later, when Mrs Merchison received news that he had been drowned off Mombasa, on the East African coast, while on a voyage from Bombay to Durban. This was positive news—I may say, sir, that I am in a position to bring before you the evidence of proof which Mrs Merchison received. From that time forward Mrs Merchison believed herself a widow, and in due course she married again, and became Mrs Elphinstone. Now I come to the cause and reason of my application. Yesterday, Mrs Elphinstone was visited by two gentlemen now present, who have, I understand, just given evidence—Mr Holt and Mr Crole. On the invitation of Mr Crole, Mr Holt informed Mrs Elphinstone that on the second evening after he and Mr Mazaroff arrived here at the Woodcock, Mr Mazaroff told him that though he had a perfect right to the name he was now known by, having legally adopted it some years ago, he was in reality the Andrew Merchison who had married Miss Jean Linton, and had left her. According to Mr Holt's story to Mrs

Elphinstone, Mr Mazaroff brought forward strong circumstantial proof of this. I need hardly say, sir, that this is a very serious matter for my client. She has consulted me about it, and I think it will be well for all parties if Mrs Elphinstone is allowed to view the body of this dead man, in order that she may see if she can recognise it as that of Andrew Merchison."

"That seems, obviously, the very thing to do," agreed the coroner. "Perhaps you'll accompany your client, Mr Wetherby?"

There was considerable hushed excitement in that room during the absence of Mrs Elphinstone and her solicitor. Some of the older folk amongst the spectators whispered—the name Merchison had evidently roused sleeping memories. But most of us waited in a tense silence—once, glancing covertly at Sheila, I saw that she was sitting with her eyes fixed steadily on the door through which her mother must reappear, a look of concentrated expectancy on her face, and I knew what she was waiting for.

But when Mrs Elphinstone, followed by Wetherby, again walked through that door her face was expressionless as if it had been carved out of marble. There was not one trace of emotion or discomposure in eye or lips—she was the incarnation of absolute self-possession. At the coroner's suggestion, she went into the witness-box and gave evidence. It compressed itself into this—she could not identify the dead man as Andrew Merchison. Had the features remained unmolested, she said calmly, she might have done so, but as things were—impossible! She could not say that the man was Merchison, but, on the other hand, she could not say that he wasn't.

Crole, in his professional capacity, rose to ask Mrs Elphinstone a question.

"Mrs Elphinstone," he said, "had Andrew Merchison a cast in his left eye?"

Mrs Elphinstone bowed a ready assent.

"Certainly, he had," she replied. "A decided one!"

Crole turned to the coroner.

"Numerous witnesses can prove that the unfortunate gentleman into whose death you are enquiring had such a cast—a squint—in his left eye, sir," he remarked. "He also had a birthmark, in the form of a brown mole, or blemish, on his right forearm. That, however, is not an uncommon mark, I believe, and I don't attach great importance to it. But I am strongly convinced that further proof of the identity of the deceased as Andrew Merchison will be found, and I should suggest——"

"There need be no doubt about it!" exclaimed a sudden voice from the spectators. "The man was Andrew Merchison!"

I knew whose voice that was before I looked round. Old Mr Hassendeane, whom I had noticed when Crole and I entered the room, had risen from his seat, and was smiling informingly at the coroner. He went on again before the coroner could speak.

"I wasn't going to say anything in this affair until I saw what happened, Mr Coroner," he continued. "But as Mrs Elphinstone can't be positive, I may as well say that I am! I knew Andrew Merchison well enough in the old days, when he used to come here, and afterwards when he was a young man—I knew him, too, after he'd married Miss Linton, now Mrs Elphinstone. And my memory for faces is remarkably keen, and I recognised him easily enough when I saw him the other night. Andrew Merchison, without doubt!—twenty-two or three years older, to be sure——"

"Where did you see this man, Mr Hassendeane?" interrupted the coroner, obviously surprised at the turn which things were taking.

"I saw him the night on which he evidently met his death," replied the old gentleman. "It was in Birnside village street, near my house. I had been out to my gardener's cottage, and as I returned up the street, I saw a tall man lighting his cigar in the doorway of John Metcalfe's house—there was a bit of wind blowing. He held the match well up to his face, and I saw it distinctly, and noticed the cast in the eye, which I remembered well enough."

"You didn't speak to him?" suggested the coroner.

"I did not," replied Hassendeane. "I was half-minded to, but he turned sharply away, having lighted his cigar, and went off in the direction of Reiver's Den and High Cap Lodge."

"And you are quite positive on this matter of identity?"

"I am absolutely positive! The man was Andrew Merchison, whatever he may have called himself of recent years."

The coroner glanced at the solicitors gathered about the table at the head of which he sat.

"I think we had better adjourn for a fortnight," he said. "During that time——"

Just then a policeman opened the door of the room, ushering in a young, spectacled man who, from his eager and enquiring look round, appeared to be anxious lest the proceedings were over. The coroner paused and glanced enquiringly at him.

"Are you here in relation to this enquiry, sir?" he demanded. "We're just about——"

The new-comer pulled out a card-case and advancing to the head of the table, whispered a few words in the coroner's ear. I saw a look of something between surprise and perplexity cross the coroner's face; a word or two more, and he glanced down the table again.

"We seem to be dealing with a strangely mysterious matter, quite apart from the death," he remarked. "This gentleman"— he glanced at the card—"Mr Stephen Postlethwaite, solicitor, from York—tells me that he saw accounts of this case in the papers yesterday, and has hurried here to give some information. I suppose we'd better have it now?—perhaps you'll go into the box, Mr Postlethwaite, and tell us what it is you've come for?"

Mr Postlethwaite entered the improvised witness-box, and formally described himself as a solicitor, practising in York, at number 293, Lendall Street. He produced a diary, and exhibited an entry dated September 23, which recorded a call from Mr Salim Mazaroff.

"Mr Mararoff," he continued, "who was a total stranger to me, though I had noticed him about the city a day or two previously, accompanied by a young gentleman whom I now see present, introduced himself as staying in York for a few days at the North Eastern Hotel. He said that he had motored from London in his own car, and was going on a trip further North; to this he added that he was a North-countryman, but had been out of England for many years, and had now returned, and was thinking of settling in London. He then informed me that he was a very wealthy man; that he had made his money in various trading concerns in the East, and lately in extensive diamond dealings in South Africa; that he had now retired from all this, had realised his various properties, and lodged all the proceeds in cash at his London bank, the Imperial Banking Corporation of South Africa, pending investment in this country. Then, in a rather jocular fashion he remarked that up to then, as he had no children, and no relations, he had never made a will, but he now desired to do so, and had walked out from his hotel that morning to look for a solicitor to aid him. He then produced a sheet of paper on which he had written out his wishes, handed it to me, and asked if I could put it into ship-shape form? I produce that sheet of paper," continued Mr Postlethwaite, drawing an oblong envelope from his pocket. "It has been in my possession ever since. On reading it over I told Mr Mazaroff that there wasn't the slightest necessity to make a professional copy of it—it was perfectly clear, and there was nothing to do but for him to sign it in the presence of myself and one of my clerks as witnesses. That, however, didn't seem to suit him—he evidently wanted something more formal and elaborate. I therefore read his draft over to him, received his assurance that it embodied precisely what he wanted said, told him that I would have the will prepared for him, and he was to call and execute it at any time after three o'clock that afternoon. He returned to my office at half-past three, when the will was ready for his signature. He duly appended that in the presence of myself and Herbert Wilkins, my clerk, and after paying my fees, carried the will off with him. It was not until some days later that I found that I had omitted to give him his own original draft, which I found lying amongst some papers on my desk. I went round to the North Eastern Hotel with it myself, but learnt then that Mr Mazaroff and his friend Mr Holt had left for Durham and the North, leaving no address. I therefore locked up the draft. Yesterday I read in the newspapers the various accounts of what had happened here, and as I particularly noticed that Mr Mazaroff had been robbed of his papers as well as his money and valuables, I thought it my duty to come here at once and tell what I knew."

Mr Postlethwaite ended as abruptly as he had begun. Every eye in that room was fastened on him; he alone of all the men and women there was in possession of a secret; he knew to whom, or to what, this undoubtedly wealthy man had left his money. I think everybody was hoping that the coroner would make immediate enquiry on that point—but the coroner was elderly and old-fashioned and given to getting at facts in his own way. He began a leisurely exchange of question and answer with the witness.

"Much obliged to you, I'm sure, Mr Postlethwaite," he said. "Now according to you the deceased man carried off this will in his pocket. It appears from the evidence that everything he had on him—money, valuables, papers—was stolen, most likely by the murderer or murderers: presumably the will has gone with the rest. However, it's something to know that such a document was in existence. Now there's a question or two I should like to put to you. Did Mr Mazaroff tell you—he seems to have been communicative—did he happen to tell you that he had ever been known by another name than that under which he introduced himself to you?"

Mr Postlethwaite made an emphatic gesture of dissent.

"No, he certainly did not!" he replied.

"He didn't say that he had assumed the name of Mazaroff!"

"No!"

"Didn't it strike you that it was an uncommon name for an Englishman?"

"It did. But I have known of still more uncommon ones."

"Did you ask him what made him come to you?—in York?"

"No—because he said, at the beginning, that he'd just taken it into his head that morning to do this, and that when he took things into his head, he carried them out there and then."

"You say he told you he was a wealthy man. Did he say how wealthy?—I gather he was a very candid, outspoken man?"

"Yes. He did say. He told me he was worth about eight hundred thousand pounds."

The coroner leaned back in his chair, put the tips of his fingers together, and looked round the court. Then he turned again to the witness.

"I think we'll trouble you to read that draft, Mr Postlethwaite," he said quietly.

Postlethwaite drew a sheet of paper from the oblong envelope and read—amidst a dead silence.

This is the last will of me, Salim Mazaroff, of the Hotel Cecil, London, in the county of Middlesex and of 941, Darling Street, Cape Town, South Africa. I devise and bequeath all my estate and effects, real and personal, which I may die possessed of or entitled to unto Mervyn Holt, of 559a, Jermyn Street, London, absolutely, and I hereby appoint the said Mervyn Holt Sole Executor of this my will, and I revoke all former wills and codicils.

That was all. But I was suddenly conscious that all eyes had turned from the witness to me.

CHAPTER 11 THE POLICE THEORY

The first thing that I was accurately conscious of after the crushing shock of the York solicitor's announcement (for, if truth be told, it produced a more stunning effect upon me than I had ever experienced through the bursting of a shell in any of my war experiences) was Crole's voice, close to my ear.

"Keep quiet, Holt!" he was whispering intently. "Keep quiet—calm!"

I don't think I did more than hear him—I was watching the coroner, feeling now, that he, somehow, crystallised in himself all that the various people in that room were thinking and wondering. He suddenly put a sharp question to Postlethwaite.

"The actual will, duly executed by the deceased, was in these very words?"

"Precisely!" assented Postlethwaite. "This is the draft—in the deceased's handwriting—from which the actual will was copied."

The coroner looked round—at nobody in particular.

"I understand that the will has not been found," he said. "The theory is that it was stolen by the supposed murderer, with other of the deceased's papers. Nobody knows anything about it, eh?"

Wetherby was suddenly on his legs, with a sidelong glance at me.

"As Mr Holt, the beneficiary, is present, sir," he said, "I should like to ask him if he knows anything about it?"

I felt Crole tug at my sleeve, but I jumped up.

"I know nothing about it!" I exclaimed. "I never heard of it!"

Wetherby gave me another look; there was something cynical in it which I strongly resented, and I felt the blood flame in my cheeks.

"You and the deceased gentleman were very close friends, I think?" he said quietly. "Isn't that so?"

"We had come to be close friends; very good friends," I answered. "But——"

He interrupted me with a wave of the hand and another disagreeable smile.

"Such close friends that he leaves you all his money—a vast fortune!—and appoints you sole executor of his last will and testament—and yet never even mentions the matter of his good intentions and your extraordinary luck to you!" he said, with what was almost a sneer. "You're sure about your memory?"

"I'm sure of something else than my memory!" I retorted hotly. "I know nothing whatever about Mazaroff's will, I never knew he'd made one. And I'm very sure that if Mazaroff really was Merchison, and his will is found, and I have to handle his money, I shall just transfer it to whom it belongs—to his widow and daughter. Do you hear that, Mr Wetherby?—if not. I'll say it again!"

But Crole had got a hand on my arm by that time, and was dragging at me.

"Sit down. Holt, you damned young ass!" he muttered strenuously. "Sit down!—leave this to me." He, too, got on his legs—his voice sounded suave and placatory as he turned to the coroner.

"I think, sir, that this has scarcely anything to do with the object of this enquiry——"

"With all respect to Mr Crole, I'm not so sure of that," interrupted Wetherby. "If——"

"I am in possession, if you please," said Crole. "I suggest that the inquest be adjourned until——"

"I'm about to do that," broke in the coroner. "During the next few days, more light will doubtless be thrown on all these matters."

He turned to the open-mouthed jurymen. "This day fortnight, gentlemen, and in the meantime——"

I paid no heed to the coroner's platitudes about keeping open minds—my own mind was in a whirl of indignation against Mrs Elphinstone's solicitor. But when I turned in her direction, I saw that Mrs Elphinstone herself had crossed over from her seat and was talking earnestly to him. Presently he came up to me, with a half-amused, half-ingratiating smile.

"You're a bit hot-tempered, Mr Holt," he said. "Come, come! —I was only speaking professionally, you know—professional manners, after all. are——"

"Confoundedly offensive, sir, if that's a specimen of them!" I retorted. "You were inferring that——"

"Now, now, I wasn't inferring anything!" he interrupted soothingly. "I've the interest of my client to consider—Crole there, and Postlethwaite would have done the same. I say again, it's an odd thing that Mazaroff or Merchison didn't mention his will to you. But the whole thing's odd," he went on, looking round, "and what I suggest is that we legal gentlemen and the parties concerned just have a talk, if we can find a place to talk in."

I took them into the private sitting-room which Mazaroff and I had chartered and I still retained—the three solicitors, Mr and Mrs Elphinstone, and Sheila: Maythorne was already in conference with the police in a quiet corner of the room in which the inquest had been held. The solicitors did most of the talking that followed: it was all about the chances of recovering the missing will and the possibilities of setting up the original draft —which was wholly in Mazaroff's handwriting and also bore his signature—if no recovery was made. The discussion didn't interest me: I was resolved, after what I had heard, that I should never touch one penny of the dead man's money. And I made a blunt interruption in the midst of the legal jargon.

"You're all forgetting," I said, "that when Mr Mazaroff—or, as

I think we ought to call him, Mr Merchison—made that will at York, he didn't know that he had a daughter."

They all turned and looked at me.

"You think that if he had known that, he'd have made a different will, Mr Holt?" suggested Wetherby.

"I can only say what I know," I replied. "When Mazaroff, or Merchison, told me what he did about his marriage, and his running away, and all the rest of it, he said that if his child had been born before he went he was sure he'd never have gone. Well, he came back—years later—and found he had a child—a daughter. He saw her! And I think it's only common sense to suppose that finding he had a daughter, he'd have left his money to her. Besides——"

I paused there. A sudden notion had struck me—one that I was glad to have.

"Well?" asked Wetherby good-humouredly.

"Considering that after coming here he discovered that he had a daughter," I continued, "I should think it's very obvious what he did with the will he made at York."

"Aye—and what, now?" enquired Wetherby.

"Burnt it, of course!" I answered. "Why should he leave his money to me, when he'd a daughter of his own? He didn't know he had one when he was at York—but he knew within an hour or two of arriving here."

"There's something in that," muttered Wetherby. "He may have done. The question is—was he going to reveal himself as Merchison?"

"Was he Merchison?" suggested Postlethwaite.

There was a pause after that. Suddenly Crole smote the table at which he was sitting.

"Who murdered this man?" he exclaimed, with emphasis. "That's the question! Who murdered him, and why? It may have been a common, vulgar crime—for mere robbery. But—there may be more in it. He was a man of mystery, evidently. And as I've asked before—was he murdered as Mazaroff, or as Merchison? I think we may have to go back—perhaps a long way. But it seems to me that the murder must be cleared up as a start."

"Supposing he is not Merchison at all?" suggested Postlethwaite once more. "Supposing——"

I don't know what his second or third supposition was: he seemed to be anxious to consider several, none of them very pertinent, to my thinking. Just then Maythorne came in, closing the door behind him.

"Gathered anything?" asked Crole.

"Well—something," answered Maythorne. "No secret about it, either. Manners tells me that a certain man named Parslave, Ralph Parslave, better known as Ratty, who lives in a cottage on the outskirts of Birnside, has never been home since the day of that fair. He's a man who lives by himself and seems to be a sort of odd-job man; occasional drover, game-watcher, rat-catcher——"

"Everybody knows Ratty Parslave!" interjected Sheila. "He's a local celebrity."

"Just so," said Maythorne. "Well, Ratty Parslave was known to go to this fair they talk about, after his usual habit, but he never came home again. However, the police have ascertained that he came in here, in company with other men, drovers and so on, returning from the fair, on the evening of the murder. He was one of the company to which Mazaroff stood drinks and cigars. Those who were present—such of them, at any rate, as can remember any details—are under the impression that Parslave left the room, where Mazaroff entertained them, a little before Mazaroff himself went out, but up to now they've failed to find anybody who actually saw Parslave leave this house, or saw him again that night. It's absolutely certain, however, that he was in here that evening—and since then nothing has been seen or heard of him. That's all."

"Might have gone off to some other fair," suggested Postlethwaite. "These fellows do go from one to another."

"Yes," agreed Maythorne. "But there are no other fairs being held just now—nothing until next month. And of course the police have already got a theory—they think that Parslave, who, they say, has been in what they call trouble before, saw Mazaroff make a display—unconsciously—of his money. They think he slipped out of the bar-room, perhaps with no very definite intention; that chancing to pass the open door of this private room he saw Musgrave's gun hanging on these hooks, stepped in, took it down and cleared off with it; that he afterwards followed Mazaroff across the moor, shot him dead, and robbed him; after that throwing the gun away where it was found, and clearing out with the proceeds of his crime. That, I say, is the police theory."

"And what do you think of it?" asked Wetherby, with some curiosity. "We know you by repute, Mr Maythorne. How does it strike you?"

"It's a good theory—from a policeman's point of view," said Maythorne. "There may be a great deal in it. But speaking for myself, I should like to know more about the dead man's personal, private history, recent as well as past. One matter in particular needs clearing up. He told Mr Holt that he wanted to see some man here at Marrasdale. Who was that man? Did he see him?"

Nobody, of course, could answer that question, and the conference broke up. Maythorne and the three solicitors began talking together; I went with the Elphinstones and Sheila to the door of the inn. Mr Elphinstone was inclined to be sceptical about the identity of Mazaroff with Merchison; the letter from Sinclair, the return of the cabin trunk, the monument in the church appeared to him proof positive that Merchison was dead long since, and that Mazaroff, knowing something of his history, had told me a cock-and-bull story. He maundered away about it as I walked up the road with them; Mrs Elphinstone and Sheila said nothing. But when I was about to turn back, Mrs Elphinstone showed more graciousness of manner than I had yet seen in her, and it emboldened me to say once more what was in my mind—rankling in it, as a matter of fact.

"You understand," I said, "that if what old Hassendeane positively asserted to be a fact turns out to be so, and if that will turns up, I'm not going to touch one penny of that money! I very much resented your solicitor's manner——"

"Don't think any more of that!" exclaimed Mrs Elphinstone, with whom I just then happened to be shaking hands. "Mr Wetherby is, of course—a lawyer. I'm not! I am quite sure you would do what you feel to be right, Mr Holt, under any circumstances—quite, quite sure!"

She and old Elphinstone turned away; Sheila lingered for a moment. She gave me a direct, questioning glance.

"Look here!" she said. "Do *you* believe that poor man was my father—Andrew Merchison? Honour bright, now?"

"Very well—I do!" I answered. "Can't think anything else. I haven't the slightest doubt of it."

"Then," she said, unconsciously coming nearer to me, "if his will turns up, please stick to the money—please! To—please me, if nothing else."

"Good Lord, why?" I exclaimed. "I haven't the least right to a penny!"

"Yes, you have," she retorted. "It was his wish."

"But—he didn't know about you, then," I said. "If——"

"Never mind," she interrupted. "I—I want you to stick to it. I do *not* want it to come into my mother's hands or mine—I know what that would mean. Anyway, please promise me that—if the will's found—you won't do anything rashly, in that way."

"I'll promise you that!" I replied eagerly. "I won't do anything at all without consulting you. But——"

She motioned me to say no more, and moved away.

"Thank you for promising," she said over her shoulder. "I'll say more—afterwards."

I went back to the Woodcock, wondering. I was quite sure that Mrs Elphinstone would rejoice greatly if the dead man's fortune came to her and her daughter: I was equally certain that her daughter didn't want to touch a penny of it. I was therefore in a fix, for I had declared publicly that if it came into my hands I should pay it over, and yet I was most certainly in love with Sheila and bound to obey her wishes—which were that I should stick to it. This bothered me—until I remembered that I was cudgelling my brains about something that might not materialise. My previous conjecture might be correct—the will had been destroyed after Mazaroff or Merchison's discovery about his daughter.

We buried him that afternoon, very quietly, and in the evening Webster drove Crole, Maythorne, and myself to Black Gill Junction, where we caught the night mail for London. For Maythorne was unusually keen on seeing the officials at the Imperial Banking Corporation of South Africa, and on finding out all he could about Mazaroff in general, and the receipt for the registered letter endorsed Bl.D.1., in particular. At half-past ten next morning we were all three closeted with an important personage of the bank, who, as soon as he knew our business, became keenly interested about Mazaroff and the circumstances of his death, and cross-examined us inquisitively on the reports he had already seen in the newspapers. I believed he was going to prove a valuable aid, but as soon as he saw the receipt and its date he shook his head.

"Ah!" he said. "The man who would deal with Mazaroff's account and letters, at the date of this receipt, is no longer here. He was Mr Armintrade—he left us six months since, to become manager of Courthope's."

CHAPTER 12 THE CYPHER LETTER

I think it was greatly to my credit that I controlled my features and the rest of me when this sudden announcement was made, neither staring nor starting at the mention of Armintrade's name. Even Crole, old and hardened man of law that he was, could not refrain from a very slight start of surprise. But the highly-placed person we were interviewing was not looking at Crole, nor at me; he was giving his attention to our companion, with whose name and reputation he was evidently quite familiar. And Maythorne, of course, showed no surprise; his face, always cheerful and bright, betrayed nothing.

"Oh!" he said. "I see. You mean that such correspondence as you would get from Mazaroff, when he was in South Africa, would, in the usual course of business, fall into a Mr Armintrade's hands, and that Mr Armintrade has now left you?"

"Precisely!" answered the important personage. "Armintrade would attend to anything that came from Mazaroff. And as I said just now, Armintrade left us six months ago, to become general manager of Courthope's. That's an old-established private banking concern, you know—Courthope, Daintree & Co, in Mincing Lane."

"Oh, I know Courthope's—by reputation," remarked Maythorne. "Then—you yourself can't tell us anything very much about Mazaroff!"

"I can tell you what I know," replied our informant, evidently quite willing to talk. "We know Mazaroff as a very wealthy man who had extensive dealings in trading affairs, and latterly in diamonds and other precious stones, in the East, and in South Africa. He kept his principal account at our Cape Town headquarters, but for years he has had a smaller account here as well. Lately, he transferred his Cape Town account here; he also realised all his various properties and paid the proceeds in here, with a view to re-investment in English securities."

"Then you hold a considerable sum of his?" suggested Crole. "We understand—in fact, he mentioned the amount to Mr Postlethwaite, the York solicitor who drew his will—that it is about eight hundred thousand pounds?"

"About that, I dare say," assented the manager, almost indifferently. "Rather more, I fancy. Oh, yes—a wealthy man! And the will, you say, is lost?"

"Missing—temporarily, we hope," said Crole. "But Postlethwaite has the original draft, in Mazaroff's own handwriting, and signed by Mazaroff. We have a copy here."

He handed the copy over, and the great man read it slowly.

"This young gentleman is the Mr Mervyn Holt referred to," observed Crole.

The manager eyed me shrewdly over the tips of his gold-rimmed spectacles and made me a friendly bow.

"Congratulate you, Mr Holt," he said, with a smile. "A desirable fortune!"

"He hasn't got it yet," laughed Crole. "There are things to be done. But now—can you tell us anything of Mazaroff—personally?"

"Next to nothing," answered the manager. "He called here, just once, some time after his arrival in London. I saw him—in this very room. He wasn't here five minutes. He said that he'd merely called in to let us know that he'd arrived in town and had taken rooms at the Cecil. He said he was just going for a tour in the North of England, and would look in on his return, a few weeks hence. And—that's all."

"I suppose you've cashed cheques of his since then?" asked

Maythorne.

"Well, I can find out," said the manager. He rang his bell, and gave some order to the clerk who appeared in answer to it, and who went away and returned a few minutes later, duly informed.

"No cheque of Mr Salim Mazaroff's has been presented, sir, since Mr Mazaroff himself called here on August 29," he said. "He then cashed a cheque personally for two thousand pounds."

The manager nodded and the clerk was retiring, but Maythorne stopped him, and glanced at his principal.

"Mazaroff would take that amount in notes," he said. "And your people will, of course, have the numbers of those notes. Now, may I have them?"

"No objection to that, certainly," assented the manager. "Get them," he said to the clerk. "You think," he continued, turning to Maythorne, "that Mazaroff was murdered for the sake of robbery?"

"Well," replied Maythorne, "there's this about it. From all I can gather—from Mr Holt here, and from others—Mazaroff was one of those careless men who, without any thought of ostentation, you know, but from sheer thoughtlessness, display the money they have about them. Pull out a handful of notes, you know—loose."

"Aye, and not only notes!" muttered Crole. "He carried diamonds and things! In his waistcoat pockets. Tempting!"

"Oh, well, as regards diamonds," observed the manager, "I suppose he regarded them pretty much as a farmer regards samples of barley. Still—as Mr Crole says—it's a temptation to dishonest folk. But now"—he laid his hand on a small pile of newspapers that lay on his desk—"what is all this that I read in the papers, in the report of the inquest yesterday, about Mazaroff's identity with some Andrew Merchison? What is there in that?"

Crole explained to him—they continued discussing the affair in all its aspects for some time. The clerk came back with a slip of paper: the manager, after a glance at it, handed it over to Maythorne, who carefully placed it in his pocket-book. A few minutes later we all left. And once outside the great door of the bank, Crole gave Maythorne a sharp glance.

"Um!" he said. "Armintrade!"

"Just so!" said Maythorne. "As you say—Armintrade!"

Then they walked a few yards in silence, while I, a neophyte in these matters, wondered what they were thinking.

"A man might have reasons, when a man he knows is murdered under his very nose, for not coming forward to say that he knows him," observed Crole at last. "But—I think, considering everything, that if I'd been in Armintrade's position the other day I should have said, 'I know this man—he's So-and-so, and I'll tell you all I know about him.' Eh?"

Maythorne made no answer—just then. He produced a cigarette-case. Crole shook his head; he was an old-fashioned man about tobacco. And Maythorne and I had smoked for five minutes, and we had strolled a good way amongst the City crowd before Maythorne spoke—this time with an air of conviction.

"I'll tell you what I think," he said suddenly. "Armintrade is the man whom Mazaroff wanted to see at Marrasdale Moor! Now then!—did he see him? Holt doesn't know—nobody knows —at least nobody that we've heard of. But—Armintrade's the man! Armintrade, as we've just heard, did all Mazaroff's business at the bank we've just left—it was into Armintrade's hands that the registered letter of which I've got the receipt in my pocket would fall. We must have a little talk with Armintrade. But before that"—he paused and waved his hand to a passing taxi-cab—"before that we're going to examine Mazaroff's rooms and belongings at the Hotel Cecil."

We had no difficulty about this stage of our proceedings. The hotel management, thanks to the publicity which had been given to what was already known as either the Mazaroff Affair or the Marrasdale Moor Murder, knew all about what had happened, and the three of us were presently in the rooms wherein I had first met the dead man. Crole and I looked on while Maythorne made a systematic search. It produced little: Mazaroff was not the sort of man who accumulates things: I had noticed during my acquaintance with him that when he had read such letters as he received at various points of our journey he invariably burnt them. Nevertheless, Maythorne made some discoveries that were of use, if of no great apparent moment. In an old trunk he found some school-books: on the fly-leaf of each was written the name *Andrew Merchison*, with dates: these he handed over to Crole.

"There's no doubt whatever that he was Merchison," said Crole, turning these things over. "It's not likely that he'd have kept these books else. These will come in handy to show to Mrs Elphinstone. But I wish there were more papers."

Maythorne, however, found some papers—in a letter-case that lay in a drawer, unlocked, in Mazaroff's writing-table. These were letters—private letters, all, with one exception, written recently from Cape Town by a Mr Herman Kloop, who appeared to be a close personal friend of Mazaroff. There was next to nothing about business affairs in them—they were chiefly filled with gossip, club gossip, personal details, and suchlike matters: the sort of stuff exchanged by old cronies. But they had this value, observed Maythorne—he now had a name and address in Cape Town to which he could cable for certain information about the dead man.

The one letter not written by this Mr Herman Kloop proved to be the only thing that particularly impressed my companions. It was in the same case that held the Kloop letters, but in an envelope which bore on its flap the impressed seal of the Imperial Banking Corporation of South Africa, with the address of the London branch. Maythorne immediately drew attention to the postmark and date: the letter had been posted in London on the previous January 3.

"From Armintrade to Mazaroff, without doubt," said Maythorne. He showed some eagerness as he drew out the enclosure. Then his face fell.

"Written in cypher!" he exclaimed. "That's a sell!"

The sheet of note-paper was almost filled with writing, the

writing of a man who, as Maythorne was quick to point out, used a fine-pointed pen, had been trained—originally—in what is commonly called commercial penmanship, and made his figures as only a man who is continually dealing with figures does make them. But to us the wording was all so much unmeaning jargon: we could make neither head nor tail of it. There were, however, certain things on the sheet of paper which were plain enough. The paper itself was the ordinary letter paper of the bank, with its title and address engraved at the top of the front page. The letter began in understandable English—*Dear Mr Mazaroff*. And it ended in plain English—*yours faithfully, John Armintrade*. But all that went between, a hotch-potch of cabalistic words and figures, was so much double Dutch to all three of us.

"A cypher!" repeated Maythorne. "Mazaroff, of course, would have a key. In his pocket-book, no doubt, and therefore stolen. Well!—it's more evident than ever that we must have a little conversation with Mr John Armintrade. But first—something else."

We left the hotel. Maythorne immediately hurried off to the nearest telegraph office: he was keen on cabling to Mr Herman Kloop for some highly necessary news of Mazaroff. And as it was then well past noon, Crole and I turned into Romano's for some lunch; we were both tired by our night journey and our goings to and fro since our arrival.

"This is a queer business, Holt," said Crole as we settled down in a comfortable and quiet corner. "I mean—what we've found out this morning. You've seen this man Armintrade?"

"For a few minutes only," I replied. "At Courthope's shooting-box, when Miss Elphinstone took me there to make enquiries about Mazaroff's disappearance."

"What sort is he?" he asked. "I don't know him at all."

"A sly sort of chap, I should say," I answered. "Looks as if he'd hear all and say nothing."

"Well, he's kept that up, so far," observed Crole. "You'd have thought that he'd have come forward and said that he'd had business dealings with Mazaroff. Instead—not a word!"

"He looks the sort of man who would probably reply to that that Mazaroff's death was no concern of his," I suggested. "He gives one that impression."

"Aye, well," remarked Crole, "we shall just have to find out a few things—leave it to Maythorne. I wish we could lay hands on that will—for your sake."

"I don't!" I replied. "I've said so already—and why."

"Don't be foolish," he retorted. "Never refuse money, my lad! It was this man's wish that you should have his money. Take it! —if you can get it. It'll maybe turn out a far better thing for you to have it than for the widow—as she legally is—and the daughter."

That made me think of what Sheila had said the day before. And then, knowing already that Crole was a shrewd man, I told him of that brief conversation.

"Why is she so anxious that the money shouldn't go to her mother and herself?" I asked.

Crole laid down his knife and fork just then, leaned back in his chair, and after reflecting a little, laughed quietly.

"Smart girl!" he said.

"What do you mean?" I demanded. He bent forward, confidentially.

"Between ourselves, Holt," he said. "Quite apart from this Mazaroff's will matter, what's your financial position?"

"Oh, well," I answered, "I've about five hundred a year of my own, and I believe I shall have about an additional five or six hundred when my father dies."

"Just so!" he assented. "A thousand-a-year man. Now then, I'll ask you another, my lad! If Mrs and Miss Elphinstone—especially the mother—came into a fortune of eight or nine hundred thousand pounds, d'ye think Mrs Elphinstone, who, in my opinion, is a bit of a worldly and ambitious woman, would be inclined to give her daughter to a comparatively poor man? This is a world of fact, not fancy, young fellow!"

"What are you driving at?" I exclaimed. "What's the riddle?"

"No riddle," he answered, laughing. "I think Miss Sheila is in love with you—and she'd far rather the money was in your hands than in her mother's and her own! Don't you be an ass, young Holt!—if we can get hold of the will, you get hold of the money. And when you've got hold—hold tight!"

I left him after lunch and went home to my rooms in Jermyn Street. It seemed as if I had been away from them a thousand years. I spent a quiet afternoon there, and a quiet evening, and I went to bed early. And at nine o'clock next morning, in came Maythorne.

"Had a cable late last night from Cape Town," he announced. "Mr Herman Kloop is in London—at the First Avenue Hotel. Come along—we'll collect Crole, and interview Kloop at once."

CHAPTER 13 THE DIAMOND WORLD

We found Mr Herman Kloop at half-past ten, leisurely finishing a late breakfast in the almost deserted coffee-room of his hotel: a little, dapper, Hebraic-looking gentleman, very scrupulously and fashionably dressed, but with rather more evidence of gold and diamonds about him than is quite usual with Englishmen. He seemed in no wise surprised to be visited by three strangers, and he pointed from the cards which we had sent in to a pile of newspapers that lay by his plate.

"I have already seen all your names in them," he said, as he motioned us to be seated round his table. "Which is Mr Crole?—Mr Maythorne?—Mr Holt?"

He appeared to take unusual interest in me as we revealed our separate identities, and I remembered then that the details of Mazaroff's will had come out in Postlethwaite's evidence at the inquest, and that newspaper reporters had been present.

"I only arrived in London last night," he continued as we seated ourselves. "I read about Mazaroff in the paper, coming from Harwich—I have been in Amsterdam and Antwerp for the past week—and as soon as I reached this place I sent out for the papers of the last few days, and have read them this morning. A strange affair, gentlemen!—and yet not so strange as it seems. Mazaroff was a careless man—he lacked a certain quality which I have always found almost too pronounced in most of you Englishmen."

"You mean he was too open?" suggested Crole. "Just what I myself have said a score of times."

"He was too ready—sheer thoughtlessness, you know—to let people see what he had on him," replied Kloop. "And he carried things that I should have kept under lock and key. However—but tell me—how did you find out that I was here?"

"We found these letters of yours in Mazaroff's rooms at the Hotel Cecil," replied Maythorne, producing the letter-case which he had discovered and brought away with him, "and judging from them that you were a very intimate friend of his, I cabled to your address in Cape Town yesterday morning, and received a reply at night that you were here. You have read up the case, Mr Kloop?"

"All that there is in these papers," replied Kloop, laying his ringed fingers on the considerable pile. "I see the police suspect some local man—a villager of no very good reputation. May be so—but I should say, knowing what I do of Mazaroff, that there is something deeper in the case than a mere vulgar murder and robbery. Now, as I learn from these newspaper accounts that Mr Holt was Mazaroff's companion in his North-country excursion, and with him all the time at this Woodcock Inn, I should like to ask Mr Holt to tell me two or three things—questions that occur to me, you know?"

"Anything I can," said I.

"Well," he continued, "during your journey North, you would doubtless stay at various places and hotels *en route*?"

"Several," I answered.

"Did you ever notice anything to make you think that you—that is to say, that Mazaroff was being followed—tracked?" he enquired.

"I can't say that I ever did," said I.

"You never, for instance, noticed a man, or men, who turned up with some regularity at the hotels you stayed at?" he suggested. "I mean, you didn't notice a man, say at Stamford, whom you afterwards saw at—shall we say, Grantham?—and then again at York, and perhaps later at Durham? You take my meaning?"

"I do!" exclaimed Crole. "Worth considering, too! Think, Holt."

I was thinking—hard. I let my mind go back to the start-out of my tour with Mazaroff and re-traced our whole route from London to the Border moorlands. We had made several stoppages: I tried to re-create the events of each.

"Well," I answered at last, "I can only think of this—that seems to have anything to do with your suggestion. We stayed a night at Huntingdon—our first night. I saw Mazaroff talking, evidently confidentially, to a man in the smoking-room late that night: I myself was just going to bed—I left them talking. Then, one day at York, I saw him in conversation with the same man in York Station, near the bookstall."

"Did he mention the man to you, afterwards, on either occasion?" asked Kloop.

"He didn't. They seemed—well, intimate, as if they knew each other," I said. "Indeed, my impression at the time was that this was probably some man Mazaroff knew in London."

"You'd know the man again?" suggested Kloop.

"Oh, yes—a young, fair-haired, fresh-complexioned man, very smartly dressed," I said. "A man of probably twenty-five or so."

"Were there any other guests than yourselves at this Woodcock Inn?" enquired Kloop.

"Staying there—no," I replied. "People came in, though, for lunch—people who were motoring North or South. On the evening of the murder, when the whole place was very busy, every room thronged, in fact, with men coming from the fair, there were motoring people there—I heard Mrs Musgrave, the landlady, complaining that she couldn't attend to them properly because of the fair people. I know, for instance, that there were people in the coffee-room—motorists, whose cars were outside—but I didn't see them; Mazaroff and I had a private room."

Kloop folded his hands on the table and looked from one to

the other of us.

"What is in my mind," he said, "is that Mazaroff may have been tracked to this place, caught on that moor by the man who had tracked him, and done to death."

"For what he had on him?" suggested Crole.

"That—or something like it," answered Kloop. "I see it's stated in the papers—from Mr Holt's evidence—that he probably had a lot of money and his valuables on him—that goes without saying—Mazaroff was one of those men who do carry a great deal of ready money, and his jewellery was worth a lot. But —do you know if he had anything else—anything that would make a man resort to actual murder to gain possession of?"

"We don't," answered Maythorne. "The fact is, Mr Kloop, we came to you hoping that you, as a close friend of his, could throw a lot of light on Mazaroff. What, now, was he likely to have on him?"

Kloop consulted his watch. Then he rose, gathering up his armful of newspapers. "Let us go into the smoking-room," he said. "We will smoke a cigar. And I will tell you what I know of Mazaroff. It may do some good—but I think," he continued, with a significant glance all round, "I think the secret of this business will be unearthed only by getting at Mazaroff's own doings between the time he arrived here in London and his murder at Marrasdale Moor. However—let us have a cigar on it."

Kloop was evidently as much of a connoisseur in tobacco as he afterwards proved to be an expert in diamonds. He was not the sort of man who buys a cigar in an hotel; installing us in a quiet corner of the smoking-room he sent a page-boy up to his room for a certain box of cigars, which, when brought, he recommended to us with almost fatherly solicitude: it was easy to see, when he lighted his own, that he was one who derived great satisfaction and mental comfort from the cigar habit. He smoked for three or four minutes in silence before he summoned us to attention with a flash of the big diamond on his fat little finger.

"Now about our poor friend Mazaroff," he said. "I have known him—intimately, closely—for many years—we were what you call here in England great pals. He and I——"

"A moment, if you please, and while it occurs to me," interrupted Maythorne. "You have read what was said at the inquest about Mazaroff being in reality one Andrew Merchison? Very well—do you know if he was Andrew Merchison?"

"I do not," replied Kloop. "But," he added with a quiet smile, "I dare say he was. In fact, I should conclude he was the Andrew Merchison spoken of at the inquest. He was a bit of a mystery man, Mazaroff. One thing was certain—he was a native of your Northern parts. If he wasn't a Scotsman, he was a Border man—by his speech. I have travelled in those parts, and I know. His accent, of course, was unmistakable. But I never knew him as anything else than Salim Mazaroff, and he never said a word to me about his antecedents, during the whole time of our friendship."

"You were saying——?" suggested Maythorne with a nod.

"I was saying that he and I saw much of each other in Cape Town during the past ten years," continued Kloop. "We were members of the same club; our offices were adjacent; at one time we did a good deal of business together. When he first became known to me, Mazaroff was what you might term a general trader, or general speculator in commerce. He bought and sold things—chiefly in the East—that is, he bought in the East and sold in the West. At one time he did a big trade in Persian carpets and rugs—he used to collect unusually fine specimens of these things and get big prices for them in London and in New York—luxury business, you know. Then he traded also in spices, and in Chinese curiosities—rarities, and so on—he had a genius for making money in that way. But of late years, he had given up all that and had turned his attention exclusively to diamonds. He did well in diamonds, but he retired from that, too, about last Christmas. Still, when he retired, and when he came to England, he had a certain deal, or venture, or speculation on, and I am inclined to believe that it has more than a little to do with his murder."

He paused at that and smoked thoughtfully for a while before resuming his story.

"Up to now," he continued at last, pointing to the papers, "there has been nothing—there—that seems to relate to what I am going to tell you. Last winter Mazaroff got hold—never mind how, for that was his own secret, one of many in his diamond dealings—of a truly magnificent blue diamond. Now, a blue diamond is a blue diamond!—if you look at the coloured illustrations of famous stones in the popular books about diamonds, you will see that there are yellow diamonds, and orange-yellow, and green, and rose, but not so many blue diamonds—that is, of a real rarity. This blue diamond that Mazaroff got hold of was exceptionally fine. I have myself seen the famous Blue Hope—Mazaroff's stone was finer, both in size and quality. It weighed fifty-five and a half carats: its colour and brilliancy were superb! I don't think—indeed I am sure—that it was seen by anyone but myself in Cape Town: Mazaroff sent it off to England. He——"

"To whom?" interrupted Maythorne.

"That I do not know," replied Kloop, smiling at the quick enquiry. "He didn't tell me all his concerns."

Maythorne produced the receipt for the registered letter posted at Cape Town and passed it over to Kloop.

"Do you think that receipt has anything to do with the sending?" he asked. "Look at the endorsement on the back—in Mazaroff's writing."

Kloop examined the bit of paper carefully, on both sides, and finally passed it back with a satisfied nod.

"Oh, no doubt!" he answered. "That would be about the date. Sent it to the London branch of his bank, to be sure. The endorsement proves it, too—what could be clearer? Bl.D.1. Blue Diamond One, of course."

"Why Blue Diamond One?" asked Maythorne. "Is there, or was there, a Blue Diamond Two?" Kloop smiled knowingly.

"Precisely what I am about to tell you!" he answered. "There was!—in the end. And I feel convinced that Mazaroff had Blue Diamond Two, and perhaps Blue Diamond One, on him when he was murdered on the moor!"

We three looked at each other wonderingly. And presently Kloop continued.

"After Mazaroff got hold of that first blue diamond, he developed an almost feverish craze to get a second. I know"—here Kloop gave us something very closely resembling a wink, as if he could tell certain trade secrets did it suit him to do so—"I know that Mazaroff got Blue Diamond One for what you call, I believe—in your English phrase—a mere song. But he was so intent on getting another blue diamond to match it that he told me he was prepared to go to a great length, a big price. He set agents to work—everybody knew Mazaroff in the diamond-producing areas; he set to work himself. Well, in the end he got what he wanted."

"Another?" exclaimed Crole.

"Another. And equally fine," replied Kloop. "And of about the same weight—fifty-five or six carats. I don't know, for he wouldn't tell me, what he gave for it. But he got it—and not very long before he sailed for England."

"You saw it?" asked Maythorne.

"I saw it—yes," assented Kloop. "So—I have seen both. I don't think anybody else has. Unless—which I suspect—Mazaroff has shown them here, since his coming. When I say I don't think any other person has seen them than myself, I mean that I'm sure no one—except the people who sold them to him—in South Africa saw them. Mazaroff had his eye on buyers in Europe."

"Did he mention any particular buyers?" enquired Maythorne.

"He did not. But he did tell me that he had a man here, in London, who did things for him, and who was in touch with European and American people of high degree that might be inclined to give a very fancy price for the pair—if he could get a pair, for that," added Kloop, "was before he secured Blue Diamond Two."

"And you feel sure that he first sent Blue Diamond One to London, and then brought Blue Diamond Two in his own pocket?" suggested Maythorne.

"I feel sure of that," said Kloop. "I may say—I'm certain of it. And since I have learnt these particulars of his sad fate, I have wondered if Mazaroff did one of two things, or, perhaps, both? The first—did he get talkative on board ship, and show his second blue diamond to fellow-passengers; the second, did he show it here in London, amongst the fraternity?"

"The fraternity?" said Crole. "You mean——"

"I mean Hatton Garden," answered Kloop with a knowing smile. "Where, as you must know, the greater part of the diamond transactions of this country are carried out. It will surprise me if Mazaroff is not to be heard of there! Although he had retired from active participation in diamond trading, his heart was in it still. But this is easy to find out—come, gentlemen, I will walk along the street with you . . . and we will see!"

CHAPTER 14 THE BOND STREET JEWELLER

We made a little procession along Holborn; Mr Kloop and May-thorne in front, Mr Crole and myself in the rear. I had no idea of what we were after—exactly; that quarter of the town was unknown to me. But at the corner of a hum-drum, grey street, quiet enough after the ceaseless traffic of the great thorough-fare, Crole gave me a knowing look.

"Hatton Garden!" he said, directing my attention to the sign above our heads. "As plain a place as ever they make 'em. But if you and I had the stuff in our pockets that's within these walls, Holt, we should be—multi-millionaires, I suppose!"

"Diamonds?" I suggested.

"Aye, and their like," he assented dryly. "It's all diamonds, and pearls, and rubies, and that sort of thing here, where once the Bishops of Ely had their garden, coolly appropriated from them by Queen Elizabeth for the use of her favourite, Kit Hatton. There's not much sign of the commodity about these walls, nor much evidence of the trade in the men you see hanging about, but I'll lay a pound to a penny that there isn't a man we elbow who hasn't got a sample of precious stones about him, and as for what there is in these old rooms and offices—ah, Golconda wasn't in it!"

We saw plenty of men on the pavements—it seemed to me

that they were chiefly of Semitic origin, or of foreign nationality; they were in twos or threes, sometimes in groups. Once, as we strolled along, Mr Crole nudged my arm—a man, in earnest conversation with another, was holding out to him, and turning over with a pudgy forefinger, a palmful of pebble-like looking things—diamonds, of course.

"Just as corn-factors turn over a farmer's samples of barley," observed Crole. "But—you'd have to have a lot of quarters of barley, Holt, to represent the value of a fistful of those things. These chaps—but Kloop's found somebody he knows."

Kloop, indeed, had greeted a man whose fine cloth overcoat was ornamented by a luxurious fur collar and his black satin stock by a blazing diamond pin. They were evidently well acquainted and met with much enthusiasm and hand-shaking—after which Kloop drew his man aside. When, a few minutes later, they parted, Kloop came to us, shaking his head.

"That's a man who knows this place from top to bottom and end to end," he remarked, "and who learns at once of anything remarkable or unusual. He has not heard of Mazaroff and his blue diamonds. And that inclines me to a further belief in what I've been thinking all along—which is that Mazaroff intended, and perhaps had in view—a private deal with those stones—did not intend them to come on the market. This is the market!—and that man knows nothing. But there are still other men."

After that he dived into several offices, and spoke to other men whom he met on the street; he took us down a narrow alley to a queer, old-world tavern called the Mitre, wherein we seemed to find ourselves in the sixteenth century. There were men there, smoking full-flavoured cigars, to whom Kloop spoke. But we got no news of Mazaroff.

"The fact is evident," he said as we once more sought the open street. "Mazaroff had not visited these regions during his stay in London. He would have been known here by name—the mere fact of his being in possession of a couple of stones like those would have spread all through the place. I am convinced now that if Mazaroff showed his blue diamonds here in London, it was in private."

Then, saying that he must now attend to his own business, and begging us to communicate with him at his hotel if there was anything more he could do, or anything we could tell him, Kloop left us. We three went back up Holborn, and, it being already well past midday, turned, at Crole's suggestion, into the Holborn Restaurant for lunch.

"Well, we've got some information," observed Maythorne as we settled down at a corner table. "We've found out about those diamonds. I figure up the situation in this way: Mazaroff sent the first—Blue Diamond One, as we'll call it—to his London bankers. Now then——did he send it for safety, until his coming, or did he send it that it might be shown to a likely customer? I think, to a likely customer—I also think more, in view of that cypher letter.' I think that—probably for some time—Armintrade, then at the Imperial Banking Corporation of South Africa in London, had not only had charge of Mazaroff's correspondence with the bank, but had corresponded privately with Mazaroff. I think that Armintrade took charge of Blue Diamond One till Mazaroff's arrival with Blue Diamond Two, and, probably, during the interval made enquiries for a likely buyer of the pair."

"Not in trade quarters?" suggested Crole.

"Not in trade quarters," assented Maythorne. "There are others—better quarters. Had those diamonds come on the market we've just had a glimpse of, several fingers would have itched to be in the pie. But there are private buyers—on the Continent, as well as here; in America as well as in Europe."

"Has anybody got sufficient money nowadays?" questioned Crole, half-lugubriously. "Mazaroff would want a price!"

"Plenty of people!" asserted Maythorne. "Profiteers—newly rich—pooh! we've got folk amongst us who are just itching to spend their easily made money. From all I hear of him, Mazaroff was an astute man. He probably figured in this—there are a lot of men here in England who, rightly or wrongly, have made vast fortunes out of the war. Such men—as we well know—want to set up in great style, or, rather, they do set up in great style. A big town house; a place in the country; expensive furniture; troops of servants; pictures; finely bound books which they never open, and could scarcely read if they did—you know. That's largely the man's line—the getting of these things. But the men have women—there's Lady Midas as well as Sir Gorgions. Now what does Lady Midas want?—furs, silks, satin, laces, everything that Bond Street and the Rue de la Paix can supply. But, more than any of these things—diamonds! What is a fashionable woman without diamonds? And not merely five-hundred-pound rings, and ten-thousand-pound necklaces—she wants a tiara, and, even more than a tiara, something very extra special in it. Her hair may be false, and her skin as yellow as parchment —but she's going to have diamonds glittering in one and on the other. Now I reckon that Mazaroff knew all that, and that he considered Lady Midas the customer he was looking for, eh?"

"Well—no doubt you're not far wrong," laughed Crole. "Now, if you've got Lady Midas's address in your pocket?"

"At present," observed Maythorne, "Lady Midas is found at a lot of addresses. In the meantime, there's spade-work to be done in another corner."

"It strikes me there are several corners," said Crole. "Up to now, we've had no light on that Mombasa affair. There can be no doubt that Merchison was on that ship, that he slipped away from it, leaving his things behind, and got safely ashore—to disappear as Merchison and re-appear as Mazaroff. Now, why?"

"I regard that as settled," answered Maythorne. "All the details point to a plant—of his own. He'd reasons for that disappearance—and he could effect it easily enough. When he left Bombay, he also left the past. If we could get at the truth, we should probably find that he'd already transferred his money to South Africa before ever he left India; that the leaving of his cabin-trunk and effects was all a trick—of course, he got ashore quite easily, and went off on a new existence."

"Again—why?" demanded Crole.

"I should say—because he wanted to cut clear of Mrs Merchison, left at home," said Maythorne dryly. "He *wanted* her to think him dead!—what did it matter as long as he was alive? He seems to have been alive enough, too, as Mazaroff. But I tell you he was always a bit of a mystery man, and I'd give a lot to know where he went, and with whom he talked, and so on, that day after he and Holt struck the Woodcock."

"But nobody knows!" I exclaimed. "We went into all that as soon as he was missed!—of course! We couldn't find out anybody to whom he talked—that is, particularly—nor get news of anybody who had seen him—except that two or three people had just noticed him going about, as a stranger."

"Well, that just makes the whole thing queerer than ever," said Maythorne. "Here's a certainty—he saw somebody that day who gave him some information about Mrs Elphinstone and Miss Merchison—he said as much to you, didn't he?"

"He did," I admitted.

"Well—who was that somebody?" he asked. "That somebody who's never come forward? What do you both make of that?"

Neither of us could make anything of it and we said nothing. Maythorne, who sat opposite to Crole and myself, laid down his knife and fork, and bent across the table to us.

"Suppose," he said in a whisper, meant to be mysterious and significant—"suppose—eh?—suppose it was his wife?"

"Mrs Elphinstone!" I exclaimed.

"Mrs Merchison, in strict law," he answered. "Just so! Suppose it was?"

This suggestion seemed to impress Crole even more than it impressed me—his mouth opened and he started. But before he could say anything, a young man came threading his way through the crowded room and made for him. He bent down, handed Crole a card, and whispered something. Crole looked at the card and towards the door.

"Outside?—waiting?" he said. "Bring him in here, Rollinson—ask him to join me—show him the way."

Rollinson—one of Crole's clerks—went off, and Crole threw the card on the table for us to look at. It was a very neat, beautifully engraved card, giving the name and address of Mr Adolf Frobenius, 508 Bond Street, W., and a very neat, spick-and-span gentleman who followed it—the exemplification of all that is smart and ultra-respectable in a fashionable West End tradesman.

"Swell jewellers in Bond Street," whispered Crole, as Mr Frobenius, ushered by the clerk, made his way to our corner; "client of mine, and neighbour of mine, too—lives near me at Wimbledon: smart man. Hallo, Frobenius!" he continued as he greeted his visitor. "Delighted you ran me to earth. Lunched?—then join us at a cigar and coffee. Let me introduce my friends—Mr Maythorne; Mr Mervyn Holt. I dare say," he added, with a sly smile, "you've heard of both, before now."

"Of Mr Maythorne, often," answered the jeweller, with a polite bow. "And of Mr Holt—since I read in the newspapers of the Mazaroff affair. Which affair, Mr Crole," he continued, seating himself by the solicitor, "is what I have come to see you about."

"I thought so," said Crole. "Guessed it at once. We shall be glad of any information. We came to town to enquire into things about Mazaroff, and, between ourselves, we've spent an hour in Hatton Garden this morning, asking about him—fruitlessly. Did you know him?"

Frobenius, who had just taken a cigar from Crole's case, lighted it and smoked a little before answering this question.

"I have read a great deal in the newspapers about this affair," he said at last. "The various accounts, sent, I presume, by local reporters; also I read, more carefully, the report of the inquest. Of course, I see your name mentioned, Mr Crole—and Mr Holt's. And I came along to see you, Mr Crole, because I am almost sure that not very long ago, under rather unusual circumstances, I met Mr Mazaroff."

"Good!" exclaimed Crole. "But—you either did or you didn't. Why 'almost'?"

"Because," answered Frobenius, "the man whom I met was not introduced to me by any name. I just met him. However, he was a notable man—and the description of Mazaroff in the papers corresponds with my recollections. But I will give you the facts. You, Mr Crole, are well aware of what my business is, and of my connections in the West End. Well, during the past twelve months or so I have had business dealings with a Sir Samuel and Lady Leeke. Sir Samuel is a self-made man; to be plain, he made a vast fortune as a contractor during the recent war; he is, I gather, a multi-millionaire. About a year ago he bought Lord Mulworthy's house in Park Lane; he has also, I am told, a very fine place in Buckinghamshire. He and Lady Leeke—chiefly her ladyship—have had extensive dealings with me in jewellery and plate—you will understand," he added, with a quiet and knowing smile, "that it was—er—necessary to fit themselves out with things which they didn't possess in the old days. Lady Leeke, for example, has bought a good many jewels from me, and, I venture to think, has formed a high opinion of my taste and experience."

"Speaks well for *her* taste, Frobenius!" interjected Crole politely.

"Well," continued the jeweller, with a smile, "to come to the important part of my story. About a month or five weeks ago I was called to the telephone one afternoon, and found Sir Samuel Leeke speaking to me. He wanted me to go round to Park Lane there and then, to look at and estimate the value of a diamond that had been offered to him. I told him I would be with him in a few minutes, and so I was, with the help of a taxi-cab. I found Sir Samuel and Lady Leeke in their library; they had with them a stranger whose appearance, as I recollect it, corresponds with the description of Mazaroff given in the newspapers—I particularly remember the cast in the left eye. He was not introduced to me by name—Sir Samuel and Lady Leeke, in spite of their wealth, are not exactly acquainted with—you know. It appeared, however, that the stranger was one who was interested in diamonds in a large way, had heard of Sir Samuel and his wife as possible buyers, and was willing to sell them something of very special value; to wit, a remarkable pair of blue diamonds, of which he had one in his pocket. It was this that I was asked to see. He produced it."

"A blue diamond?" asked Maythorne, always particular as to exact facts.

"A blue diamond—and an unusually fine stone," asserted Frobenius. "Its proprietor told me that it was one of a pair—the other was equally fine. He further said that he had been in the diamond trade for some years, in South Africa, had now retired, and this would be his last deal. He and I talked—professionally —for a while: our conversation, I could see, excited Sir Samuel and Lady Leeke to a desire to possess what was evidently something well worth having. And what they—the Leekes—wanted to get at was—what were the two diamonds worth? The would-be vendor and myself had a good deal of talk about the matter. He was very fair and reasonable, and he and I eventually came to a decision as to a proper price for the pair."

"And what might that be?" asked Crole eagerly.

"Well," answered Frobenius, "we agreed that a fair price would be a hundred and sixty thousand pounds."

CHAPTER 15 THE NEWLY RICH

Although the jeweller mentioned this vast sum of money as casually as a greengrocer might mention the current market price of gooseberries, the rest of us were not quite so phlegmatic, and Crole let out an exclamation of astonishment.

"One hundred and sixty thousand pounds!—for a couple of diamonds!" he said. "Whew!—that's a bit exceptional, isn't it?"

"You have to bear in mind that the diamonds are exceptional," answered Frobenius, with the quiet smile of superior knowledge. "Of course, I only saw one. But the would-be vendor assured me that the other was equally fine, if not finer. Now, you don't get such a pair on the market every day, nor every year—perhaps not once in a generation. The sum we agreed upon was a reasonable price—not an extravagant one."

"You'd have given it yourself?" asked Maythorne sharply.

"Well," replied the jeweller, "I'd have given ten thousand less."

"Without much doubt about making a nice profit, eh?" suggested Crole.

"I should have made a profit," admitted Frobenius. "However, the diamonds were not offered to me. I was merely a valuer."

"And what happened?" asked Maythorne. "Was the deal carried out?"

"That I do not know," replied Frobenius. "I perceived that after having agreed with the seller as to what would be a fair price, my part was played, and I left seller and buyer talking the matter over. My impression was that Sir Samuel would probably buy."

"You've heard nothing since?" enquired Crole.

"Nothing. I haven't seen Sir Samuel Leeke, nor Lady Leeke, since that afternoon," said the jeweller. "And of course I haven't seen the blue diamond man. But I feel sure that he was the man who is referred to in the newspapers as Mazaroff."

"I don't think there's much doubt about that," assented Crole. "Well, now, we'd better get in touch with these Leeke people," he continued, glancing at me and Maythorne. "What sort of folk are they?" he asked, turning to our informant.

Frobenius smiled and gave us a confidential look.

"Oh, well!" he said. "They're of a class which didn't exist—at any rate, noticeably—before the war. Newly-rich! The man was, so I have been told, a grocer, or provision merchant, somewhere in the North, who made an immense fortune out of contracting during the early years of the war, and at the same time did a lot of local work in furthering recruiting. So he got one of the titles that have been dealt out so lavishly and blossomed into Sir Samuel. Good-natured, friendly, simple people—who have more money than they know what to do with. That's about it."

"We must see them," said Crole. "Park Lane, you said?"

Mr Frobenius gave us the exact address of Sir Samuel Leeke and left us. Crole and I, as if by common impulse, looked at our companion.

"Well?" said Crole. "What's Maythorne asking himself?"

Maythorne looked up from a pattern which he was mechanically tracing on the tablecloth

"Only one thing to ask—at present," he said. "Did Mazaroff sell those diamonds to Sir Samuel Leeke?"

"That's what we want to find out," observed Crole. "A plain question! And——"

Maythorne interrupted him with a significant glance.

"Aye!" he said. "And easily answered, as no doubt it will be. But —if he didn't——"

"Well?" demanded Crole.

Maythorne got up, with a gesture that suggested action.

"Then, in that case, Armintrade's got them—in my opinion," he said. "And—the job will be to prove that he has! A quiet man, Armintrade, evidently—secret as they make 'em. And where have we got the slightest clue to what we want to establish— that he and Mazaroff met on that first day after Mazaroff and Holt arrived at the Woodcock?"

"There must be somebody about there who knows what Armintrade's movements were on that day!" I suggested. "He's Courthope's guest—Courthope would know. And the doctor chap—Eccleshare. They would all be about together—shooting. Those two must know where Armintrade was."

"How are you going to get them to speak—if Armintrade's a pal of theirs?" asked Maythorne. "From what I saw and heard of them at the Woodcock, they're both men who'll keep their knowledge to themselves. But we're getting at something here —and it all points to Armintrade. Now let's see this Sir Samuel man and get a step farther."

We chartered a taxi-cab outside in Holborn and were driven to Park Lane, where we pulled up in front of an imposing mansion, at the door of which we were encountered by footmen whose liveries were rather more gorgeous than the usual run of things in that way. In fact, everything that we met was of the rather more, rather overdone order, and suggested that in their painful anxiety to hit the precise mark Sir Samuel and Lady Leeke had consistently overshot it. The room into which we were ushered after we had sent in our cards looked as if some very high-class upholsterer had been given *carte blanche* to wreak his own will and fancy on it; also, it looked as if the furnishings had never been touched or used since the upholsterers' men had placed them in position: the whole apartment resembled one of those models which you see at furniture exhibitions, and was plainly intended for show rather than for use. Mr Crole muttered sarcastically that the chairs were much too grand to sit upon, and we all remained standing, staring at gold clocks, priceless china, and apparently very expensive pictures until a little, apple-cheeked, rotund man, who wore mutton-chop whiskers and a ready smile, came bustling in, a big half-smoked cigar in one podgy hand and our cards in the other.

"I know what you chaps have come for!" he exclaimed, beaming from one to the other of us. "This Mazaroff affair!—I've read it all in the papers, and your names too, same as what I see on your cards—just so. Now then, which is which? Mr Crole? Just so! Mr Holt? Just so! Mr Maythorne?—to be sure. Now then, we know who we are—and what's it all about, gentlemen?"

"We have the honour of seeing Sir Samuel Leeke?" enquired Crole with great politeness.

"You have, sir!—that's me, Sir Samuel Leeke, KBE, in the flesh," agreed our host good-humouredly. "And none the worse, I hope, for a bit of a handle to my name! But this Mazaroff affair, now—egad, it's a queer business, I think—what?"

"You're aware of it, then, Sir Samuel?" suggested Crole. "Well up in things as far as they've gone?"

"Who isn't?" exclaimed Sir Samuel. "Been plenty in the papers, anyway. Of course me and her ladyship's read all we could set our eyes to. It was only this morning she says to me, 'Sam!' she says, 'as sure as fate somebody'll be coming to us about this here affair!' And—there you are! But I'll tell you what—come this way, gentlemen, and then her ladyship can hear all you've got to say—women, you know, is curious, and news is better at first hand than at second—this way!"

We followed Sir Samuel out of the cold grandeurs of our first haven into the less formal and more comfortable harbour of another and smaller room, where we found Lady Leeke, in a deep chair by a big fire, toying with a piece of fancy-work. She was as rotund as her husband; her dress was of the latest fashion, and she had many rings on her fingers, and it struck me that she was somewhat sharper of intellect than Sir Samuel, not quite so open, and infinitely more watchful. She sized us all up as we were formally presented to her, and she marshalled us all into chairs facing her own, so that while the light fell on our faces it left hers in shade.

"Of course I knew we should have enquiries made here," she observed in a slightly affected tone. I said so, this morning to Sir Samuel."

"As I've just told 'em," said Sir Samuel, who, hospitably bent, was handing his cigar-case round amongst us. "Though, to be sure, I've no idea as yet as to how they got here. Nobody knows about our transactions with Mazaroff outside ourselves—so far as I know. Of course, Mazaroff may have talked. But now—how did you come to hear of us?"

"My dear Sir Samuel," replied Crole solemnly, "there are mysteries within mysteries! A man of your position, and your knowledge of the world, will understand me when I say that this is a big thing. You've already read a good deal about it—now, to be brief, what can you tell us?"

Sir Samuel settled himself in a chair adjacent to his wife's, and rubbed his hands on the knees of his trousers: it seemed to me that he was one of those men who highly enjoy telling a story.

"Well, I don't know that there's anything to keep back," he said, with a glance at Lady Leeke. "Nor that there's such a great deal to tell, either. This Mr Mazaroff called here one day—just as you've done—and introduced himself as a man that had had big dealings in diamonds and the like in South Africa. He'd heard, so he told us, of Lady Leeke as a likely purchaser of something exceptional in diamonds, and he'd thought she'd like to see a particularly fine bit of property that he'd got in that line o' goods. Then he told me it was a pair of very fine and rare blue diamonds, and he produced one."

"Only one?" enquired Maythorne.

"Only one. The other," continued Sir Samuel, "he said was in the possession of his agent, a Mr Armintrade, of Courthope's Bank, who was just then away holiday-making—shooting, in fact, with Mr Courthope, in Northumberland. He said he should be seeing Mr Armintrade very soon, as he was going motoring that way, and he would get the fellow diamond from him——"

"Unless!" interrupted Lady Leeke. "There was an unless about it."

"So there was," admitted Sir Samuel. "Yes—unless Armintrade had got a definite offer from some other customer—Armintrade, he said, had had the first blue diamond in his possession for some months and might have found an advantageous customer for the pair."

"Then you didn't buy?" asked Maythorne.

"No—we didn't buy," replied Sir Samuel. "What we did was this—I telephoned our regular jeweller, Frobenius, and got him to come here and examine the diamond that Mazaroff had with him. They talked—professional jargon, of course—and they agreed that a reasonable price for such a pair of blue diamonds would be a hundred and sixty thousand pounds. After Frobenius had gone, Mazaroff and I came to this arrangement—if his agent, Armintrade, hadn't got a better offer, or made some arrangement to which they were committed, Mazaroff was to get the second blue diamond from Armintrade, and, on his return to London, show me and her ladyship the pair. If we then decided to buy, we were to have the pair at the price I've just mentioned to you. And of course," concluded Sir Samuel, with a comprehensive glance from one to the other of us, "of course, that's where it ended. We've never seen the diamonds since."

"Did you ever see Mazaroff after that first call?" asked Maythorne.

"Oh, yes, we did!" answered Sir Samuel readily enough. "He was a very friendly, sociable, pleasant sort of man, and we asked him to come and dine with us. He came—would it be the next night, Maria?"

"The next but one," replied Lady Leeke.

"Came here and dined with you," said Maythorne. "Had you any other guests, Sir Samuel?"

"No, we hadn't, that night," replied Sir Samuel. "Leastways, there was her ladyship's nephew, young Jim Mallison—but we don't reckon him a guest. Nobody else."

"Any more talk about the diamonds?" suggested Maythorne.

"There was some talk—yes," said Sir Samuel. "Nothing much. He showed it to us again—had it in his pocket, you know. But the talk that time was more in a friendly way, like—not business."

"Was that the only time you saw Mazaroff—except the first one?" asked Maythorne.

"No, there was another," said Sir Samuel. "As we'd asked him to dine with us, he asked us to dine with him. We did—at his hotel, the Cecil. A night or two after—a rare good host he was, too!"

"Just you and Lady Leeke, I suppose?" suggested Maythorne.

"Nay, there was Jim Mallison as well," replied Sir Samuel. "He asked the three of us, and a very pleasant evening we had."

"Any talk of diamonds that time?" enquired Maythorne.

"No—I don't remember that they were mentioned that time at all," said Sir Samuel. "The arrangement was made, d'ye see. We were to inspect the pair when Mazaroff came back from his jaunt."

"And you never saw him again after that dinner at the Cecil?" asked Maythorne. "Never met him anywhere about London?"

"No—never saw nor heard of him again," replied Sir Samuel. "Until we saw all this in the papers."

"Your nephew, Mr James Mallison, I think you said," remarked Maythorne. "Did you ever hear him mention seeing Mazaroff in town—after that dinner?"

Sir Samuel looked at his wife.

"I never heard Jim mention that," he answered. "To be sure, Jim knocks about a good deal in fashionable places, and so on —he's away just now, or he could tell you himself. But I never heard him speak of meeting Mazaroff again—did you, Maria?"

"No—I never heard him say anything of that," replied Lady Leeke. "Besides, I think Mr Mazaroff was just going away when we dined with him at the Cecil."

We had a little more conversation with this worthy couple, and then left them. I was anxious to get out of the house: I had an announcement to make which I could not make before. I made it as soon as we got clear of the gorgeous footmen.

"I say!" I exclaimed, seizing my companions' elbows. "You remember that—this morning—I spoke of seeing Mazaroff in conversation with a man, first at Huntingdon, then at York—a man who was a stranger to me, but whom Mazaroff evidently knew? Well—there's a photograph of that man—the very man!—on Lady Leeke's mantelpiece!"

CHAPTER 16 THE KNOCK AT MY DOOR

The two men stopped, staring at me—Crole with an ordinary glare of surprise, but Maythorne with a sudden flash of the eye and an alertness that I had never noticed before in him: it was as if my remark had acted as an illumination. Just as suddenly his quick look shifted back, sidewise, to the house we had left.

"There were two photographs of men on Lady Leeke's mantel-piece," he said. "One on each side of that apparently thousand-guinea clock. Which are you referring to?"

"The man in the rather loud check jacket and soft collar," I answered. "A head-and-shoulder photograph."

"That was the chap on the right-hand side of the clock," he went on musingly. "A youngish man, evidently fair-haired, fair-moustached. That it?"

"That's the man I saw talking to Mazaroff at Huntingdon and again at York, anyway," I asserted. "I recognised the photograph instantly."

We stood for another moment in silence, Crole and I watching Maythorne. Suddenly he moved; we walked along Park Lane a little.

"The probability is that that's the nephew we heard about—Mallison," said Maythorne, as if waking out of a reverie. "Let's see—he was referred to as Lady Leeke's nephew, and Sir Samuel spoke of him as knowing his way about town pretty well. Now then, where are we? Mallison, according to what we've just heard, twice met Mazaroff—once here at Leeke's house, again when Mazaroff entertained the three at the Cecil. Mallison heard about, and saw, one of the blue diamonds. If the photograph is that of Mallison, as you assert, Holt, Mallison is the man to whom you saw Mazaroff talking first at Huntingdon and then at York. So—does Mallison know anything about this affair? That's to find out—when we can come across Mallison."

"Ought to be no great difficulty about that," muttered Crole.

"They said that Mallison was away just now," observed Maythorne. "Away North, of course, if Holt's correct about the identification. But—I'm not thinking so much about that. What I am thinking about is that the name Mallison is somehow familiar —I've some recollection of it in connection with something or other that happened here in London, in the West End, comparatively recently. It's in my mind—though I can't fix it at the minute. Mallison?"

He paused for a moment in the middle of the sidewalk, hands plunged in his trousers pockets, eyes staring at the pavement. Suddenly he looked up, signalled to a passing taxi-cab, and motioned us to follow him into it.

"Come to my office," he said. "I've a chap there—my confidential clerk—who possesses one of the sharpest brains and most retentive memories in Europe. He'll know!"

Maythorne's office was in Conduit Street, so we were there in a few minutes. I was anxious to see what sort of place it might be, naturally associating private enquiry work with drabness and a suggestion of gloom. I found the exact opposite: the place was almost palatial. There was a front office wherein two smart-looking girls were busy with typewriters and a sharp boy evidently acted as janitor; beyond that was an inner apartment, very elegantly furnished, in which sat a youthful gentleman who, when we entered, was leisurely reading the *Sporting Times*, and did not relinquish it as he rose and made his bow; beyond that, again, evidently the strictly private part of the premises, was a room rendered utterly luxurious by Turkey carpets, deep chairs, a few fine pictures, and the very latest things in office fittings. There were doubtless dark secrets told in that room from time to time, but it was to the accompaniment of everything pleasant to the senses.

At each end of this room stood a table-desk; at that at the farther end sat, when we walked in, a young man who would have attracted my attention wherever I had met him. He was a smallish-sized chap, almost a bantam-weight, to use the language of the prize-ring, and his thinnish person was arrayed in a tweed suit of very large checks; he wore a hunting-stock instead of an ordinary collar, and its folds were gathered together by a gold horseshoe pin: he might, indeed, have been a head stableboy as far as this sort of thing went. But there were more noticeable things about him—seen as soon as he rose and turned towards his employer. He had the sharpest and queerest pair of blue eyes I have ever seen; the most inquisitive nose, and the straightest line of lip above the squarest and most obstinate of chins—and yet even these things were not, severally or collectively, the most remarkable of his features. The thing that one's eye went to first was the fellow's red hair—absolutely, genuinely red, a veritable flame of colour against the delicate shading of the walls, and this in spite of the fact that he wore it close-cropped, thereby accentuating a pair of unduly large, rather pointed ears. I don't know what Crole thought of him—he had doubtless seen him before, perhaps often—but my own mind immediately crystallised its impressions into a word at sight of the vivid fell, the sharp nose, the general aspect of ready watchfulness. Ferret!

Maythorne motioned us into two big chairs that flanked a cheery fire, threw aside his stick and gloves, and turned on his clerk, who, after rising from his desk, stood—watching.

"Cottingley!" he said, going straight to the subject without preface. "Do we know the name Mallison?"

I saw a swift flash of light in the red-headed one's queer eyes—it was as if a lamp had suddenly been lighted somewhere behind them. The thin straight line of the lips relaxed—the close-cropped head nodded.

"We do! Mallison. James Mallison."

124

The creature's voice was as odd as his appearance. It was a sort of subdued falsetto—piping. He remained staring at Maythorne, and Maythorne nodded.

"I thought you'd remember, Cottingley. In what connection, now?"

"Welminster Square affair. No direct connection—with him. One of our clients was in it, though. Mallison—his name was in the list. Memorised it. James Mallison—no occupation. Address —Park Lane. Lady Leeke's nephew—that's who Mallison is."

"And that Welminster Square affair, Cottingley? Gambling business, wasn't it?"

"Police raid in a private gambling-house in Welminster Square. About three or four months ago. Thirty or forty arrests. Mallison was one of the men on the premises. There were women, too. Fashionable women. Man who kept the place heavily fined—very heavily. Rest—frequenters—usual thing—got off lightly. If you remember, one of our clients was there—came to you in a blue funk. Nothing! Like the scrap-book?"

Maythorne nodded his head and held out a hand, and the clerk, turning to a big table that stood in the centre of the room, took up a solidly-bound volume which proved to contain newspaper cuttings, and with almost uncanny celerity found a page and handed the book over. Maythorne glanced at the extract, and then twisted the volume round towards Crole and me.

"There you are," he said. "We cut out all sorts of stuff and things from the current newspapers and paste 'em up for future reference—you never know when they'll come in handy. I find that system very useful—I haven't such a retentive memory as Cottingley there. This, you see, is a newspaper account of a police raid on a private gambling-hell in the West End—house kept by an amiable gentleman who had such troops of friends, male and female, to visit him of an evening that the police grew suspicious and decided to visit him themselves—uninvited. There's all about it, and what happened, and there are the names of the folk found on the premises, and amongst them, you see, that of James Mallison, no occupation. Park Lane—which seems to argue that Mr Mallison lives with his aunt and his uncle-in-law. But perhaps Cottingley knows—Cottingley knows a lot! Do you know anything about Mallison, Cottingley?"

The clerk pursed his lips and made a slight gesture of his shoulders—his action seemed to indicate that Mallison was scarcely worth his attention.

"Very little! Young man about town. A bit—foppish. Sporty —in a way. Lives with Sir Samuel and Lady Leeke. You can see him sometimes with them—and more often by himself in one of Sir Samuel's motors. Chucks his money about fairly freely— they've no children, those Leekes. Newly-rich—war profiteers —that sort. They say this Mallison will come in for Sir Samuel's money."

"And that's all you know, Cottingley?"

"All!"

Maythorne threw the scrap-book back on the table.

"Well, that's that!" he said. "We know a bit more now about Mallison. Doubtless he's the man Mazaroff spoke to at Huntingdon and at York. Now, there's nothing much in that, but it seems to show that Mallison was going North. And what I'd like to know is this—did he and Mazaroff ever meet again?"

"Why?" asked Crole, with a look of surprise. "And—where?"

"The second part of your question is more pertinent than the first," answered Maythorne. "It's the whereabouts of such a meeting that is important. What we want to get at is the relationship of Mazaroff's murder to the fact that Mazaroff had Blue Diamond Number Two on him when he was murdered. How many people knew that he had? Well, from all we can make out, here was a man—Mallison—who certainly knew it. Mallison had seen the blue diamond—Number Two—in Mazaroff's possession, twice. Probably, when they encountered at Huntingdon and at York, the blue diamond deal with Sir Samuel Leeke was the subject of their conversation. We'll have to get and talk with Mallison, certainly. I'll contrive to find out this evening when he's likely to return to town, or where he can be found at present—I'll get that out of the Leekes myself. But now—Armintrade? That man has got to be seen, too—he knows more than he's told; in fact, he's told nothing. And in the meantime he must be carefully watched. Holt!—is that man you left at the Woodcock, the chauffeur, Webster, a man of good intelligence?"

"Webster's a sharp, clever chap," I answered. "Smart—trusty."

"Give me some telegraph forms, Cottingley," said Maythorne. "Holt, I'm going to send Webster wire in your name, telling him of certain things I want him to do there as regards keeping an eye on High Cap Lodge. We shall have to go back there, I expect, but it mayn't be tomorrow. As for tomorrow, will you two come here at ten o'clock in the morning?"

Crole and I presently went away, leaving Maythorne concocting his telegram to Webster. Outside, Crole yawned.

"I'm going home. Holt," he said. "Home to Wimbledon—dinner and bed, my boy!—that's what I want after all this. Yourself, now?—what're you going to do?"

"Just about the same thing," I answered. "I shall dine somewhere, and then go to my rooms. I'm tired, too. And—I suppose we've got to get on the trail again tomorrow morning?"

"Meet at ten o'clock at Maythorne's," he assented with a nod. "Um!—I wonder if we've made any headway today? Who killed Salim Mazaroff?—I hope I shan't be asking myself that in my dreams all night! Well—till the morning, then?"

He yawned once more, smiled apologetically, shook my hand, and hurried off in the direction of the nearest Tube Station. And when he had gone I discovered that I was weary—more weary than I had realised. The anxiety of the last few days, the rushing about, the mental confusion—all these things were exerting their influence. I looked at my watch—it was just six o'clock. I determined to dine at once, and then to go to my rooms in Jermyn Street and fall into bed.

I dined at a certain restaurant where quietude is obtainable, even in these days, and I took care to dine well, and to spend plenty of time over my dinner. That and the resultant rest revived me: I began to have notions of seeking out my friend Harker and telling him of my adventures. But on reflection I decided that it would be far wiser to go home—for anything that I knew we should have an even busier day on the morrow, and possibly a return to Marrasdale. So I bought the evening newspapers and went off to Jermyn Street, resolved on going to bed at exactly nine o'clock. I was nodding over the papers before that arrived and I should have kept my resolution if, just as I was about to make the definite move bedwards, Maythorne had not turned up. I saw, as soon as I opened my outer door to him, that he had news.

"I've seen Sir Samuel Leeke again, Holt," he said when I had got him inside and installed him in an easy chair with a whisky-and-soda and a cigar. "I made a plausible excuse, and called there once more. I've found out a certain fact that may or may not be relevant. About this chap Mallison, of course."

"Yes?" I said.

"Mallison," continued Maythorne, "went up North just about the time you and Mazaroff did. He went in one of Leeke's automobiles—they seem to possess a fleet!—and for a definite purpose. Old Leeke wants to rent a shooting next year—grouse moor, you know—and he thought it would be a good notion if Mallison went and inspected some shootings while guns were actually at work. From what he told me, I'm pretty dead certain that Mallison was in the immediate neighbourhood of Marrasdale at the very time you and Mazaroff reached the Woodcock Inn. Eh?"

He was watching me closely, and I saw that he expected me to make some comment. I had no comment to make: all I could say was that I had never seen anything of Mallison in those regions. He smiled.

"Why, no!" he answered. "Of course you didn't—or, I might say, wouldn't, if—but still, that's all in the clouds. Yet—Mallison was certainly there or thereabouts. And——"

He paused at that, and remained silent so long that I spoke what was in my mind.

"I wonder if we shall ever find out all about it!" I said.

He gave me a queer, knowing look.

"We shall find out all about it, Holt," he replied. "And—when we do, there'll be a fine surprise! Look here! Do you remember that when we were at Reiver's Den I picked up something close by where Mazaroff's body was found? You do? Well, now——"

He broke off short. Somebody was knocking, gently but persistently, at my outer door. We both turned in its direction, listening. The knocking came again. And at that I walked out of the room, across the little hall, and opened the door—to start back amazed.

Sheila stood there—alone!

CHAPTER 17 HOW WAS IT GOT?

Her name sprang to my lips involuntarily as I stood there, staring at her—she had been in my thoughts a good deal during the evening. She laughed, half-shyly, as I let it out, but she was more collected than I, and she stepped into the hall as readily as if there were nothing strange in this—to me—surprising visit.

I had left the door of the sitting-room open; she glanced through and saw Maythorne, and her first words were business-like enough.

"You've Mr Maythorne there? That's better!" she said. "Well ____"

I followed her into the room and closed the door. Maythorne had jumped to his feet; for a second or two the three of us stood gazing at each other. As for myself, I felt utterly at a loss: Maythorne was readier. He drew a chair in front of the fire, silently motioning Sheila to it.

"Miss Merchison is here because—something has happened," he said.

"Exactly!"

She was in a big travelling coat—a thick, fur-lined thing—and as she sat down in the chair between us she half-undid its fastenings, thrust her hand into some inner pocket and drew out a folded paper. As quietly as if she were giving me an ordinary letter to read she held it out to me.

"Mr Maythorne is right," she said. "Something has happened.

That's the will! I brought it to you—myself."

In the silence that followed on this two slight sounds forced themselves on my notice, as insignificant sounds will at supremely critical moments. One was the striking of a match by Maythorne, who had been just about to light a cigar when Sheila's knock came at the door; the other was the slight rustling of the paper as I unfolded it. I gave one glance at the signature at its foot—here, without doubt, was the will, made at York, of which Postlethwaite had spoken at the inquest. I handed it across to Maythorne; he looked it over, refolded it, and holding it in his hand, turned quietly to Sheila.

"Where did you get this, Miss Merchison?" he asked.

The answer came promptly and sharply—with a certain hardness of tone.

"Stole it!"

"Stole it? From—whom?"

"No use beating about the bush now! I stole it from my own mother!"

Maythorne and I exchanged glances: Sheila looked from one to the other. Then suddenly her glance went round to the sideboard behind my chair.

"I say," she said, "I wish you'd give me a glass of wine—I see you've got some port there. I had lunch on the train, of course, and I've had some sort of dinner at Euston since, but I want a glass of port and a biscuit, if you've got one handy—and then I'll tell—lots!"

I had some excellent port, a present from my father, and I hurried to get her some and to put a box of biscuits before her. She had nibbled half through a biscuit and taken a sip or two of port before she turned on Maythorne with an odd, half-defiant laugh.

"I dare say you've heard, perhaps known, of cases where daughters have had to tell the truth about their own mothers, Mr Maythorne?" she said. "Well—whether it's wrong or not, I'm going to tell the truth about mine. I stole that will from her this morning, because I knew she'd no right whatever to be in possession of it, and when I'd got it, I jumped on my bicycle and made off to Black Gill Junction, and caught the next train going South—to hand it over! If I hadn't, who knows what would have become of it?"

Maythorne was watching her attentively, nodding his head understandingly at each point she made: as for me, I could only sit like an oaf, wondering. It was all beyond me—so far.

"Yes?" said Maythorne. "Exactly. But—you know a lot more than that, Miss Merchison. And—we three are alone."

She ate the last of the biscuit which she had been crumbling, drank off the wine remaining in her glass, and throwing back the heavy collar of her coat, put her fingers together in her lap—I noticed they trembled a little.

"Yes," she answered. "I know a lot more than that, and I'm going to tell you. As I said at the beginning—no use in beating about the bush now! Well, it's this. I knew, from the very moment we heard about it at that inquest, that my mother was keen as she could be about news of that will, but of course I never suspected that, missing as it was, it could possibly come her way. Let me tell you, for it's no use denying it, that my mother is one of those women who love money—money, to her, means all sorts of things—never mind what. I saw from the beginning that as soon as it was put into her mind that Mazaroff was really Merchison, the idea of getting hold of his fortune began to shape itself. Mervyn!" she suddenly broke off, speaking my name for the first time, and laying her hand on my arm in a sort of natural appeal, "didn't I tell you when we walked away from the inquest that morning that I—I!—didn't want you to give up this fortune?—that I didn't want it to come into our hands?—didn't I say so, with what you might have seen to be real earnestness?"

I could only nod—there was something in the emphasis of her tone and in the pressure of her hand on my arm that seemed to stop my tongue; clearly, there were matters behind her words at which, so far, I could only guess.

"Well," she went on, "I didn't know what my mother might do: I don't know now, I tell you both, and at once, what she has done—I only know that somehow or other she became possessed of that will, and that I've stolen it from her and given it up to you. That came about in this way. Night before last, latish in the evening, my mother did a most unusual thing for her. Some little time after dinner she went out, saying that she was going to see an old man who is lying ill in the village. Now my mother is not by any means an anxious sort about old men and women who are ill, and I was surprised that she should take so much trouble in this particular instance. She went—and she was away some time; so long, indeed, that my stepfather, who is usually the least observant of men, noticed it, and suggested that I should go to the old man's cottage and walk back with her. I went—she had been there, they said, some time before, and had stayed only a few minutes. I went off, and met her near our lodge gates—she said that, being out, she had called to see some other old folk—not a very likely thing, seeing that all our old folk are in the habit of going to bed at eight o'clock. I tell you both I suspected something then, but I didn't know what! Could I help it?"

"Go on," said Maythorne quietly. "Tell us everything."

"Well, last night the same thing occurred again," continued Sheila. "She went out on the same excuse, and she was away still longer. Mr Elphinstone, who had a slight cold, went to bed; eventually I went, too. At last I heard her come in—I went down in my dressing-gown and slippers to see if there was anything I could do for her. And it was then I made a discovery. Now please don't think I was spying or eavesdropping—I was doing neither: it was all accidental. She was in the inner library—I saw her through the curtains that shut it off from the big library. There was a small lamp on the table in the centre; she stood by it examining a sheet of paper. And—I don't know if it was intuition, or what—it flashed across me that what she was looking at was the missing will! So—well, then I did watch her—I'll confess it. She read the paper through, folded it up, looked round, and then went over to one of the bookcases and slipped the paper into a big folio volume—Drake's *Eboracum*—in a corner.

Then I went off—and I didn't sleep. I knew there was—mischief. I was certain—dead certain!—that paper was the will, wherever and however she had got it. And in the middle of the night I got up and went down, and straight to the folio, and I got the paper out in the dark, and then just struck a match—and of course one glance was enough. I put it back, and went back to bed. And then there was no more sleep. I felt—oh, I don't know what I felt! There was devilry somewhere—close at hand. My own mother or not!—what business had she with that will? Where did she get it? By what means? Was she mixed up with?—but I didn't dare to think about what she might be mixed up with. What I did realise was this—the probability was that if the will remained in her possession, she'd destroy it, and then—well then, all sorts of things would happen that I didn't want to happen. And so I determined to take matters into my own hands. I got up early—long before anybody, even the servants, was astir. I made myself ready for the journey, I took the will, got on my bicycle, and set off for Black Gill Junction—it was still dark when I set out. I got down to Carlisle—and then, of course, it was plane-sailing up to town. And—you've got the will!"

Maythorne, whose whisky-and-soda stood at his elbow all this time untasted, suddenly picked it up, and made Sheila a bow in which there was more than formal politeness.

"You're a good plucked 'un!" he said, with obvious admiration. "You know at any rate how to act without hesitation. Well!—this is a queer tale. Holt. How does it strike you?"

I had been thinking hard during the last half of Sheila's story. Perhaps my ideas run on old-fashioned and conventional lines—but I said what I thought.

"It may be," I answered, "that Mrs Elphinstone could give a perfectly proper and valid explanation as to how she became possessed of the will."

Sheila turned on me like a flash.

"Mervyn!" she exclaimed, "I believe you think I should have asked her that before I stole the will and ran off with it—to you!"

"No-no!" I protested. "I——"

"I believe you do—I believe you do!" she exclaimed. "A pretty fool I should have been if I'd as much as let her know that I knew it was there! I know what would have happened if I'd told her that I knew what was hidden in that folio!"

"What, then?" I asked.

"She'd have burned it before my very eyes," she replied. "I know! No!—knowing what I did, there was only one thing to do, and that was to place it in safety."

"Miss Merchison's right," said Maythorne. "That was the only thing to do. And here it is, and tomorrow morning I'll hand it over to Crole. Mind you, Miss Merchison, your mother, as Holt suggests, may have a perfectly good explanation as to how she got the will. But, under the circumstances, you took the best step you could. Here's the will, affecting nearly a million of money—safe!"

Sheila jumped up suddenly and began to button her big coat.

"Then that's all right," she said. "I've done my bit, anyway—and now I'm off—I'll sleep tonight."

"Where are you going?" I asked as Maythorne and I rose. "Wherever it is, you must let me see you there, safely?"

"Oh, you can do that," she answered, half-carelessly. "I'm going to my old school-friend, Rhoda Apperley. She lives in a flat of her own in Ashington Mansions, in Maida Vale. I wired to her from Carlisle that I should turn up tonight. I'm all right—but you can get me a taxi and ride there with me if you like."

"And tomorrow?" asked Maythorne, with a suggesting look. "Tomorrow?"

"I'll think about tomorrow in the morning," said Sheila.

"Well, tomorrow, in the morning, let Holt call for you and bring you to my office," continued Maythorne. "Crole will be there, too, at ten o'clock, and we shall have a talk which will interest you. And by the by, before we go out, I've got something in my pocket, Miss Merchison, that I'd like to show you. Come to the light."

Suddenly, from some inner pocket, he produced and laid on the table, in the full glare of the lamp, an old-fashioned cairngorm brooch, set in fine, much-worn silver. He gave me a meaning glance as he set it down, and then looked closely at Sheila.

"Have you ever seen that before?" he asked. "Think!"

"No!" replied Sheila. "Never! Whose is it?—What is it?"

Holt picked up the brooch, and began to finger it. Turning it over, he pointed to the pin at the back, which was considerably worn, and fitted loosely to its socket.

"It would easily slip out of any woman's gown," he said. "That pin's almost worn out. As for the rest of it, that's beautiful old silver, very old, and quite thin now, here and there, and the stones are of the best quality of cairngorm, full of transparency and colour. This has been considered a brooch of value in its day, and has doubtless belonged to somebody of consequence. And—I picked it up at Reiver's Den, close to the spot where Mazaroff's dead body was found."

He was watching her still more closely as he said this. She turned on him a quick, questioning glance that shifted from him to the brooch, and he picked up the brooch again, and restored it to his pocket.

"So—to the best of your recollection—you've never seen it before?" he said.

"Never!" she repeated. "Never!"

Presently we all three went downstairs, and into the street. I got a taxi-cab, and Sheila and I got into it. Maythorne, with another admonition to us to be at his office at ten o'clock next morning, said good night and went off; we, too, set out on our ride to Maida Vale. In the lights of Piccadilly Circus we turned and looked at each other. She suddenly laughed shyly.

"Mervyn!" she said. "Were—were you glad to see me?"

"Will it be an answer," said I, "if I tell you that I'd been thinking about you all the evening?"

"That's a nice answer," she laughed. "Oh, well—now don't let's talk—we'll talk tomorrow, or next day, or some other day. But you can hold my hand, if you like, till we get to the end of the ride."

We held each other's hands—in silence—all the way to Maida

Vale. I saw her safely in charge of her friend, and went back home in the same cab. Wondering, of course—wondering . . . what next?

CHAPTER 18 THE MISSING MAN

I was back at Ashington Mansions soon after nine o'clock on the following morning, and by half past Sheila and I were walking down Edgware Road on our way to Maythorne's office. It was a fine, crisp autumn day, but that was not the reason why we walked instead of riding the mile and a half that lay between Maida Vale and Conduit Street. I think that we both had a mutual feeling of wanting to be together as long as possible, in full enjoyment of our liberty. There, amidst the crowded London streets, we were alone in a sense in which we could not have been alone in the solitudes of Marrasdale, and the sensation was as novel as it was delightful. Yet I knew it could not last, and we had not been walking far when Sheila voiced exactly what I was feeling.

"Mervyn!—I'll have to go back, you know!" she said. "I've done what I came for—given you the will—and now I'll have to go home—soon, anyway—and face the music. Of course, my mother has guessed long since what's happened. And—there'll be a nice row!"

"I shall have to go back there, too," said I. "So will Maythorne—and perhaps Crole. Couldn't we all go back together. And then ____"

"To sort of buck me up?" she laughed. "That won't save me. I shall have the liveliest quarter of an hour I ever had in my life. And I shall only have one retort to make—not a nice one to make to one's own mother—and that's to ask her what she was doing with that will and how she got it? And, if I know her, she won't say."

It was on my lips to retort that Mrs Elphinstone would probably have to say, whether she liked it or not, but I refrained.

"There may be developments before it comes to that," I remarked. "The fact is, we none of us know where we are. I don't, anyhow! Maythorne says we shall find out, and that then there'll be a tremendous surprise. As for me, I feel as if I didn't know what on earth's going to turn up next."

"Anything may," said Sheila. "I suppose the thing is, in these cases, to be ready for anything and surprised at nothing."

And at that very moment a surprise was within touching distance of us. We had walked down Edgware Road as far as Church Street; thereabouts the traffic in road and sidewalk was thick, for the road itself is a main artery, and business people were hurrying along the pavements towards the Tube stations. Suddenly Sheila stopped dead and clutched my arm; turning sharply on her I saw that she was staring as if fascinated at the open door of a tobacconist's shop, a few yards ahead of us.

"Mervyn!" she whispered. "Parslave! Gone in—there!"

I, too, stared—incredulous.

"Parslave!" I exclaimed. "The man missing from Marrasdale? Impossible!"

"I tell you Parslave has just gone into that shop—the tobacco shop! Parslave! Do you think I don't know Parslave? As well as I know my own mother! Parslave is in that shop! Come back!"

We drew back a little, against the window of another shop: there were so many people hurrying by, one way or the other, that we had a reasonable chance of seeing without being seen.

"You're certain?" I said.

"Dead certain! Parslave is in there! Listen!—did he ever see you at the Woodcock?"

"Not that I know of. He may have done. I don't remember him, of course. What's he like?"

"Tallish, thin, wiry man—rather gipsyish in appearance—

dark. He's in a blue serge suit—new. I was sharp-eyed enough to notice that. Watch for him—let me stand in this shop-door."

"He'll know you?"

"Of course! If he comes this way. I'll slip into this shop and buy something—anything. If he goes the other—follow. Good Heavens!—what is he doing here!—in London?"

It was a drapery establishment by which we were standing, with a deep doorway. Sheila slipped within its shelter, and affected an interest in the goods displayed behind the plate glass; I, half-hidden, kept an eye on the tobacconist's door. And presently out came such a man as she had described, a tall, wiry fellow in a ready-made suit of blue serge, obviously a countryman, bronzed in cheek and neck; he carried a packet of tobacco in one hand and was already opening it with the other; absorbed in this, he looked neither to right nor left, but turned along the pavement, away from us.

"Look again!" I said. "He's out—going in the other direction."

Sheila came out of the doorway and glanced down the street.

"That's Parslave!" she said. "But I knew it was. What next?"

"We must follow him," I answered. "No matter where he goes, I'm going to track him. Look here!—I'll keep a little way behind him; you keep a little way behind me. Whatever you do, keep me in sight. Now then—careful!"

So we began our chase of this man who had disappeared from Birnside on the night of Mazaroff's murder, and for whom the police had already instituted a hue-and-cry. They were wanting him badly at Marrasdale—and here he was, quietly buying tobacco in a busy London street!

Parslave went slowly away in front, and just as slowly Sheila sauntered after me in the rear. I took stock of my man as I shadowed him at ten or twelve yards distance. He was a muscular, sinewy fellow, well set up, springy of step; his slop suit did not obscure the general athletic bearing of his figure. Yet it was easy to see he was the countryman in town; he showed hesitation in crossing streets; now and then he cannoned into hurrying passers-by. But he was cool enough and leisured enough: as he walked along he transferred the contents of his packet of tobacco to an old skin-covered pouch; he filled and lighted his pipe, making a shield against the light wind with both hands, after the countryman's fashion; pipe in lips, and in full blast, he thrust his hands in his trousers pockets and trudged forward again, looking to neither right nor left—another trick of habit common to countrymen. Certainly, he was an easy man to follow, and it needed little watchfulness on my part to see that he had not the ghost of an idea that he was being followed.

By this time we had crossed the end of the Harrow Road, where it debouches into the Edgware Road, and here the crowds on the sidewalk grew thicker than ever. Parslave went straight on, keeping well to the front of the shops, and never once looking round; the smoke of his pipe trailed steadily over his shoulder. But he turned at last—to his right sharply, into Praed Street. Fifty yards along that, after a moment of hesitation at the traffic, he crossed the roadway, and a little further along the other side, turned again, down one of the mean streets which lie between Praed Street and Oxford and Cambridge Terrace. It was quieter down there; only a few slatternly women and crawling children were about on the side-walk, and I hesitated as to following him, for he had only to turn in that street to spot me at once. But he did not turn, and sauntering after him, at a considerable distance, I saw him enter the side door of a house— a rather bigger, more pretentious house than those that flanked it. Then he disappeared. And realising then that if I wanted to know something I must act quickly, I hastened my steps, walked swiftly past the house he had entered, and on the side-door, on a dirty, uncleaned brass-plate read, to my utter amazement:

DR ECCLESHARE Surgery Hours: 9.30 to 11 a.m.; 7 to 8.30 p.m.

I turned on my heel as I read that, and hurried back to the top of the street, where Sheila was already hanging about. She saw the excitement in my face, no doubt, and she joined me quickly.

"Got him?" she asked.

I touched her arm with one hand, pointing with the other to the house at the further end of the street.

"You see that house down there?—the one that stands out from the rest?"

"I see it!"

"That's Eccleshare's! Eccleshare's, do you understand? Dr Eccleshare. Surgery hours 9.30 to 11 in the morning, and 7 to 8.30 in the evening. Eccleshare's—good Lord! And—Parslave's in there!"

She stood staring at me for a moment, open-mouthed—a queer little pucker formed itself between her eyebrows.

"Eccleshare's? Then——And—Parslave went in there?"

"Parslave went in there. He's in there!"

Then silence fell upon us. We stood, mutually questioning each other. It seemed a long time before either spoke. But Sheila spoke first.

"Eccleshare's house!—and Parslave in it? Then here's some devilry at work. Mervyn!—what's to be done? Of course, I see how things are. Eccleshare sent Parslave here—to hide!"

But I had been thinking during that moment of silence—thinking fast.

"There's only one thing to be done," I said. "Look here—you do just what I tell you. Get a taxi-cab at the corner of Praed Street there. Go straight to Maythorne's—103b Conduit Street—got that?—and tell him exactly what's happened. Get him to come back here with you, and to bring his clerk, Cottingley. Meanwhile, I'll keep an eye on Parslave and that house. Now—hurry!"

She went off on the instant, without as much as a word, and I turned to watch the house fifty yards away. And I had not watched long before Parslave came out again, and came my way, too. I shifted my position, going across the roadway in Praed Street, and affecting an interest in a second-hand book shop. But I watched Parslave all the same, out of the tail of my left eye. He came up the street, still smoking his black pipe—he was now carrying a rush basket, such as servants use when they go shopping. And Parslave was going shopping—I sauntered after him (on the opposite side) along Praed Street. He went to a greengrocer's shop; he bought potatoes and a couple of fine cauliflowers. And that little domestic mission fulfilled, he went leisurely back to Dr Eccleshare's. I pictured him and some housekeeper woman in there—Parslave would doubtless be peeling the potatoes, like any tame family man, and exchanging pleasant talk with the female presiding genius—and yonder in the Northumberland wilds, three hundred miles away, the police were wanting him . . . on suspicion of murder!

I was laughing softly over this when a hand was laid on my arm—so quietly, but so firmly that the very uncanniness of the touch made me jump. I looked sharply round—to see Maythorne's queer clerk, Cottingley. His eyes were brighter, his lips grimmer, his entire appearance more ferrety than ever: he jerked a thumb over his left shoulder, silently, and following the gesture I saw, a few yards away, Sheila, Maythorne, and a strange man. I looked at the strange man first, wondering who on earth he was. Then I had a sort of dawning comprehension—he was somebody or other got up for the part of the confirmed loafer, the type that just hangs about, and hangs about—and is still found hanging about, doing nothing.

"Guv'nor!" said Cottingley, as if introducing Maythorne. "Here!"

I went up to Maythorne and Sheila, Cottingley at my heels. The loafer person made a slinking movement to the rear, and began to study the contents of a shop-window: his whole attitude was that of a man who awaits orders with philosophic indifference. Maythorne gave me a glance that meant more things than I could realise.

"Now then, Holt," he said, plunging straight into business, "Miss Merchison's given us a description of this man Parslave— just you give us another, so that Cottingley and this other man of mine will know him to the last detail. Here—Johnson!"

The loafer individual slid close to us, like a shadow shifted by a moving light, and he kept his eyes on me without blinking while I rapidly but thoroughly detailed a description of Parslave. So, too, did Cottingley—and Cottingley, when I had finished, first glanced at Maythorne and then at me: his glance at me was accompanied by another jerk of his curiously-turned-out left thumb, in the direction of Eccleshare's house.

"Still in there?" he asked.

"He's not come out again since he went in ten minutes ago with a basket of potatoes and cauliflowers," I answered.

Cottingley nodded at Maythorne, nudged the loafer, and turned away, with seeming utter indifference. He pulled a cigarette-case out of his pocket, gave a cigarette to his companion; they began to smoke, wandering away from us. Sheila stared after them in obvious wonder.

"What are they going to do?" she asked. "Queer, odd creatures!"

Maythorne laughed and motioned us towards the end of Praed Street.

"You two young people can go off duty now," he said. "Parslave is as safe as if we'd got him inside the jewel case at the Tower! Take my advice—go somewhere and have the day to yourselves. Leave all this to me—the only thing is that I want you. Holt, to look in at my office at six o'clock sharp this evening. Now—I'm off! Business! Go somewhere and enjoy yourselves—never mind anything else."

He was in the taxi-cab which he had kept waiting and was being driven away before we could say anything, and for a minute or two we stood aimlessly staring around us, wondering at this strange development. Then we both looked at each other and laughed.

"That's good advice of Maythorne's, anyhow," I said. "Let's follow it. Hang all this business! Let's go somewhere where we can talk about——"

"What?" she said as I hesitated.

"Ourselves!" said I. "We've had enough of other people."

We went somewhere else—to be exact we motored out to

a certain little village north of London. We had a delightful lunch in a delightful, old-fashioned inn; we spent the afternoon amongst the autumn-tinted lanes, and . . .

But that, after all, has nothing to do with this story, though it has all to do with Sheila and myself. At half-past five I took her back to her friend's flat, and then went on to Conduit Street and Maythorne. He immediately waved a telegram at me.

"Here you are, Holt," he said. "More developments. A wire from your man, Webster."

CHAPTER 19 THE
BLANK WALL

There was no great amount of wording in Webster's telegram, but such words as were there conveyed a good deal of highly important information. The telegram itself, addressed to me at Maythorne's office, had been despatched from Black Gill Junction at ten minutes past ten that morning. And this is what Webster said in it:-

Courthope, Armintrade, Eccleshare, Mr and Mrs Elphinstone all left here for Carlisle by eight o'clock train this morning. No other developments here and Manners says no news whatever of Parslave.

I handed back the telegram without comment, and Maythorne, placing it amongst other papers in a separate compartment of his desk, pointed to a Bradshaw which lay open close by.

"Carlisle, of course, means London," he said. "I've been looking out the trains. They'd reach Carlisle from Black Gill Junction at nine-thirty, in nice time to catch the ten o'clock express. That would get them to Euston at five minutes past six—which means that they're all in London now. The scene of operation's shifted, Holt!—we've got some of the chief actors close at hand. Now, I don't attach much importance to the return of the three men from High Cap Lodge—that simply means that their shooting party's broken up, and that they're returning to their respective avocations. But Mrs Elphinstone's journey to London is a different matter."

"Mrs Elphinstone, of course, has come after her daughter," I suggested.

"And the will," he answered. "Or to find out what her daughter's done with the will. Well—there are two men we'll have to have a pretty straight talk with tomorrow. Crole's been here, and you and I are to meet him at his office in the morning. Then we're going to have it out with Armintrade. After that, we're going to interview Eccleshare—and Parslave, possibly with a little police assistance, if need be. But tonight you and I are going to see Mrs Elphinstone. We know where she's to be found —and we'll go now and find her."

"Where?" I asked, wondering if he had some further information.

"Can you doubt?" he answered with a laugh. "She'll be found at Ashington Mansions—where, I suppose, you've just left her daughter. That's the first thing Mrs Elphinstone would do, Holt, as soon as she struck Euston! Come along!—we shall be up there in Maida Vale about the same time that she gets there. Look here —what sort of person is this Miss Apperley that Miss Merchison is with?"

"Very self-sufficient, cool-headed, modern young woman, I should say," I replied. "Teaches science at some woman's college or other."

"Not the sort to let Mrs Elphinstone drag her daughter off before we arrive?" he suggested, with a laugh.

"Not at all," said I, "but I don't think Miss Merchison is the sort to let herself be dragged off, either. I think she'll probably give her mother as good as she gets."

"That's all right," he remarked. "I want to see those two to-gether—and to ask Mrs Elphinstone a question or two. And I may as well tell you. Holt—she won't answer 'em! Tonight, at any rate."

"That I quite expect," said I.

"Just so! But she'll answer 'em tomorrow—or next day—or the day after that," he said, with a significant glance. "The thing is, first, to put them to her. Now let's get a taxi-cab."

We rode up to Maida Vale and got out of our cab some twenty or thirty yards short of Ashington Mansions. Maythorne immediately nudged my elbow.

"What did I tell you?" he said. "They're here, now!"

In front of the main entrance to the flats a taxi-cab stood. There was luggage on it—suit-cases, portmanteaux. And within it, as we were quick to see when we came abreast of its door, sat a woman—a tall, angular, elderly woman, dressed in somewhat rusty black, who stared straight in front of her until, attracted by our momentary halt and seeing our eyes turn in her direction, she gave us a quick side-glance only to withdraw it sharply and to look ahead again, still more steadily. We passed on and entered the door.

"I've seen that woman before," remarked Maythorne, as we crossed the hall to the elevator. "At Marrasdale."

"So have I," I answered. "I saw her about the Woodcock—in fact, I took her for the cook. She was certainly in the kitchen there, cooking, one day when I looked into to ask some question of the landlady. What can she be doing—here?"

"Mrs Elphinstone will know," he said. "But—I shan't ask her that, now. Well—what's this Miss Apperley's number?" he went on, as we were whirled upwards. "Twenty-seven? Right! Now then, Holt—we walk straight in! We'll excuse ourselves to Miss Apperley afterwards. But—open the door, and straight forward."

I did as he bade me. Without ceremony or as much as a tap, I opened the door of Miss Apperley's sitting-room, and Maythorne and I entered, abreast. We plunged into the middle of things. An acrimonious debate was already at its full height. The setting was almost stage-like. The owner of the flat, her pince-nez balanced on the bridge of a rather supercilious nose, sat, hands folded in her lap, on a Chesterfield in the window, glancing, half-amused, half-speculative, alternately from Sheila, who stood, indignant and defiant, by the centre table, to Mrs Elphinstone, enthroned, obviously in a fine temper, in an elbow

148

chair by the hearth. As for Mr Elphinstone, he was perched on the edge of a chair in another corner, nursing the handle of his umbrella and apparently as uncomfortable as a nervous and peaceable man can be. At sight of us he looked up and groaned—audibly. But it seemed to me that in spite of his groaning, the advent of two persons of his own sex gave him some comfort.

"—not one word, good mother, till you tell me how you came into possession of that will!" Sheila was saying, and saying with emphasis, as we strode in. "It's up to you to speak first—you're..."

She broke off there, or, rather, Maythorne broke things off for her. He had quietly closed the door as we entered, and without a sign or sound of preface, he strode forward and took the words out of Sheila's mouth.

"Your daughter's in the right, Mrs Elphinstone," he said in cool, even accents. "It's up to you to give explanations. Now, come, Mrs Elphinstone—how did you obtain possession of Mazaroff's will—which is now safe, let me tell you, safe—in Mr Crole's strong room. Come?"

Mr Elphinstone groaned again—wearily. But Mrs Elphinstone showed temper—and fight.

"How dare you speak to me—me!—like that?" she demanded. "What right——"

"My dear lady!" interrupted Maythorne. "Be calm, and don't be foolish. Think a little. Here is a very wealthy man murdered under most suspicious circumstances. He has his will in his pocket, with other papers, and with valuables, and with money. He is not only murdered, but he is robbed of everything he has on him. Nothing can be discovered about his missing property. Then a few nights later, your daughter accidentally finds out that the will is in—your hands! What do you suppose the police authorities will say to that, Mrs Elphinstone? I'm asking you."

But I saw at once that however and whatever Maythorne might ask, he was not going to get an answer out of Mrs Elphinstone—just then, at any rate, if ever. She looked at him half-wonderingly, as thoroughly obstinate and slightly stupid people will look at a questioner: I could see quite well that she was wondering how he dared to be so plain-spoken and unceremonious. And as she kept silence, he became still more outspoken.

"I said—I'm asking you, Mrs Elphinstone! I also referred to the police. Which do you prefer?—to tell me, or to be questioned by them. It can easily come to the latter. One word—from me—and then . . . but I think you understand——"

Mr Elphinstone groaned once more—audibly. He shifted uneasily in his chair, clinging desperately to his umbrella.

"Most distressing!" he murmured. "Most—unpleasant. Really —I—I think, Marion, that—er—you know—if I were you—I—I think I should say how you got this—er—document—I should— really."

"Mrs Elphinstone will have to say how she got it and from whom," observed Maythorne. "That will was without doubt abstracted—stolen—from Mazaroff's pocket by the man who murdered him. And, Mr Elphinstone, it is later discovered in Mrs Elphinstone's keeping. How came it there?"

Mrs Elphinstone suddenly gathered up her wraps and her umbrella and rose from her chair. It seemed to me that she was the most self-possessed person there—even Miss Apperley was beginning to show signs of concern.

"What right have you to ask me questions?" she demanded, facing Maythorne. "You're not a policeman, as far as I'm aware, and I don't know that you've any authority. If I were Miss Apperley, I should ask you to walk out of my flat! As for me, I am going, and whoever wishes to see me will find me at Short's Hotel. You'll find me there, Sheila—I shall not run after you again."

"That's a useful thing to know, Mrs Elphinstone," said Maythorne, still pertinacious. "You will no doubt be called upon at Short's. And as to our intrusion upon Miss Apperley—I should think Miss Apperley has already heard enough to feel sure that we were justified. This is a matter of murder! And whether you like it or not, Mrs Elphinstone—or, as it should be, Merchison— I am going to know who murdered Mazaroff. If you know, you're already an accessory after the crime."

That was useless. Mrs Elphinstone moved towards the door, motioning Mr Elphinstone to follow. He got up from his chair, irresolute, frightened.

"I think—er—I think, really—there may be some—some explanation, don't you know," he faltered, looking appealingly at Maythorne. "Mrs Elphinstone may have come into possession of this—er—will in a quite——"

"Mrs Elphinstone has only to speak, sir," said Maythorne. "You cannot get over the fact that things are as I have just set them out. I repeat—this is a matter of murder! If Mrs Elphinstone chooses to allow herself to come under suspicion, it is her own fault. Things can't remain where they are. If Mrs Elphinstone came into possession of the will in any innocent way, why does she not say straight out in what way, and help us, instead of hindering us, in our work?"

Mrs Elphinstone was at the door by this time, and her eyes were as hard as ever as she swept us all with a half-contemptuous glance.

"Do your own work!" she retorted. "Are you coming, Malcolm? As for you, Sheila, if you want me again, you'll have to come to me. Otherwise——"

She made a gesture which seemed to indicate that she washed her hands of her daughter and of everybody present, and without waiting for Mr Elphinstone she marched off down the corridor. But he, lingering, turned another appealing look on Maythorne.

"I—I do hope you won't go to—to the police!" he said. "Most unfortunate and most unpleasant, all this, but I'm sure—certain!—there's some explanation. It was, I think, very unkind, thoughtless, of—er—my step-daughter to run away with that document before she asked her mother any question about it, and——"

"Miss Merchison did the only thing that could be done," interrupted Maythorne. "Drastic, no doubt, but the only thing. Had that will remained in your house, Mr Elphinstone, it would have been destroyed—sure enough! And the best thing you can do is to give your wife some sound advice. Let her speak! Get this into your mind—neither she nor you seem to appreciate the fact, so far—this is a case of murder! Why trifle with it?"

Mr Elphinstone shook his head—wearily and despondently. He looked round at all of us as if he wanted to speak, but no words came, and he presently turned and went after his wife. Maythorne closed the door, and glanced at us.

"You may think I was too explicit—perhaps brutal—with Mrs Elphinstone," he said, "but I don't believe any of you understand. Knowing what I do—and Crole, of course, knows it now—I cannot keep this information from the police! It's impossible! We know—the police know—that Mazaroff was robbed as well as murdered. That will was on him! How did Mrs Elphinstone get it?"

"There's one thing doesn't seem to have struck you, or any of you," said Miss Apperley, suddenly speaking for the first time. "I think it might have struck Sheila, if she were not so notoriously impulsive. Mrs Elphinstone may have found the will."

"In that case," retorted Maythorne, "why does not Mrs Elphinstone say so? Let us suppose she did find it?—let us suppose she picked it up on the moors. Knowing all the circumstances, why does she refuse information? No—Mrs Elphinstone did not find the will! I know, precisely, what the real truth of the matter is—where it lies!"

His tone was so certain, so full of assuredness, that we all looked at him.

"Mrs Elphinstone is shielding somebody," he said. "That's the truth! Now, then—who is it?" Then, without waiting for any reply or remark, he tapped my shoulder and set off. I lingered a moment, to exchange a word or two with Sheila, and then followed him. We marched side by side down the corridor.

"You think that, Maythorne?" I asked as we paused at the door of the elevator.

"Of course!" he exclaimed. "Doesn't need half-an-eye nor an ounce of brain to be dead certain of that! She knows—*knows*!

And, as I said in there—who is it? Here's one thing certain. Holt —if she won't speak. I'll have to tell the police. But between now and tomorrow she'll have time to reflect. And in the meantime ____"

He broke off abruptly. We went down and into the street, and in silence walked quickly down Edgware Road. I knew what he was after—Cottingley. And Cottingley suddenly appeared before us in Praed Street, as if he had shot out of the earth.

"He's come!" said Cottingley. "Come in a taxi from Euston; about six-thirty. Alone. I've settled everything for the night— relief for Johnson and all that. We've seen the other man once since morning. They're both in the house, now. All's arranged."

Maythorne nodded; they whispered together a moment; then Maythorne and I turned away.

"Did he mean that Eccleshare had come?" I asked. "And that— they'll watch him?"

"Eccleshare, of course," answered Maythorne. "Who else? Watch him?—Aye, they'll watch him—they'll watch both of 'em!"

CHAPTER 20 OPTION

I went back to my rooms in Jermyn Street that evening thoroughly muddled in mind by the day's events. The presence of Parslave at Eccleshare's house in Paddington, showing some extraordinary connection between him and Eccleshare—the advent of Mrs Elphinstone and her amazing callousness to the position in which she was placing herself—the determined revolt of Sheila against her own mother—the possibility that Mrs Elphinstone actually did know something about the murder of the man who, after all, was her legal husband—all these things were more than a mystery; they were the broken-up and widely distributed bits of a psychological puzzle. It seemed hopeless to try to piece them together, and yet I could scarcely refrain from the attempt. And underneath everything lay an uncomfortable suspicion, which forced itself upon me however much I fought against it—was Mrs Elphinstone an accessory to Mazaroff's murder, and if so, after or... before? It was—possible. That there was some secret in Mazaroff's comings and goings after he and I reached the Woodcock seemed certain—was she connected with it? Had those two, separated for so many years, met? Had she been playing a part when Crole and I interviewed her? Out of all these speculations one clear fact emerged—she had come into possession of that will, which, without doubt, was in Mazaroff's pocket when his murderer shot him.

All this was still seething in my mind when I met Maythorne next morning, at Crole's office in Bedford Row. We were shown into Crole's private room at once; there, by Crole's desk, sat Mr Herman Kloop, spick and span from his morning toilet, and already smoking one of his choice cigars. He gave us a knowing look as we walked in, and Crole nodded at him, as much as to say that whatever was to be said first was to come from the diamond merchant.

"News!" remarked Crole laconically. "Another development!"

We sat down and turned on Kloop. Kloop airily removed his cigar, and blew out a cloud of fragrant smoke.

"I came round to Mr Crole as soon as I had breakfasted—to tell him," he said. "Now I tell you. It is what I learned last night —late. From some of my friends in our trade. Common knowledge, I fancy, by now—across there in Hatton Garden. Mazaroff's pair of blue diamonds have been sold!"

"To whom?" demanded Maythorne.

"The precise details are not quite available," answered Kloop. "But I think what was told me will be found to be substantially correct. They have been sold to a syndicate of three well-known dealers—men, I say—well known in our circles. A fancy price, too!" he added, with a chuckle.

"What price?" asked Maythorne.

Kloop chuckled again and waved his cigar.

"It is said—and I dare say it's quite correct—two hundred thousand pounds," he replied. "Of course—they're worth that— and more. Sufficiently more to give the buyers a nice big profit— when they sell. As—equally of course—they will."

"Frobenius mentioned—how much was it?" asked Crole. "Not that, anyway."

"One hundred and sixty thousand," said Maythorne promptly. "A difference!" He turned on Kloop again. "Well?" he asked. "But—who sold?"

Kloop laughed, glancing at Crole.

"To be sure!" he replied. "A pertinent question! Armintrade sold. No concealment about that. The deal was talked of frankly. Armintrade—the bank man."

"Armintrade only returned from the North last night," said Maythorne. "Where and how was this deal carried out?"

"Yes," answered Kloop. "I can tell something of that, but not precise details. I should say—by correspondence. Anyway, this syndicate came into possession of the stones yesterday morning, and by noon they had been shown to a favoured few. I was told by my informant that they were offered an advance of ten thousand on the purchase price by one dealer at once. The fact is —if you want to know—the two diamonds together are worth a quarter of a million."

Maythorne looked at Crole: Crole shook his head.

"What concerns us," he remarked, "is the fact that Armintrade sold these things—Mazaroff's property. We know that Armintrade was in possession of what we'll call Blue Diamond Number One, and we also know that Mazaroff had Blue Diamond Number Two on him when he went North. So—Mazaroff must have met Armintrade and handed over to him the second diamond. They must have met—unknown to anyone—at Marrasdale."

Maythorne turned again to Kloop.

"Armintrade's name was openly, freely mentioned to you in connection with this?" he asked. "He was spoken of as seller?"

"Oh, yes!" replied Kloop. "Quite openly."

"Was Mazaroff's name mentioned?"

"Oh, to be sure! As the source from which the diamonds came."

"Was Armintrade spoken of as—what now?"

"Well, I suppose as agent. But that's immaterial—obvious, anyhow. The thing is that Armintrade has effected the deal."

"And got the cash?"

"And got the cash—oh, yes!"

Maythorne got up from his chair and began to button his overcoat.

"There's only one thing to be done," he said, glancing at Crole. "You and I and Holt must see Armintrade at once."

"Exactly!" remarked Kloop, with a chuckle. "But—you'll find he's all right."

"How do you mean all right?" demanded Maythorne.

"Just that a man of any common sense wouldn't carry out

a deal of that sort openly and above-board unless he was all right," replied Kloop. "A two hundred thousand pound deal!—come!"

"We want an explanation, all the same," said Maythorne. "As far as I'm aware, those diamonds, since the moment of Mazaroff's death, have been the property of Mr Holt here. Isn't that so, Crole?"

"Yes," answered Crole laconically. He got up from his desk, crossed over to a safe in the corner and, unlocking it, took from some inner receptacle an oblong envelope. "Here's the will," he said. "I'll take it with me. But I think Mr Kloop will be found to be correct in his opinion—Armintrade will be all right. And by that I mean that Armintrade will have acted within his rights. How, I don't know. But—come along."

We parted from Kloop in the street outside; Crole, Maythorne, and I got into a taxi-cab and set off for Courthope's Bank. Crole, grasping the will, sat grim and brooding; Maythorne seemed to be thinking hard. He looked up at last.

"It seems pretty clear—now!—that Mazaroff wasn't murdered for the sake of those diamonds," he muttered, as if somewhat dissatisfied at the new turn of affairs. "And I'm not sure that I ever thought he was. But in that case—what was he murdered for?—what was the motive?"

"He'd other valuable property on him, you know," observed Crole. "And there are other people to question when we've done with Armintrade. Eccleshare, for instance, and that man Parslave. Your people are keeping a strict watch on 'em, I suppose?"

"They'd have to escape through drain-pipes or rat-holes to get away from my men," answered Maythorne. "They're safe enough!—were when I left my office, anyway. Oh, yes, we'll go round to Eccleshare's when we've finished in the City. But Armintrade first—we must know where we are as regards that business."

We entered Courthope's Bank together and sent in our cards to Armintrade. Without delay we were ushered into a waiting-room, and then left, to nurse our impatience, for a good ten minutes. Then a door suddenly opened, and Armintrade himself appeared on the threshold of what was evidently the private parlour of the management. I have already said that he was a sly-faced, bearded man, of a supercilious manner—he looked slyer, more supercilious than ever as he stood there in his fine City clothes, inspecting us. But his eyes smiled—a bit sardonically, I thought—and his manner was outwardly courteous.

"Sorry to keep you waiting, gentlemen," he said. "Come in, if you please."

We went into the room; Armintrade seated himself at his desk and motioned us to chairs around him. He took small notice of Maythorne and myself; his attention gave itself to the solicitor.

"Well, Mr Crole?" he began. "What can I do for you?"

"You can give us some much-needed information, Mr Armintrade," replied Crole promptly. "You are aware, of course, that, having acted as the late Mr Mazaroff's solicitors here in London, I have employed Mr Maythorne to enquire into the mystery of his murder. Now, we have ascertained from Mr Herman Kloop of Cape Town, a close personal friend of Mazaroff's, now in London, that Mazaroff possessed two extremely valuable diamonds, one of which was in his possession when he went North, to Marrasdale, and the other of which had been in your keeping, as Mazaroff's agent, for some months. Kloop tells us, too—has just told us, in fact—that you have sold these two diamonds to a syndicate for two hundred thousand pounds. Is that correct!"

Armintrade, whose smile, sardonic and inscrutable, had never left his eyes, nodded.

"Quite correct!" he answered. "You have the details to the full."

Crole gave him an understanding look.

"Do you mind telling us all about it?" he asked. "I gather the whole thing is plain enough—when explained."

"Plain as a pikestaff," replied Armintrade, with a laugh. "I have acted as agent, or intermediary, or whatever you like to call it, for Mazaroff for some time—I knew him, by correspondence, through my association with my former bank. Well, now, as regards these blue diamonds—great rarities. As you say, I have had the first in my hands for some time. The second he handed to me personally at Marrasdale the day after he arrived at the Woodcock."

"Ah!—you met him there?"

"Certainly I met him there!"

"By appointment?"

"To be sure—by appointment."

"Precisely where?"

"At Birnside cross-roads, at noon. We were together only ten minutes or so."

"Well? And what happened?"

"We discussed the sale of the diamonds, and came to an arrangement."

"May I ask what it was?"

"Certainly! He gave me an option on them."

"Ah! I see! An option? Just so. You were to have them at a price?"

"Of course. But I'll show you the terms, in Mazaroff's handwriting. He had brought me this, already written and signed—there you are!"

From a drawer in the desk before him he produced a sheet of letter-paper and handed it to Crole, who took and read it attentively.

"I see!" he said, handing it back. "He gave you the option for one month of buying the diamonds for a hundred and seventy-five thousand pounds. And—you have taken it up?"

"I have taken it up, and I have sold the two diamonds, as you said, to a syndicate, for two hundred thousand. That's all!"

Crole nodded. Then he leaned forward a little, looking Armintrade steadily in the face.

"Just so! Then—what about the option money? One hundred and seventy-five thousand pounds? Which, of course, should and would have been paid to Mazaroff."

"Exactly! The money is at the disposal of the late Salim Mazaroff's rightful heir or heirs, beneficiaries, residuary legatees, or whoever has a proper right to it."

Crole pointed to me.

"Mr Holt there is Mazaroff's residuary legatee," he said. "He comes in for—everything!"

Armintrade laughed, and gave me a shy smile.

"Lucky for Mr Holt!" he remarked. "But—are you sure of that? What about these queer facts relative to the identity of Salim Mazaroff with Andrew Merchison, and Mrs Elphinstone being in reality Mrs Merchison—and so on? Besides, I understand that the will made at York is lost?"

"The will is here!" said Crole, holding up his envelope. "You can see it and read it."

Armintrade's face underwent a change as he took and read the will. He gave a long, careful look at the signature; another at Crole as he handed back the paper.

"What," he asked, "what do you, a solicitor, say about that will?" he asked quietly.

"That nothing whatever can upset it," answered Crole promptly. "It won't be contested, either. Everything that Mazaroff died possessed of belongs to Mr Mervyn Holt. So——"

"So I owe Mr Holt one hundred and seventy-five thousand pounds," said Armintrade with a laugh. "Very good!—shall I send the cheque and the papers along to you, Mr Crole? Just so—it shall be done at once. Glad you've found the will."

We all rose. For the first time Maythorne spoke—addressing Armintrade.

"You didn't think it necessary to give evidence at the inquest?" he suggested.

"What evidence had I to give?" asked Armintrade. "My affairs with Mazaroff had nothing to do with his murder."

"Have you any theory, yourself, about his murder?" continued Maythorne.

"I have had two. One was that he may have been followed from London by somebody who knew that he had the second blue diamond on him—he was a very careless, thoughtless man!

—the other that it was just a common, vulgar murder for the sake of robbery by one or other of those men whom he had been treating at the Woodcock. For instance, where is that man who disappeared—Parslave? So far, I believe, the police have failed to track him. Possibly he murdered Mazaroff, robbed the body, and cleared out. Anyhow—he's vanished."

Maythorne nodded silently, and without more words we took our departure.

CHAPTER 21
FRESH LINKS

We took our departure—silently and unceremoniously, as if we had been very ordinary customers, doing very ordinary business. But outside, in Mincing Lane, Maythorne halted, and looked questioningly at Crole.

"Satisfied?" he asked.

"As far as that goes—yes," replied Crole. "There's no doubt about the option—that's clear enough. No getting past Mazaroff's own handwriting and own terms! I suspected something of the sort—I couldn't believe that Armintrade would sell those diamonds unless he'd a legal right to do so. All that remains now is to receive his cheque for the amount of the option. You'll see I shall get it as he promised—at once. And that settles that part of the case."

"Very well—if you're satisfied," said Maythorne. He moved forward a few yards and again stopped. "I wish we knew a bit more about Mazaroff's movements on the day following his arrival at the Woodcock," he muttered. "It's all vague, shadowy, uncertain—and yet bits keep coming out. You didn't know much of his doings that day, did you Holt?"

"Next to nothing—in fact, nothing," I answered. "He told me after breakfast that he wanted to have the day to himself. He set out soon afterwards, carrying a stout walking-stick, and wearing a pair of blue spectacles—I think he put those on as a sort of disguise, for I never saw him wear eye-glasses of any kind at any other time, and I know his eyesight was unusually good. He was out all day—I never saw him at all until evening. I don't know where he went, nor whom he saw."

"Of course, he knew the country—intimately," remarked Maythorne. "We don't know where he may not have gone, nor whom he mayn't have seen—nor (a most important thing!) what appointments he mayn't have made for the next day or evening."

"The next day he was with me," I said. "That is, for practically the whole of the day. We were motoring round about—examining churches, ruins, and that sort of thing. It was not until evening—after half-past seven—that he disappeared."

"Went to meet somebody, without doubt," muttered Maythorne. "And met his death! Well—the next job is Eccleshare and Parslave. If we can't get some light through those two . . ."

He paused, looking round for a taxi-cab; as he signalled to one a little distance away, Crole spoke, shaking his head.

"My impression is that Eccleshare will have as straight a tale to tell us as we've just heard from Armintrade," he exclaimed. "We're off the track, Maythorne!—or, rather, we've never been on it. I've got an intuition that neither Armintrade, nor Eccleshare, nor Parslave know anything about nor have anything whatever to do with Mazaroff's murder. We haven't got deep enough!—we'll have to dig down a good many feet yet."

"All the same, we're going to have things out with Eccleshare and Parslave," answered Maythorne. "We may get a hint; a bit of a clue; anything. Perhaps," he added, as we settled ourselves in the cab, "perhaps I've got a pretty good idea of how things are, myself, Crole—but I want all the contributory information I can get. And I want to know why Parslave has been lying safely hidden in Dr Eccleshare's house in London ever since this affair happened. Conduit Street!" he called out, as the driver closed the door on us. "I just want to call in thera for a few minutes before we go on to Eccleshare's."

At Maythorne's bidding we got out at the corner of Conduit Street and walked along to his office. Outside his door stood a fine, obviously brand-new Rolls-Royce car, in charge of a chauffeur whose livery was just a little too grand: Crole smiled at the sight of it.

"One of your aristocratic clients, eh, Maythorne?" he observed chaffingly. "A duke or a duchess at least—what?"

"On the contrary, if you want to know," answered Maythorne, who had given car and chauffeur a sharp glance, "that's Sir Samuel Leeke's car—or one of 'em—and his livery. And I've a pretty good idea as to whom we shall find upstairs."

"Who?" asked Crole. "Lady Leeke?"

"No—but his nephew, Mallison," retorted Maythorne. "A thousand to one on it! I've been expecting him these last twenty-four hours. Come in!"

We went upstairs to Maythorne's palatial rooms. One of the girl clerks came forward as we entered the outer office.

"Mr Mallison—waiting to see you, sir," she said.

We went forward to Maythorne's private room. There, dressed in the very height of fashion, his silk hat tilted to the back of his head, his hands in the pockets of his beautifully creased trousers, stood, examining a picture, the young man whom I had seen Mazaroff talking to at Huntingdon and at York. He turned sharply as we walked in, and a flicker of his quick eyes showed that he recognised me. But he instantly picked out Maythorne.

"Oh—er—Mr Maythorne?" he said. "I—er—just dropped in to see you, don't you know—this Mazaroff affair. My uncle. Sir Samuel Leeke, you know——"

"I know!" broke in Maythorne cheerily. "Very good of you, Mr Mallison, I'm sure. Take a chair. Mr Crole—Mr Holt."

Mallison dropped into a chair and grinned at me.

"Seen you before," he said. "Saw you at Huntingdon—with Mazaroff."

"And—later—at York," said I.

"Just so—at York, too," he assented. "Queer business, ain't it?"

"What do you know about it, Mr Mallison?" asked Maythorne. He took a box of cigarettes from his desk and passed it round.

"We're anxious to get any information we can. And if you can tell us anything——"

Mallison sought inspiration in his cigarette.

"Oh, well—I—I scarcely know anything at all!" he said. "Of course, I met Mazaroff in Park Lane, and then we dined with him at the Cecil. And I saw one of the blue diamonds, and heard about the pair of 'em—the other was in the hands of a chap named Arm—something—not Armstrong, though—a banking man. And between you and me. Lady Leeke was jolly keen about getting hold of the pair—she was so!"

"Really wanted them, did she?" asked Maythorne.

"She did!—though she didn't say much about it just at the time. But I know," continued Mallison, with an ingenuous smile. "I know her!—she was all for Sir Samuel buying 'em there and then. That's what I gave Marazoff the tip about when I met him as I was going North."

"I see!" said Maythorne. "You were both going North about the same time, eh? To be sure. And what were you going North for?"

"Inspect some shootings," answered Mallison promptly. "Sir Samuel wants a grouse moor next year, and we thought it would be a good business idea for me to go and see some, personally, while guns were actually at work on 'em. Looked over a lot while I was up there—both sides the Tweed."

"Capital idea!" agreed Maythorne. "And you met Mazaroff—accidentally? At Huntingdon, first; then at York. Exactly. But—did you ever meet him again?"

"Oh, yes," replied Mallison. "That's what Sir Samuel wanted me to tell you. I met him at Gilchester."

Maythorne gave Crole and myself a swift, almost imperceptible glance as he settled down to questioning his caller.

"At Gilchester, eh? That's the market-town for Marrasdale—a few miles from the Woodcock. How did you come to meet him there?"

"Accident! I'd motored over from Jedburgh to look at a shooting near Gilchester. I went into the hotel there to get some lunch, and stopped a bit afterwards. Mazaroff came in—we had a drink or two together."

"What date was that?"

"Can't say! Bad at dates. But he told me that he'd arrived at the Woodcock the previous afternoon. Perhaps you can fix the date?"

"We can fix it. What's important for us is—you met Mazaroff at Gilchester the day after he arrived at the Woodcock. Can you remember the exact time?"

"Yes—about two o'clock in the afternoon."

"Well—-did you talk about the diamonds again?"

"Of course! He told me what he'd done. He said he'd seen this agent of his—Arm—something——"

"The man's name is Armintrade."

"That's it!—Armintrade. He said he'd just seen Armintrade, who was shooting in the neighbourhood, and they'd come to an agreement. Armintrade had already a big deal in prospect. So Mazaroff had given Armintrade an option—for a hundred and seventy-five thousand. He believed Armintrade would take it up. But, if he didn't, then, Mazaroff said. Lady Leeke should have the pair at the price first named—a hundred and sixty thousand."

"That corroborates Armintrade," remarked Maythorne in an aside to Crole and myself. "Well," he went on, turning again to his caller. "That, I suppose, was about all?—you'd no further talk about the diamonds?"

"Oh, none! That settled it. Of course, if Armintrade took up his option, the thing was done—if not, well, Lady Leeke would come in. That's all there was to it."

"You parted at Gilchester?"

"Of course! I went off in my car, over the border again, back to Jedburgh—went further North after that. Then I heard about Mazaroff's disappearance and murder. I say!—have you got any idea what he was murdered for?"

"Not quite," replied Maythorne. "Have you?"

Mallison bestowed a knowing wink on all three of us.

"He was a silly chap!" he said. "You see, I've been with him in two or three public places—had drinks and cigars with him. He showed his money too freely amongst strangers—and not only money, but other things. Why, that day at Gilchester, he and I, we were in the smoking-room—there were a lot of Toms, Dicks, and Harries about us that you didn't know from Adam! And Mazaroff pulled out a fistful of loose diamonds from his waist-coat pocket!—just to illustrate something he was telling me! Why, I ain't a fool!—he was asking for trouble! Done in for what he had on him!—that's my notion!"

"You may be quite right, Mr Mallison," said Maythorne, with affected solemnity. "He was evidently a thoughtless man. Well —I'm much obliged to you for calling."

"That's all right," replied Mallison artlessly. "Thought I'd just drop in, you know—always glad to be of help."

He went away presently, and the three of us looked at each other. Crole spoke first.

"As you said just now, Maythorne, that corroborates Arm-intrade," he remarked. "And I'm beginning to think that there may be something in what that youngster suggested—that this is a simple case of murder for the sake of robbery. Mazaroff may easily have been tracked, and, as Mallison put it, done in for what he had on him."

"That's no new theory," observed Maythorne. "It's the ori-ginal one—but it may have all manner of variations. Well, now —Eccleshare and Parslave! That's the next——"

The door opened just then—a girl-clerk appeared.

"Sergeant Manners and Detective-Sergeant Corkerdale to see you, sir," she announced.

"Show them in!" said Maythorne. He turned wonderingly on us as the girl withdrew. "Manners!" he exclaimed. "Here in London? What's that mean? Something fresh! Well, Manners," he continued, as the sergeant and another man, both in plain clothes, came into the room, staring curiously at their sur-roundings, "what brings you here? Take a seat!—you know these gentlemen."

Manners grinned at Crole and myself, dropped into a chair, and unbuttoned his overcoat. He jerked a thumb at his companion, a quiet-looking, observant man.

"Detective-Sergeant Corkerdale, of the Yard, gentlemen," he said. "Well, Mr Maythorne, I'm here on business you can guess at. The fact is, I learnt something yesterday, and I hurried up to town, by orders, and I've been to New Scotland Yard, and told all we know. They've put Corkerdale here on to help me—and we just thought we'd drop in on you and see if you'd heard anything fresh—of course, I know you're working at this case."

"We've heard a good deal, Manners," replied Maythorne. "But —it'll simplify matters if you say what you've learned."

"Well—this," answered Manners. "Two or three things happened our way yesterday. All the folks—Elphinstone's—left Marrasdale Tower for London, sudden. Then, the High Cap Lodge party broke up and came here, too—same train. All that was talked about, of course. And later in the morning that old chap Cowie, that lives in a cottage close by Reiver's Den, came to me and said that he'd something to tell—something, he said, that he'd kept to himself until the gentlemen had gone away from Mr Courthope's. Then, when I'd assured him that no harm would come to him, he went on to tell me that on the night of Mazaroff's murder, some little time after hearing a shot fired near his cottage, he went out, and from behind his garden hedge, saw two men, close by. One, he said, was the big fat gentleman from High Cap Lodge: the other was Parslave. Do you follow me, gentlemen?—Parslave! And, says Cowie, he saw 'em go away together, talking, sort of whispering, in the direction of Courthope's. Now, as we know, Parslave's never been seen since —in our parts. Where is he?"

"Is that what you've come to see Mr Eccleshare about. Manners?" asked Maythorne.

"That's it, sir!—me and Detective-Sergeant Corkerdale here are going to see Dr Eccleshare and hear what he's got to say," answered Manners. "If Parslave was with him that night, then I want to know why—and I want to know where Parslave is now!"

"Then I'll save you some trouble, Manners," said Maythorne. "I'll tell you where Parslave is now! Parslave is where he's probably been ever since the night of the murder—or, rather, since the day after. He's in Dr Eccleshare's house, at Paddington!"

CHAPTER 22 WHO IS SUSPECT?

The two policemen looked at each other. But that was only for a second; each turned sharply on Maythorne. The man from New Scotland Yard spoke.

"You're sure of that?" he asked quickly.

"Dead sure!" replied Maythorne. "I repeat—Parslave is in Dr Eccleshare's house, which is in a side street off Praed Street, Paddington. And I repeat further—he's probably been there, lying safe, ever since the day after the murder."

"That looks like some sort of collusion between him and this doctor," said the detective. "They'll have to be seen."

"We were just going to see them when you came," remarked Maythorne. "You'd better come with us. I may as well tell you that Parslave was seen, accidentally, by Miss Merchison and Mr Holt, yesterday morning, in Edgware Road. They tracked him to Dr Eccleshare's house. Since then I've had two men watching the house: one of 'em's my head clerk, a chap from whom the cleverest criminal in Europe couldn't get away. Come along!—we'll go see him, and hear the latest."

We all five filed out and squeezed ourselves into a taxi-cab; Maythorne bade its driver to set us down at the corner of Chapel Street. Arrived there, he turned a little way down Edgware Road, looked at his watch, and beckoning the rest of us to follow, entered the saloon bar of a pretentious-looking tavern. There, in a quiet corner, a tankard of ale and a plate of bread-

and-cheese before him, sat the queer clerk, Cottingley, quietly munching, and reading a newspaper.

We grouped ourselves round Cottingley; beyond a nod to his employer, Cottingley took no more notice of us than if we had been so many lay-figures. And Maythorne, instead of plunging straight into business, invited us all to take a drink, and said nothing until each of us had a glass in his hand. Then he turned on his clerk.

"Well?" he said.

Cottingley's odd eyes took us all in, then: he leaned closer, over the little table at which he sat.

"Eccleshare," he answered in a low voice, "came home, from Euston, about six-thirty last night. Three suit-cases and a gun-case. Parslave came out and helped to carry them in. At seven o'clock Eccleshare came out, alone. He went to Riggiori's, round the corner here in Chapel Street. He dined there. He left there just after eight, and went home. About nine o'clock Parslave came out. He went to a public-house, higher up the street, and had a pint of ale there. Then he went back. Neither of 'em showed again last night: neither of 'em have left the house this morning: at least, we'd seen nothing of either of 'em up to half-an-hour ago, when I left Johnson there. But about nine o'clock a van came there and left six trunks—the sort of trunks people use that are going long-distance travelling; those strong, zinc-lined affairs. They were carried in by the men who came with the van. The door was opened by a woman who looked like a working-housekeeper. That's all."

"Plenty!" observed Maythorne. He glanced significantly at the man from New Scotland Yard. "Eccleshare is going to clear out!" he said. "What do you think, Corkerdale?"

Corkerdale, who had listened to Cottingley with close attention, nodded.

"What I think," he answered, "is that the sooner we get to business the better. But—let's be clear about what we're going to do.

Maythorne turned to Manners.

"Have you got a warrant for Parslave?" he asked.

"No!" replied Manners. "You see, beyond the mere fact of Parslave's disappearance, we've no direct evidence against him. We've had bills out, asking for information about him. No—I've no warrant."

"The simplest thing to do," said Maythorne, "is to walk in there, say that Parslave's been seen to enter, and have it out with the two of them. Come on!—we'll go there and walk straight in."

We left Cottingley calmly continuing his interrupted lunch, and led by Maythorne and Manners, went off to the quiet side-street. There we saw Johnson, playing the part of loafer to perfection; he took no notice of Maythorne and Maythorne took none of him, unless some secret signal passed between them which I failed to notice: a moment later we were at Eccleshare's door. From the outside the house looked quiet enough; it was just a typical, somewhat shabby London house, the door set flush with the walls and the pavement. Maythorne knocked; the door was opened almost instantly by a tall, elderly woman in cap and apron. She showed no surprise at seeing the five of us on the step.

"Dr Eccleshare at home?" demanded Maythorne. "Just so— thank you, we'll come in."

He and Manners were over the threshold before the woman could say anything; the rest of us crowding closely behind, and looking over their shoulders, found ourselves gazing on a big, roomy hall, set in the centre of the ground floor. And there, before us, and now turning on this incursion with wondering and surprised faces, were our two men. The zinc-lined trunks of which Cottingley had spoken were open on the hall floor, Parslave, in his shirt-sleeves, was engaged in packing things into them, under Eccleshare's superintendence. Through the open doors of adjacent rooms we saw tables laden with things laid out for packing—clothes, instruments, books. Clearly, as May-thorne had suggested, Eccleshare was contemplating a departure.

Eccleshare was first to speak. He turned on us sharply as we crowded in, and the look that he gave us was one of nothing but surprise—there was no annoyance, no sign of self-consciousness; it was easy to see that all that was in his mind was just wonder at our presence.

"Hullo!" he exclaimed. "What's this? You, Manners?—and a whole company behind you? What's arisen?—some new development?"

Manners said the best thing he could have said—it did credit to his countryman's plain-spokenness. Without hesitation he pointed to Parslave, who, on his knees beside a trunk, had turned to stare at him, open-mouthed.

"Dr Eccleshare!" he said. "What's that man doing in your house?"

Eccleshare, in his turn, stared—first at Parslave, then at Manners: I could see he was now more surprised than ever.

"Parslave?" he said. "Why shouldn't he be in my house? He's in my employ—my man!"

"Your man—your servant?" asked Manners. "Since—when?"

"Since I engaged him at Marrasdale," retorted Eccleshare. He looked from one to the other of us. "I don't know what concern it is of anybody's, Manners," he went on, "but since you seem extraordinarily inquisitive, I may as well tell you that I've sold this practice and I'm going to South America—on other pursuits. I wanted a strong, capable man—preferably a countryman, used to outdoor life—to go with me, and I engaged Parslave. That's why he's here."

Manners drew a long breath and shook his head.

"You know that we've had a bill out for Parslave this last two or three days. Dr Eccleshare," he said. "Posted all about the district! Why didn't you tell us where Parslave was?"

"Pardon me, my man, I know nothing whatever about any bill," replied Eccleshare. "I was never near Marrasdale nor Birnside nor Gilchester the last few days I was in your parts. If I left High Cap Lodge at all, it was for the moors on the other side. I neither saw your bill nor heard of it."

"You knew it was talked about that Parslave had disappeared," said Manners. "It was common talk."

"I heard something of that," answered Eccleshare coolly. "But as I knew where Parslave was, and why he was where he was, I had no particular call to give you information. Why should I?"

Manners became official in aspect and tone. He jerked his head towards Corkerdale.

"Oh, very well, doctor!" he said. "This is Detective-Sergeant Corkerdale, from New Scotland Yard. I've been there this morning and laid before the authorities certain facts concerning you and Parslave, and if we don't get some satisfactory explanation from you, I shall just have to ask you to come with us and explain things elsewhere."

Eccleshare's big face flushed a little. But he made an obvious attempt to keep his temper.

"That sounds very threatening. Manners," he answered. "What explanation do you want? Here!—we won't stand talking in all this confusion. Come into my dining-room, all of you —Parslave, you come, too. Now, then," he continued, as we all filed into a big room, heavily furnished in an old-fashioned style, "sit down, and let us hear what it's all about. What are these certain facts that you've heard of, concerning Parslave and myself? Out with them!"

Manners hesitated. He had removed his hat as we entered the room, and now he ran his fingers through his hair—there was something in the gesture which made me think that he was beginning to feel uncertain about his position. A doubt was springing up in his mind; he was already suspecting that there was more behind this than he had fancied. He suddenly pointed at Crole, who had dropped into a chair at the head of the big dining-table.

"I'm no lawyer!" he exclaimed. "No hand at putting things— as they ought to be put. Mr Crole there is a lawyer. Perhaps——" He glanced appealingly at Crole, and Crole turned to Eccleshare with a smile.

"The situation is this, Dr Eccleshare," he said. "You know as well as we do that Mr Mazaroff was murdered at or near Reiver's

Den on the third night after his arrival at the Woodcock. He was also robbed—of money to a considerable amount: probably, too, of loose diamonds that he had on him; of all his valuables, and of important papers. About the same time, this man, Parslave—no implication on you, Parslave, mind, in what I say! —disappears, mysteriously. Parslave is now discovered in your house, here in London. You've given an explanation of that. But —there's more, and it is this, I think, that Sergeant Manners is particularly referring to. After you and Mr Armintrade and your host, Mr Courthope, left Marradale yesterday morning, information was given to Manners to the effect that you and Parslave were seen near Reiver's Den on the night of the murder, just after the informant had heard the shot fired which was, no doubt, the immediate cause of Mazaroff's death. Now, my dear sir, I think you should explain—anything that you can explain."

Eccleshare had taken up a position on the hearth-rug; he stood there, his hands in his pockets, listening quietly: near the door, Parslave, stolid and unemotional, sat on the edge of a chair.

"Before I give any explanation," said Eccleshare, after a pause, "I should like to know who it was that saw Parslave and myself near Reiver's Den on the night of the murder?"

Crole nodded, and turned to Manners.

"I think you should tell Dr Eccleshare that," he remarked.

"Well—it was Cowie," said Manners. "The old man who lives in the cottage near Reiver's Den. He saw you—both."

"What did he see?" asked Eccleshare.

"He saw you there, and heard you—talking. Then he saw you go away together—towards Mr Courthope's place. High Cap Lodge."

Eccleshare nodded. He was looking from one to the other of us, and for a moment or two he remained silent, evidently thinking.

"Look here!" he said suddenly. "Am I—or is Parslave—or are the two of us suspected of the murder of Mazaroff?"

No one answered. Manners moved uneasily in his chair; the

man from New Scotland Yard preserved a granite-like countenance; Maythorne showed what seemed to be indifference; Crole and myself looked on. There was a brief silence—broken by Manners.

"I should like to know what Parslave there has to say about his movements that night!" he said. "A rare lot of trouble he's given us!"

"I'm quite sure that Parslave hasn't the slightest notion that he gave you any trouble," remarked Eccleshare. "You forget, I think, that Parslave can't read—so he hasn't learnt anything from the newspapers. But—Parslave, tell Sergeant Manners what you did that evening you left Marrasdale."

Parslave, thus bidden, screwed up his face to the feat of remembrance. An idea suddenly came to him: he brightened.

"Cloughthwaite Fair day that was!" he said. "I'd been there—took some sheep there, belonging to Mr Robinson. Come away from there end o' the afternoon. Then I went home, and according to orders—Doctor's orders there—changed into my best clothes. 'Cause why? I was to go to London that night. Got my supper then, and after that, walked along to the Woodcock. I went in there and had a pint—the strange gentleman as was stopping there, he come into the room where there was a reg'lar crowd on us, drovers and shepherds and such-like. He stood treat all round—drinks and smokes. Gen'rous he was! Talked to us affable like, too. Then he went away. I stopped a bit longer, then I went off. To meet the doctor there—by arrangement. I met him. That's all as I did that night—before leaving."

"Did you ever mention to anybody that you were going to London?" asked Maythorne.

"No, master, I never did," replied Parslave. "Hadn't no cause to. I'm a lone man—neither kith nor kin, nobody to leave. Paid up, I did, where I lodged—and just went off. My way, that was. Didn't want no talk about it. 'Twarn't no concern o' nobody's but my own, as I knew of."

"Where did you meet Dr Eccleshare?" asked Manners.

"Where it had been arranged," replied Parslave promptly.

"Near Reiver's Den. He was to be there and give me my orders and my travelling money. And there he was!"

Eccleshare suddenly came from the hearth and joined us at the table.

"Just so!" he said. "There I was!—and I think I'd better tell you, as things are, precisely what happened. Possibly, I ought to have told all this before. But I had reasons—for silence."

CHAPTER 23 WHO WAS THE WOMAN?

I think that each of the men who sat round that table felt that at last there was going to be some revelation as to the murder of Mazaroff which, up to then, had never been made. I realized it myself, anyway—and I began to feel a curiously sickening sense of apprehension, not unconnected with the events of the previous evening. Eccleshare knew something!—so, too, probably, did Parslave. But—what?

"I say I had reasons for keeping silence," continued Eccleshare, settling down to talk to us. "I had!—strong enough for me. Perhaps I've been wrong—perhaps in these cases—murder!—nobody should keep silent, under any circumstances. And yet—you'll see, as men, that I had reasons, and weighty ones. Now I'll tell you—as it seems absolutely necessary—precisely what happened to Parslave and myself on the night on which Mazaroff met his death. Let me begin at the beginning. Before I went up North, to Marrasdale, to shoot with Courthope, who's a fellow club-member of mine, as Armintrade also is, I'd decided to sell my practice—had sold it, in fact—and to leave England for South America and a quite different life—prospecting, shooting, hunting, and that sort of thing. I wanted to take with me a man who'd be useful to me—preferably a countryman; a gamekeeper, used to outdoor life, was the sort of man I had in mind. At Marrasdale I came across Parslave—as you can see for yourselves, he's just the wiry, muscular sort of chap that was wanted.

He is, as he's said just now, a lone man—nothing to tie him to England. He's thoroughly up in woodcraft and that sort of thing; in short, he was the very man I was looking for. I broached the matter to him, and we very soon came to terms. There were certain things that he could do for me here in London, so I arranged that he should come up in advance of me and stay at my house until my return. We arranged further that on the night after Cloughthwaite Fair, which he had to attend on business, he was to meet me, and I was then to give him money and some final instructions and he was to leave for Newcastle and London."

"Why by Newcastle?" asked Maythorne. "It's a detail, but why not by Black Gill Junction and Carlisle?—the more usual western route?"

"I'll tell you," answered Eccleshare. "Parslave has some interest in a bit of cottage property in Newcastle; as he was leaving England he wanted to see a solicitor in Newcastle who manages that property and to give him some instructions about it. So we arranged that after seeing me, he was to cross the moor to that little branch line that runs East of Marrasdale, catch the last train to Newcastle, stay the night there, see his solicitor in the morning, and then go on to King's Cross. All of which, he will tell you himself, he did."

"Very well—and—your meeting that night?" asked Maythorne.

"I'm coming to that, now," continued Eccleshare. "I had told Parslave to meet me on the path between High Cap Lodge and the Woodcock about eight o'clock. I strolled out to meet him, as soon as dinner was over at Courthope's. That would be about ten minutes to eight. We met a little to the further side—the side nearest the Woodcock—of Reiver's Den. As far as I can recollect, it would then be just after eight o'clock. We stood a few minutes, talking. Then——"

"A moment, if you please," interrupted Maythorne. He produced a memorandum book, and laying it open on the table before him, drew Eccleshare's attention to a rough diagram pencilled on one of the pages. "Here's a sketch that I made the day of my arrival at the Woodcock," he said. "A sketch of the paths across the moor. Now there are two paths that lead from the direction of High Cap Lodge and go towards the Woodcock. One leads directly across the front of Reiver's Den, at the very foot of the rocks—we'll call that the higher one. The other is some fifteen or twenty yards lower down—amongst the heather; we'll call that the lower one. Which path were you and Parslave on?"

Eccleshare bent over the diagram for a moment, twisting it round so as to get a clear idea of its geography. He put his finger on a spot.

"We were about there," he said. "On the lower one. But—I don't know if you've made it quite plain—those two paths (one, the lower one's a mere sheep-track) almost meet on the West side, the High Cap Lodge side of Reiver's Den, near Cowie's cottage. They're only separated there by a yard or two. Then the lower one goes away through the heather to the top side of High Cap Lodge; the other one passes High Cap Lodge on the lower side at fifty or sixty yards distance and breaks into the moorland road to Cloughthwaite."

"Well," said Maythorne. "Anyway—you and Parslave were on the lower one?"

"We were on the lower one—perhaps a hundred yards from Reiver's Den. And," continued Eccleshare, "as I was saying, we stood there a few minutes talking. It was then quite dark, but a clear, starlit night. We were just moving away, in the High Cap Lodge direction, when we heard a shot fired. It seemed, as far as we could make out, to be in Reiver's Den, or just beyond it—I think it must have been in Reiver's Den, because there was a distinct echo from the rocks. We heard nothing follow—no cry, scream, anything of that sort. Neither of us took any particular notice—I think we each had the same idea; that it was a gamekeeper who was after something. In fact, we heeded it so little that we went on talking about our own business for a minute or two after the shot was fired. Then because it was time for Parslave to be getting on to catch his train we moved—coming over to the other path because it leads directly to the moorland road. We had just got on it when we heard steps coming along from the direction of Reiver's Den. There were some high, thick bushes close by, and—I really don't know why we did it, but we did!—we sort of instinctively moved into their shadow, where it was quite dark. And then, a minute later, walking very swiftly, a woman passed us."

"A woman!"

It was Manners who let out this sharp exclamation. Like all the rest of us he had been following Eccleshare closely; now he showed signs of excitement; clearly, some notion had suddenly come to him.

"A woman!" repeated Eccleshare quietly. "A woman—tall, slender, walking very quickly indeed—we heard her breathing sharply. She was past and gone, like a flash."

"In which direction?" asked Maythorne.

"Towards Marrasdale," replied Eccleshare.

"And then?" suggested Maythorne after a brief pause.

"Then Parslave and I went on again—he was getting pressed for time. We neither heard nor saw anything there. We passed Cowie's cottage. You say Cowie saw us together. Probable!—but we never saw him. We walked quickly across the moor, struck the high road, and parted. I went into High Cap Lodge, and Parslave—but let Parslave himself tell you what he did."

We all turned to Parslave, who still sat perched on the edge of a chair near the door, twiddling his thumbs.

"Went straight along the road to Petherby Station, then," said Parslave. "Caught the nine-fifteen train—last train that is—to Newcastle. Got to Newcastle at ten-fifty. Put up at a temperance, near the station, for the night. Went to see Mr Graham, the lawyer, as soon as I'd had my breakfast next morning—'bout ten o'clock, that 'ud be. When I'd done with him, got a bit of a snack and then caught the twelve-ten express to London. Got to King's Cross at a quarter to seven that evening. Came straight here—and been here ever since."

"Let me ask Parslave a question while I think of it," said Crole. "Parslave!—do you mean to say that since you left Marrasdale, you've never heard of the murder there?—from the news-papers?"

"I can't read, sir," answered Parslave. "I've no scholarship. Can't neither read nor write."

"But you've been in the company of Dr Eccleshare's house-keeper," continued Crole. "Do you mean to say that she's never read anything about it to you—out of the papers?"

Parslave shook his head.

"No, sir—she hasn't," he replied. "Don't seem a paper-reading woman, that. Her reads them story-papers—tales—such-like. But I ain't seen her a-reading of newspapers."

"Well, but you've no doubt been in the habit since you've been here, of going out to have a glass of ale at some public-house or other," persisted Crole. "Have you never heard it men-tioned at such times?"

"No, sir," answered Parslave, with solemn assurance. "Never! I always go out to take a pint of ale at the public up the street just after I've had my dinner, and again after my supper, but I ain't never talked to nobody—don't understand this London talk —'tis all so much furrin language to me. And I ain't never heard nobody talking of the murder."

"You can take it from me, Mr Crole," said Eccleshare, "that Parslave never heard of Mazaroff's murder at all until last night, when I returned home. I told him—we had a talk last night about our own experiences near Reiver's Den that evening—in the light of what we remembered, of course."

"That's just what I want to ask you some questions about, doctor," said Crole. "It seems to me that we're getting nearer a solution of this mystery than we've ever been before. Now, you won't mind if I ask you a few straightforward questions?"

"Ask me anything you like," replied Eccleshare.

"You were at the inquest on Mazaroff's body at the Wood-cock," said Crole. "You gave evidence——"

"Purely professional evidence," interrupted Eccleshare.

"Precisely—as to the cause of death," assented Crole. "Now, why didn't you tell the coroner and the jury what you've told us just now?"

"And—if I may put a word in," said Manners quickly, "why didn't you tell us—the police—all you've just told us about Parslave, when you knew quite well that we were looking for him?"

"As to your question. Manners, I wasn't aware of the hue-and-cry for Parslave to the extent you think," answered Eccleshare. "My time wasn't spent in the Marrasdale district, so much as on the East side of my host's house. As to yours, Crole—well, I've told you I possibly made a mistake—no doubt I did. But I had reasons for silence. They're easily summed up. The person that Parslave and I saw hurrying away from Reiver's Den, where, presumably, murder had just been committed was—a woman!"

Crole summoned our undivided attention with a swift glance round the table. He went forward to Eccleshare.

"Now, doctor!" he said. "Don't let's beat about the bush any longer—let's get at the truth, however unpleasant it may be. Did you form any opinion as to who that woman was?"

Eccleshare made a gesture of dislike at the situation. But he bowed his head and replied without hesitation.

"I did!—certainly!"

"Who was she?"

"Mrs Elphinstone!"

"You feel sure of that?"

"Positive—without doubt. Ask Parslave!"

Crole turned sharply on Parslave. And Parslave threw up his head with a jerk.

"What do you say, Parslave? Who was the woman that passed you?"

"Mistress Elphinstone, sir—no doubt on it! Never had no doubt—myself."

Crole turned again to Eccleshare.

"You said it was dark, then, but clear, star-lit. How did you recognise her?"

"Figure, walk, profile," replied Eccleshare. "I'd no doubt at the time, and I've none now. The woman who passed Parslave and myself just after—at least almost just after—we heard the shot fired, was Mrs Elphinstone."

"That's why you kept silence?" suggested Crole.

"I thought things out, next morning," answered Eccleshare. "I kept silence—Parslave, of course, had gone. I—well, I didn't want to give a woman away. And after all—there might be explanations."

"Explanations!" exclaimed Crole. "Ex——"

"Here's something that needs explanation," interrupted Maythorne. "Dr Eccleshare and Parslave agree that they heard a shot fired near Reiver's Den soon after eight o'clock. Old Mr Hassendeane told us, Crole, when you, Holt, and myself met him there, that he heard a shot fired about, I think, ten o'clock. Now then—which of those shots was it that killed Mazaroff? Remember!—neither Eccleshare nor Parslave saw anything of Mazaroff near Reiver's Den at eight o'clock. And yet, if the eight o'clock shot killed him, he must have been about there when they were. What do you make of that?"

"Don't know—it needs thinking out," answered Crole. "But—to my mind, the pertinent thing is this. Dr Eccleshare and Parslave are both dead certain they saw Mrs Elphinstone come away from Reiver's Den, where, afterwards, Mazaroff's lifeless body was found, robbed of money, valuables, papers, and his will. Now then, neither Manners nor Corkerdale know this—and I'm going to tell them, as police-officers. A few nights after the murder, Mrs Elphinstone was found to be in possession of the will! How did she get it?"

CHAPTER 24 MISSING!

It needed no more than a glance at the two policemen to see that this announcement produced an effect on their officially-trained minds which was equivalent to letting in a sudden flood of illuminating light on a hitherto dark subject. Corkerdale looked at Manners; Manners stared at Corkerdale; then both turned on the solicitor.

"Mrs Elphinstone!" exclaimed Manners. "In possession of the missing will?"

But Corkerdale's first remark was in a quieter tone.

"That'll need some explanation," he said, with a significant look. "As I understand matters, the will was in Mazaroff's pocket when he was murdered."

"As far as is known, it was," replied Crole. "He carried it away from Postlethwaite's office at York, in his pocket, anyway, and it certainly wasn't amongst his effects at the Woodcock, which we examined after his death. Explanation, yes!—but I'll tell you how we came to find out that Mrs Elphinstone got it." He went on to narrate the happenings of the previous night but one, on which Sheila came to me with the missing will. "Now," he continued, "the thing, of course, is—how, where, under what circumstances did Mrs Elphinstone get hold of that will? Last night, after Mrs Elphinstone arrived in London, Maythorne saw her and tried to get an explanation out of her. He got nothing!"

"Not a word!" said Maythorne. "She showed nothing but defiance I pointed out the inference that might be drawn; the suspicion that might be thrown upon her—all no good! She refused to say or tell anything."

"And that makes me think," remarked Crole, a little eagerly, "that Mrs Elphinstone, after all, may have a proper and reasonable explanation to give. I can't think that a woman of any common sense—and she's a shrewd, clever, hard woman!—would be so foolish as to behave in this fashion unless she knew she was safe. You hinted that you'd have to give information to the police, didn't you, Maythorne?"

"I did!"

"And it produced no effect on her?"

"Not the slightest! Her whole attitude was that of—mind your own business!"

Crole began to drum the table with his fingers, looking round at the rest of us as if he wondered whether anybody had got any suggestion to make. As nobody spoke, he made one himself.

"I wonder if Mazaroff, or Merchison, as he really was, met Mrs Elphinstone, or Mrs Merchison, as she really is, at any time while he was at the Woodcock before his death?" he said. "Possible!"

"I don't think he did," replied Maythorne, at whom Crole was looking particularly. "There's nothing whatever to suggest it. Of course, if Mrs Elphinstone could be got to speak it would clear up a tremendous lot."

"From what little I saw of Mrs Elphinstone at Marrasdale," observed Crole, "she's the sort of woman who will not speak—until it pleases her to do so! A hard woman—damned hard!"

"Where is Mrs Elphinstone to be found?" asked Corkerdale.

"Short's Hotel," replied Maythorne.

"Then I think Manners and I had better go there and see her," said Corkerdale. He turned to Eccleshare. "You spoke of leaving England, doctor? When?"

"I've not quite settled the exact date," replied Eccleshare. "I thought about the end of next week."

"Better put it off a bit, doctor," suggested Corkerdale quietly. "As far as I can see, your evidence will be wanted—and so will your man's. Now," he continued, "I suppose Parslave there is a native of this place, Marrasdale? Just so—then he's very well acquainted with the personal appearance of Mrs Elphinstone?"

"Known her a many years, sir—ever since she came to live at Marrasdale Tower," replied Parslave.

"You'd be in the habit of seeing her regularly, Parslave?" suggested the detective.

"Most every day, sir—here and there."

"And you've no doubt that it was Mrs Elphinstone you saw that night, coming away from the place where you heard the shot fired, and where Mazaroff's dead body was afterwards discovered?"

"Not a doubt about that, sir! Take my solemn 'davy 'twas Mrs Elphinstone."

"And you've no doubt either, doctor?—though you, of course, being, I gather, a mere visitor to these parts, wouldn't know Mrs Elphinstone so well?"

"I've no doubt," replied Eccleshare. "Although I was only a visitor, I know Mrs Elphinstone well enough. My host, Mr Courthope, is her nephew. He, Mr Armintrade, and myself dined at Marrasdale Tower two or three times during my stay. I often met Mrs Elphinstone out on the moors, or in the village. I'm positive she was the woman Parslave and I saw coming away that night from Reiver's Den. I've never had any doubt about it—whatever it all means!"

Corkerdale turned to Manners.

"I think we'd better go round to Short's Hotel," he remarked.

"That's what I think," agreed Manners. "Can't be left where it is."

We all got up. There was a brief silence. Crole was just going to say something when a knock came at the door. Eccleshare's housekeeper put her head inside.

"There's a young man outside, sir, wants to know if Mr Maythorne is here?" she said. "Come in a taxi, sir, with an old gentleman. The young man said—if Mr Maythorne's here which his name is Pickles."

"One of my clerks," muttered Maythorne. "Excuse me!" He hurried out—to return within a minute or two with Mr Elphinstone. And, for the first time since the beginning of my acquaintanceship with him, Maythorne showed evidence of something close akin to excitement and concern.

"Here's a new development!" he exclaimed as he came into the room. "Mr Elphinstone has been to my office and followed me here to tell me that Mrs Elphinstone has disappeared!"

We all turned on Mr Elphinstone. He was shaken out of his usual dreaminess; he looked perturbed, dismayed, puzzled, wholly at a loss. Standing there a little within the doorway, blinking at us as if unable to make us out or reckon us up, he nodded automatically at Maythorne's announcement. But he was sufficiently master of himself to confirm it, in words.

"Since last night!" he said. "Disappeared—completely! Most extraordinary—and unpleasant—and embarrassing—I really do not know what to think—or do! A very trying situation!"

Crole, who had given the two policemen a sharp glance on hearing the news, pushed a chair towards the new-comer.

"Sit down, Mr Elphinstone," he said. "Perhaps we can help you a bit. When did Mrs Elphinstone disappear?"

Mr Elphinstone dropped into the chair, and looked round us again. He was carrying an old-fashioned walking-cane, and he mechanically lifted its silver head to his chin and rubbed it thoughtfully.

"Just so!" he said. "The fact is, the whole thing is really most confusing. Last night, of course! We left Miss Apperley's flat and went to Short's Hotel—that's where we always stay when we come to town. We had dinner on our arrival, in our own private sitting-room. It was some little time after that that Sheila came. She——"

"Oh!—Miss Merchison came there, did she?" interrupted Maythorne.

"Miss Merchison—Sheila—my step-daughter—yes. She came. She and her mother went into the adjoining bedroom—to talk. I heard them talking. I—I went away—downstairs, you know—I thought I'd smoke a cigar in the smoking-room. I was down there perhaps an hour—I foregathered with a man who turned out to be something of an archaeologist—interesting conversation. Perhaps I was a little longer away. Then I went up to our rooms again. There was nobody there—nobody at all! I thought perhaps Mrs Elphinstone and Sheila had gone into the drawing-room, and I went there, but they were not to be seen. I waited some time. Then, as they didn't come, I made some enquiry. And I found—really most astonishing!—I found, from the hall-porter, that Mrs Elphinstone, and Sheila, and Alison Murdoch had all gone out of the hotel some time before, evidently soon after I had gone down to the smoking-room. And——"

"Pardon me, Mr Elphinstone," broke in Maythorne, "but—who is Alison Murdoch?"

Mr Elphinstone looked at his questioner pretty much as a man looks who wonders that anybody shouldn't know as much as he knows himself.

"Alison Murdoch?" he answered. "Oh, ah!—you're not a Marrasdale man, of course. Alison Murdoch is a sort of foster-sister of my wife's. Brought up together, as children, you know. Then at one time she was for many years my wife's maid—still acts in that capacity when we go travelling, as in this instance. But for some few years she has lived in a little house at Marrasdale —Birnside, really—on her own means—little competency, you know. An active woman, though—in the tourist season, for instance, she helps them at the Woodcock with their cooking—clever, bustling woman!"

"And she went out last night with Mrs Elphinstone and Miss Merchison?" asked Maythorne.

"So I learnt from the hall-porter. He said that Mrs Elphinstone and her maid—they know them both well enough at Short's, for we are always up, all three of us, two or three times a year, and Miss Merchison, whom, of course, they also know well, all went out together about—I think he said half-past nine."

"Did he call a cab for them?" demanded Maythorne.

"No—he said they turned to the left, down the street—walking," replied Mr Elphinstone. "Dear me!—I really can't think why they should go walking at that hour of the evening!"

"But the point is—did they, or any one of them, return?" enquired Crole.

"None returned!" said Mr Elphinstone. "I waited up till midnight—eventually I retired—very much puzzled—and—I was so fatigued I fell asleep at once, and slept soundly until morning. To my great amazement, I found that neither Mrs Elphinstone nor Alison Murdoch had come back—Sheila, of course, I supposed to be at Miss Apperley's. So, after getting a little breakfast, I drove to Miss Apperley's, and just caught that young lady as she was leaving for her classes. To my still greater amazement she knew nothing whatever about Sheila. Sheila, she said, had suddenly remarked, after sitting in silence for a long time the previous evening, that she would go to Short's Hotel and have things out with her mother, and had set off there and then— and had never returned! So," concluded Mr Elphinstone, waving his silver-mounted cane, "there it is! All three have vanished!— in London! I thought of Mr Maythorne and went to his office— and was brought along here to him. And I was going to ask you, Mr Maythorne—do you think it possible they have been kidnapped?"

No one laughed: Mr Elphinstone's simplicity was too apparent. He was very grave, too, in his simplicity, and Crole was equally grave in replying to his ingenuous question.

"No, Mr Elphinstone, no, I don't think it possible for three women to be kidnapped, even in London," he answered. "I think you'll find that they went out on some business of their own, and that they had good reasons—again of their own!—for not returning. But let me ask you for a little more information—when your wife and her daughter went into the bedroom to talk in private, where was Alison Murdoch?"

Mr Elphinstone considered this for a moment.

"Probably," he replied at last, "probably in the next room to that—a dressing-room, which she used as a bedroom. We always have the same rooms when we stay at Short's. There's a sitting-room, a bedroom, and a dressing-room: Alison Murdoch always has the dressing-room. I should say she'd be in there when my wife and Sheila went into the bedroom."

"Did you find out from the hall-porter if they took anything away with them?" enquired Crole. "Any light baggage—anything of that sort—as if they, or one or other of them, meant to stay away for the night?"

"I didn't enquire," replied Mr Elphinstone. "But I'm sure they didn't. The hall-porter—an intelligent man whom I've known for many years—told me this morning that his own opinion, when they went out was—well, in short, one that would never have occurred to me."

"And that was—what?" asked Crole.

"He said he thought the ladies were going to have what he called an hour at the pictures," answered Mr Elphinstone. "Of course, I didn't understand him. He explained that just round the corner from Short's, in the direction they took, is one of these new-fangled Cinema theatres, where, I am told, moving pictures are shown. But I can't think——"

"I think we may take it that they didn't go there," remarked Maythorne. He glanced significantly at the two policemen. "This'll have to be gone into carefully," he murmured. "Your line!"

"We don't know that Mrs Elphinstone mayn't be found at Short's—when Mr Elphinstone goes back there," said Crole, glancing at his watch. "It's now noon, and——"

"We don't," interrupted Maythorne. Then, in an undertone, he muttered, "But I guess he won't! Mr Elphinstone!" he continued, raising his voice, "I want to show you something—something that I have in my pocket. Here it is," he went on, producing the cairngorm brooch, and laying it on the table. "Tell me!—have you ever seen that article before?"

Mr Elphinstone peered carefully at the brooch and then looked up, quickly.

"Where did you get this?" he asked, as if in surprise. "To be sure—it belongs to my wife!"

CHAPTER 25 WHO WAS HE?

Maythorne bent over the table towards Manners and Corkerdale and for a moment or two spoke to them in a whisper: I gathered that he was telling them how and when he found the brooch which he had just exhibited. Again he turned to Mr Elphinstone.

"You've no doubt that this is your wife's brooch?" he asked. "After all, I suppose that one of these things is very like another."

"That is my wife's property!" affirmed Mr Elphinstone with more decision of will and manner than he usually showed. "I bought it for her myself, years ago, in Inverness. It is one of two —they are precisely alike. The stones are of a rather uncommon sort of cairngorm; the silver mountings are old. I bought the pair in a sort of odds-and-ends shop in Inverness—I remember the circumstances very well. But to be sure!—I haven't seen either brooch for years."

"Mrs Elphinstone didn't wear them, then?" suggested Maythorne.

"She thought them old-fashioned and rather too heavy," replied Mr Elphinstone. "She looked on them, I think, as curiosities—she said they'd been used, originally, for fastening plaids —men's plaids, you know, at the shoulders—and she put them away. I don't remember that she ever did wear them—but I have no doubt whatever that what you show me is one of the pair. Now, where did you get it?"

"Let it suffice for the moment, Mr Elphinstone, to say that I found it, accidentally," answered Maythorne. "Picked it up, you know—when I was at Marrasdale. Never mind more, just now."

He replaced the brooch in his pocket, and rose, looking round at the rest of us. "Well?" he said "What next?"

Nobody made any suggestion. The next words came from Mr Elphinstone.

"I wish I knew what has become of my wife!" he said plaintively. "Can no one think of anything to do?"

"She'll have to be sought for, sir," said Corkerdale. He nudged Manners. "We'd better be doing something, I think," he murmured. "The hotel first, eh?"

Maythorne turned to Eccleshare.

"I suppose you're on the telephone?" he said. "Just so!—let us ring up Short's and find out if Mrs Elphinstone has returned there."

He went out into the hall with Eccleshare; the rest of us waited until their return a few minutes later. Maythorne shook his head.

"No news!" he answered. "They haven't been back there—up to now. But—as they set out from there I suppose that's the best base from which to conduct operations?"

"We're going there, anyway," said Corkerdale. "Mrs Elphinstone's got to be found! Perhaps Mr Elphinstone will come with us?—we may hit on some clue from something that's been left."

Mr Elphinstone, feebly protesting that all this was very annoying and confusing, went away with the two policemen: when they had gone, Maythorne, with a shrug of his shoulders, looked at Crole.

"That'll do no good!" he said. "They'll find nothing! This is all a plant—between Mrs Elphinstone and somebody else—Alison Murdoch, very likely. The only thing that puzzles me is—how did Miss Merchison come into it last night?"

That, too, was puzzling me. But Crole was quicker of thought and suggestion.

"I don't think there's much doubt about that," he remarked. "I fancy I can see the whole thing. Miss Merchison, acting on the principle that blood, after all, is thicker than water, somewhat relented last night after you two had been at Miss Apperley's flat, and betook herself to her mother's at Short's. There, I should say, Mrs Elphinstone let her daughter into whatever secret it is she's guarding, and as a result—they made themselves scarce!"

"Why?" asked Maythorne.

Crole spread out his hands with a significant gesture.

"I think Mrs Elphinstone shot Mazaroff!" he said.

"So do I!" muttered Eccleshare.

But at that—I suppose it was really for Sheila's sake—I thought it high time to put in a word myself. I had kept silence, not feeling qualified to speak in the presence of policemen and detectives, but I had been thinking and reflecting.

"I think you're both wrong!" said I, looking from Crole to Eccleshare. "Mazaroff, as we know, was shot with Musgrave's gun! How could Mrs Elphinstone get hold of Musgrave's gun? Musgrave's gun was found on the spot."

But Maythorne shook his head.

"We don't know that Mazaroff was shot with Musgrave's gun. Holt," he said. "That's a stiff point! There were two shots fired that night—the first heard by Dr Eccleshare and Parslave; the second heard by old Hassendeane, some time later. We don't know which shot killed Mazaroff; nor from what gun it was fired."

"If it was the second shot—just before ten—that killed Mazaroff," I said, "then it wasn't Mrs Elphinstone who fired it. For Eccleshare and Parslave say that they saw her just after eight. And I for one am not satisfied that they saw her! They admit it was dark—they may have seen some woman who closely resembled her——"

"No!" said Eccleshare. "We saw—her!"

"Besides," I continued, "there's another thing. Is it likely? Is it probable? Why should Mrs Elphinstone shoot Mazaroff, or Merchison—her legal husband?"

194

"Perhaps just because he was her legal husband," remarked Crole, with a dry smile. "From what I've seen of her, I wouldn't put it past Mrs Elphinstone to do anything."

"This is murder!" I said. "Anyway—if Mrs Elphinstone did this, and let out the secret to her daughter last night, I'm certain Miss Merchison wouldn't aid and abet by further concealment."

"Are you, my lad!" retorted Crole. "Well, then, all I can say is, you don't know life, nor human nature—nor women! Now, I should say that's precisely what Miss Merchison would do!—as I've remarked before, blood's thicker than water. Miss Merchison—a very impulsive young woman—no doubt felt very indignant with her mother about the will, and rushed off to return it to its rightful owner—in whom, my dear Holt, she feels a strong—very strong!—interest. But—if it came to this: that Mrs Elphinstone was forced to confess to her daughter that she is implicated in the actual murder, well, then, I make bold to say, Miss Merchison's feelings as a daughter would assert themselves and she'd do all in her power to help her parent! And I guess Maythorne agrees?"

"Of course!" said Maythorne, half-carelessly. "No doubt about it—human nature! Shouldn't think much of Miss Merchison if she didn't fight for her own mother! However, this is all talk—let's do something." He turned to Eccleshare. "I suppose you'll take Corkerdale's tip and stop here until you find out if your evidence, and Parslave's, is wanted, doctor?" he suggested.

"I suppose I'll have to," responded Eccleshare. "A week or two makes little difference, except that the man I've sold my practice to wants to come in. However, that can be arranged. Needs must, eh?"

"I think so," answered Maythorne. "Well," he continued, turning to Crole and myself, "let's get a move on."

We left the house. Outside, across the street, Johnson was still loafing about. He caught Maythorne's eye; what Maythorne did in the way of signalling to him I did not make out, but Johnson loafed away, and still further away, and faded out of sight.

"No need to keep that chap hanging round," observed Maythorne. "Now for Cottingley—I think I shall put Cottingley on to the track of Mrs Elphinstone—he'll find her a lot quicker than any professional police will."

"Where's he going to pick up a clue?" enquired Crole sarcastically.

"Leave that to Cottingley!" retorted Maythorne. "He'll see a clue where no one else would. All he wants is clear—and concise—instructions to start out on."

We found Cottingley at the top of the street. He was eating an apple, in supplement to his lunch of bread and cheese. Phlegmatic as ever, he turned with us towards the nearest cab-rank, Maythorne talking to him as we went along.

"What next?" asked Crole as we reached Edgware Road again.

"I'm just going round by Short's Hotel," answered Maythorne, "to hear if those chaps have made anything out, and to give Cottingley a start. Better come, both of you."

"I won't," said Crole. "I must get back to my office. I can do no good at Short's, and you can ring me up if you've any news. Oh, by the by!" he added, as Maythorne signalled to a taxi-cab driver. "I forgot to mention it before. Holt. Armintrade's cheque duly arrived this morning. So that's all right, and I suppose we've finished with his part in all these mysteries."

"Finished with nothing, Crole!" exclaimed Maythorne. "The curtain is still up—well up!—on everything. Coming, Holt?—you'd better."

I went with him. I was not so much concerned about Mrs Elphinstone as about Sheila. That some new and very serious situation had arisen when Sheila called on her mother the previous evening there could be no doubt—nothing else, I was sure, could have occasioned the strange departure and disappearance of which Mr Elphinstone had told us. What was it?

It took little time to run round to Short's—a famous, if somewhat old-fashioned hotel in the West End, greatly in favour with county family people. While we rode there Maythorne occupied himself in posting up Cottingley in all our doings that morning, and especially about the disappearance of Mrs Elphinstone. Cottingley soaked it all in without saying a word; he was still eating apples, and he munched them steadily while his employer talked. But as Maythorne made an end Cottingley also finished his last apple, and tossing the core out of the cab window, rapped out a word or two.

"Steamship offices!" he said. "Likeliest place, first."

"Good!" assented Maythorne. "There may be something in that. All right!—you get on to it. But first, we'll see if anything's turned up here."

We left the cab a little way from Short's, and walked along towards the principal entrance. Manners and Corkerdale were just coming out as we reached it—I thought I saw in their manner that they had heard something.

"Well?" asked Maythorne as we joined them. "Any news?"

"Nobody's returned," replied Corkerdale, "and there's nothing in Mrs Elphinstone's or the maid's rooms to suggest why they ever went away. But we have heard a bit that the old gentleman hadn't found out when he set off to you this morning."

"What's that?" asked Maythorne.

"Odd circumstance, to be sure!" answered the detective. "I'd like to know what it means. Got it from the under hall-porter. He says that some little time after Mr and Mrs Elphinstone and the maid arrived last night—he knows all three well enough, he says, as they come there two or three times a year—a man came into the entrance hall and asked him if they—naming them— were stopping there? He said they were, and he believed they were then having dinner. The man went away. But this under hall-porter also says that he noticed the same man hanging about the hotel front after that, and that he was there, as if watching, when Mrs Elphinstone and her daughter and the maid went out—in fact, he's positive that the man followed them down the street and round the first corner. And—that's all!"

"And a good lot!" remarked Maythorne. "Could he describe the man?"

"Oh, yes! A little, thin man, about thirty or so; slight brown moustache, wore spectacles; very respectably dressed; wore a

Trilby hat—looked like a clerk or commercial traveller—something of that sort," replied Corkerdale.

"Did he say anything to the under hall-porter as to why he wanted the Elphinstones?" asked Maythorne.

"No—the man asked him if he could take up any message," said Corkerdale. "He replied no—it didn't matter: he wouldn't disturb them if they were at dinner; he'd look in again."

"And he didn't look in again?"

"No—the last the under hall-porter saw of him, he was following the three women down the street."

Maythorne remained silent for a minute or two.

"Well," he said at last. "I suppose you'll follow things up in your own way. If I can be of any help, let me know. If I hear anything. I'll let you know, Corkerdale. May as well help each other."

He turned away, Cottingley and I following him. After going a short distance, he motioned to the clerk.

"Try your line—the shipping offices, Cottingley," he said. "May be some good."

Cottingley went off, and Maythorne and I walked on in silence for a while.

"This is a queer business, Holt!" he said, after some time. "That Mrs Elphinstone is either guilty or is privy to somebody else's guilt seems dead certain! But—where on earth has she disappeared to? And when and where are we going to get news of her?"

I got no more light on that problem for more than two days. Nobody heard anything, nobody discovered anything. I called continually at Short's; Mr Elphinstone, after being first at his wits' ends, settled down to a sort of philosophic calm, waiting. And nothing happened, until, on the third night after the disappearance, Maythorne rushed up to my rooms and thrust an evening newspaper before me. "For God's sake, Holt!" he exclaimed excitedly. "Read that!"

CHAPTER 26 WE KNOW THAT MAN!

I snatched at the newspaper eagerly enough: there was that in Maythorne's manner which showed me that here was news of importance. I saw it at once—there it was, in big letters in the stop-press space.

STARTLING DISCOVERY IN THE HARROW ROAD
SUPPOSED ROBBERY AND MURDER

About half-past four this afternoon Mr Kilthwaite, Grocer, of 623x, Harrow Road, having occasion to visit a yard at the back of his premises, in search for some crates stored amongst a quantity of similar odds and ends, came across the dead body of a man which had evidently been dragged across the yard through the rear entrance and partly concealed by loose timber. He at once summoned the police, and on examination it was found that the man had been murdered by repeated blows on the head with some heavy instrument. He is a man of presumably thirty years of age, small of stature, of slight build, wearing spectacles, the lens on the right being shattered; he is respectably dressed, and a new Trilby hat was found lying beneath the body. He had evidently been robbed after being struck down, as there was nothing on him in the way of money or valuables, nor were there any papers that could lead to identification: everything, in fact, of this sort had been carefully removed, and the only articles found in the clothing were a fountain-pen and two recently pointed lead pencils. New Scotland Yard was at once communicated with and detectives are making a careful investigation. Anyone recognising the dead man from the foregoing description should at once communicate with the police authorities.

I laid the paper down and stared enquiringly at Maythorne. He slapped his hand heavily on the paragraph I had just read.

"Holt!" he exclaimed. "That's the chap who followed these three women away from Short's Hotel the other night! A million to one on it!"

"You think so?" I said incredulously. "But—there are lots of men who'd correspond to that description."

"That's the man!—I'll lay anything!" he declared. "And this thing's getting more of a mystery than ever Look at it!—Mrs Elphinstone, her daughter, and her maid, without a word to Elphinstone, suddenly clear out of Short's, late at night. They are seen to be followed by a man who had previously enquired if the Elphinstones were staying at Short's. They never return, the women; from that moment to this—all this time having elapsed —seventy-two hours!—nothing whatever has been heard of them. And then this discovery is made—the man who was seen to follow them is found murdered—head battered to pieces— and robbed! Now—why?"

"If he is the man!" I exclaimed.

"It'll surprise me more than I've been surprised, so far," he retorted, "if he isn't the man. But we'll soon settle that. Come along—I've got a taxi outside. We'll go round by Short's, get hold of that under hall-porter, and go up to the Harrow Road."

"To see—him?" I asked.

"What else?" he answered. "Come on!—you don't know what depends on it. Nor—where those women are. In danger, for anything we know."

I went willingly enough, then. Somehow, it had not struck me up to that time that Sheila might be in real danger: I had fancied, rather, that she was probably assisting her mother in flying from justice, or, at any rate, from distasteful enquiries.

"You really think that?" I said as we hurried downstairs.

"Where are they?" he demanded. "The police have been after them for three days and nights. Not a trace! Cottingley and I have been working, in our way. Dead failure! Holt, I'm so convinced that this is the man who followed them that we must see him at once: And if he is——"

"Well," I asked impatiently, as he paused. "What then?"

"Then, if he is, and if he can be identified," he muttered, "we may—at last—be on the right track towards—more! Come on!— let's get to it."

We rode round to Short's, and after some slight delay, carried off the under hall-porter. Once in the cab again, Maythorne showed him the newspaper description of the murdered man.

"Does that answer to the man you saw following Mrs Elphinstone three nights ago?" he asked.

The under hall-porter, a sharp-eyed fellow, nodded.

"I should say it did, sir, myself," he answered. "Yes, it's a good description of him, taking it altogether. It doesn't mention that he'd a slight brown moustache, though. If this dead man has ——"

"We shall soon see that," said Maythorne grimly. "A few minutes——"

Mr Kilthwaite's grocer's establishment was away up at the poorer end of the Harrow Road—a very modest establishment, too, catering for a humble class of customers. But when we got out of our cab and walked towards it, we found that for once at any rate it was a centre of vast interest, if not of trade. The pavement outside was thronged with people, and a posse of policemen was engaged in getting them to move away or move along, not over successfully: two policemen stood at the shop-door, evidently with orders to admit none but *bona fide* customers. A word from Maythorne procured us instant admission, however, and we entered—to find Manners and Corkerdale standing inside, in conversation with the grocer, an excited and voluble person who was obviously re-telling his story for the *xth* time. Corkerdale nodded significantly as Maythorne advanced on them.

"Same notion as ourselves, eh, Mr Maythorne?" he said with a smile. "We thought this man might be the man who was seen at Short's, so we just came round. We didn't think of that, though," he added, pointing to the under hall-porter. "Good notion of yours to bring him!"

"Have you seen the man?" asked Maythorne.

"We haven't, yet," replied Corkerdale. "He's at the mortuary, of course. We'll go round there. Well," he continued, turning to the grocer, "we'll look in again when we've been to the mortuary, and perhaps you'll show us the premises where you found him?"

"Anything you please, Mr Corkerdale," replied the grocer, rubbing his hands. "Always glad to assist the police, sir. These gentlemen, I suppose, are in your line, too?"

"Bit that way," answered Corkerdale, with a smile at Maythorne. "Well," he went on, motioning us to follow. "We'll just step round—it's not far."

He led us along the dismal road to a still more dismal, if more spick-and-span building, the gloom and sombreness of which was accentuated by its air of officialism and formality. We trooped one after the other, under the guidance of a police-constable, into a white-washed chamber. There, on a centre table or slab, was laid out, stiffly evident under a white covering, what we had come to see. The police-constable began to turn back the sheet: Maythorne and Corkerdale motioned the under hall-porter to go nearer.

"Look well!—see if you can identify him," whispered Maythorne.

But the identification did not come from the hall-porter. We had all crowded close to the still figure; we all looked steadily at the dead man's face. And in that instant Manners and I, after a single glance at it, turned sharply on each other; a look of mutual understanding flashed between us, and we let out the same simultaneous exclamation.

"We know that man!"

The others turned on us, then, questioningly.

"You know him—both of you!" exclaimed Maythorne. "Then, who is he?"

"Newspaper reporter from up our way," answered Manners. "Name of Bownas. I don't suppose you ever saw him when you went up there—his work was more to the other side of Gilchester. But Mr Holt here knew him. That's Bownas, right enough!"

"He came to see me, at the Woodcock, with Manners, after Mazaroff's disappearance," I said. "I saw him, just once, afterwards—in Gilchester. But that is Bownas, without doubt!"

"And murdered here in London!" muttered Manners. "Good Lord!—what's it mean! There's more in this——"

"A moment!" interrupted Maythorne. He turned on the hall-porter. "Don't make any mistake!" he said. "Is that the man who came to Short's Hotel, and whom you afterwards saw following Mrs Elphinstone and her daughter and the maid? Look well at him, now!—be sure!"

But the hall-porter shook his head as much as to imply that all the looking in the world wouldn't make him surer.

"Oh, that's the man!" he exclaimed. "I knew him at once. There's no doubt about it! Recognised him as soon as I set eyes on him. Of course he's lost his colour, but——"

We went out of the mortuary, and into an office where there were more officials. They evidently knew Corkerdale, and after a few minutes' whispered conversation with him they produced some clothing. Corkerdale immediately placed his finger on a label within the Trilby hat.

"That wasn't mentioned in the newspaper account," he said. "See—Border Clothing Company, Carlisle. New, too. Let me have a look at his other things." I stood by, watching curiously while Corkerdale and Manners and Maythorne went through the dead man's garments. They found but one thing of any note—a tailor's label sewn within the inside breast-pocket of the coat, showing that the suit had been made in Newcastle. It had a date and a number on it, and Corkerdale remarked that there was a clue to identification, if necessary.

"It's not necessary," remarked Manners. "I know the man well enough. Bownas—reporter of the *Tweed and Border Gazette* at Gilchester. And I'd like to know what he was doing here!"

"What was he doing at Short's Hotel?" suggested Maythorne. "That's more like it. Manners! But that's obvious—he was after Mrs Elphinstone. He followed her, too, when she went out. Where? Now, then, did she, and her two companions, come to this quarter of the town? If they did—why? And where are they?"

"Let's go back to the grocer's," said Corkerdale.

We went out again into the gloomy road. The under hall-porter, having done what was required of him, was anxious to go back to the hotel. Maythorne sent him off in a taxi-cab: the rest of us returned to Kilthwaite's shop. Maythorne and I walked side by side—at first in silence.

"What do you make of this, Maythorne?" I asked at last.

"God knows!" he answered. "It seems evident that the poor fellow we've just seen followed the Elphinstones—Mrs Elphinstone, of course!—to London, tracked them to the hotel, went after Mrs Elphinstone when she went out that night, but—as to the rest——"

"Do you think he followed them here?" I suggested. "If so, what could they want in this neighbourhood?"

"Shabby and sordid enough for anything, hereabouts, isn't it?" he answered, with a shrug of his shoulders. "Again I say—who knows?—who knows anything? Let's have a look at the place where he was found, however—we may get some idea of something."

The grocer took us through his shop into his backyard. It was a dismal place, all the more dismal because that was an unusually fine Spring evening It seemed to be a sort of dumping ground for boxes, barrels, chests, old tins, crates, all the refuse of a chandlery shop, and it was of some extent, running from the back of the premises to a high wall in which there was a crazy door.

"Here's where I found him!" whispered Kilthwaite in a half awe-struck whisper. "I wanted some planking out of this pile of old wood: I pulled some aside, and there was a man's arm! And then—well, then I found the rest. I saw no signs of a struggle. But," he added, "some of your people that have been here already, Mr Corkerdale, they say that there are clear indications that he'd been dragged in here, across the yard, from the door there."

"What's outside that door and the wall?" asked Corkerdale.

We all went to look. There was a narrow, stone-paved lane there, running from a side street between the backs of the Harrow Road houses and those of some street or terrace, set further back. It was fenced in by high walls for all its length: there were only two feeble gas-lamps to light it; it was dark, silent—its very gloom seemed to suggest murder.

"One of your men says there are blood-stains on the stones—just there!" whispered the grocer. "Of course, you know, I never heard anything and I've not heard, either, of anybody who did, so far."

We went back to the shop and stood discussing the matter and its probabilities for some little time. Then the grocer's telephone bell rang. He went to answer it, and from the box looked round at us.

"If one of you gentlemen's Mr Maythorne," he said, "he's wanted."

Maythorne crossed over and took up the receiver A moment later, he, too, turned on us.

"From the under hall-porter!" he exclaimed. "Mrs Elphinstone and Miss Merchison are back!"

CHAPTER 27
ACCUSED!

I had been pretty much of a passive spectator and observer up to that point, but as soon as Maythorne made his startling announcement I leapt into action. I was half-way to the shop-door before his last word had left his lips; he himself was scarcely less rapid of movement and his hand was on my arm as I crossed the threshold.

"Where are you going?" he exclaimed.

"Where? Short's, of course!" I answered. "Aren't you?"

"To be sure!" he said. "But—a moment. These other two had better come, as well. And—a word with this grocer chap."

I waited impatiently outside the shop until the three men joined me. We had some little difficulty in finding a taxi-cab; they were not plentiful in that dreary quarter; when at last we had packed ourselves into one I chafed all the time its driver was running down to a more palatable neighbourhood. My three companions had relapsed into silence: each seemed to be following some train of thought of his own. Nobody spoke, indeed, until we were close to Short's Hotel: then Manners suddenly gave voice to what he was evidently thinking.

"That poor fellow Bownas must have come up to London by the same train that the Elphinstones came in!" he said, in the tone of a man who thinks that he has made a startling discovery.

"Evidently!" remarked Maythorne, in his direct manner. "Evidently!—since he presented himself at their hotel very soon after they got there."

"What I meant," said Manners, "was this—if he did, as he must have done, he was tracking them—or some one of them."

"That, too, seems evident," rejoined Maythorne. "I should say he was! Especially as he followed the three women when they went out!"

"Why?" asked Manners. "Why? That's what licks me!"

There was a brief silence on that. Then Corkerdale spoke.

"Newspaper man, you say he was," he remarked. "Reporter. Those chaps have a trick of poking their noses into places and things where they've no right to be. Poachers, as it were. I've had more than one game of mine spoiled by that sort! Get it into their heads that it's a fine thing to do a bit of detective work for their papers. Gets 'em credit with the editors. I should say this chap's been going on a line of his own since that murder—and you see what it's brought him to! Murdered, himself!"

"Ah!" said Maythorne, with a touch of sarcasm that was lost on our companions. "I shouldn't wonder if you're right, Corkerdale. But what a pity we didn't get on his line, too! For, if he was murdered to silence him, you may bet your life he was on the right line! But here we are."

The under hall-porter hurried down the steps at Short's and opened the door of our cab, glancing knowingly at Maythorne.

"Came in just as I got back, sir," he announced in an undertone. "Both of 'em! In a taxi. So I telephoned up there to you, at once."

"Good!" answered Maythorne. "But—only Mrs Elphinstone and Miss Merchison? Not the Maid?"

"No, sir. Only the lady and her daughter. I think Mrs Elphinstone's ill, sir. There's a doctor gone up."

"Ill, eh? Heard any particulars?"

"No, sir. She went up in the lift all right—except that she looked very tired. But they sent out for a doctor, just after."

Maythorne turned to the two policemen. But before he could say anything, a woman in the uniform of a professional nurse came hurrying round the corner and sped up the steps into the hotel: we watched her accost the hall-porter, who immediately took her to the lift.

"The doctor's evidently telephoned for a nurse," observed Maythorne. "Um!—we can't very well break in on illness."

But Corkerdale shook his head and his face grew inflexible.

"Illness or no illness, Mr Maythorne," he said, "I'm going up! Things are a bit too thick, too serious. And there's the young lady. She'll know where her mother's been and where they've come from. And—where's that other woman, the maid. We'll go up, Manners."

Maythorne and I followed them. We went up to the floor on which the Elphinstones' suite of rooms was situate. At the door Corkerdale paused and turned to me.

"Mr Holt knows the family," he said in a suggestive whisper. "Go in, Mr Holt, and just see how the land lies! We don't want to intrude, you know, nor to make any bother, but we must have some explanation. Get the young lady to yourself and——"

He broke off with a meaning nod at the door, and, anxious enough to see Sheila and to make sure that she was safe, I tapped at the panels and walked into the room. I saw Sheila at once; she was standing on one side of the hearth; Mr Elphinstone, in his usual semi-distressed, semi-perplexed state, stood at the other; between them, his hat in his hand, stood a tall, professional-looking man whom I at once set down as the doctor we had just heard of. He was speaking as I entered, and with a mere glance at me, he went on—

"—after a good night's rest, quite all right, I think. But I will call again, Mr Elphinstone, in a couple of hours, and perhaps give Mrs Elphinstone a sleeping draught. Keep the nurse all night— she'll save you a lot of trouble. I think that's all at present."

He turned and made for the door, and as I was still close by it, I opened it for him, let him out, and shut it on him, at the same time slipping the latch—those three outside were not coming in until I was sure of something. I turned: Sheila was already advancing towards me.

"You're all right?" I said eagerly. "Safe?"

"Safe—yes!" she answered. "All right, too. But—everything

else is all wrong! Maythorne?—where is he?"

"Outside," I said. "The police, too! Two of them—Corkerdale and Manners. Are they to come in?"

Mr Elphinstone had overheard all this: he came forward.

"Oh, dear, dear!" he exclaimed querulously. "I really do think, Sheila, that we can't have these people in! Your mother comes back and collapses—we have to send for a doctor and a nurse—I myself have had no explanation of your mysterious goings-on—disappearance and all that, and—really——"

"We've got to see the police at once!" interrupted Sheila. "Let them in, Mervyn. You'll hear everything that I say to them," she added, turning to Mr Elphinstone. "There mustn't be any delay, either! Open the door!"

I thrust back the latch and threw the door open—the three men outside came in, wonderingly. The two policemen, thus admitted, appeared to lose their tongues; but Maythorne, after a first keen glance at Sheila, smiled.

"I think you're none the worse for your adventures, Miss Merchison," he said. "I hope Mrs Elphinstone is not seriously the worse, either?"

"My mother's had a sort of collapse after she came in," replied Sheila. "The doctor says she will be all right after a night's rest. Sit down, all of you, if you please—I want to talk to you," she continued abruptly. "You've all been wondering where my mother, and Alison Murdoch, and myself went, and where we've been since, haven't you?"

"A good deal of search has been made for you, miss," observed Corker dale, finding his tongue. "Going on now, it is, too! What happened, if I may ask?"

Sheila looked at Maythorne and from him to me.

"Happened?" she answered. "My mother and I were kidnapped!"

Mr Elphinstone groaned—but there was a note of triumph in his voice.

"I said so!—I said so!" he exclaimed. "I suggested it—it occurred to me. But he"—here he pointed to and wagged his forefinger at Maythorne—"I could see he didn't believe it— and Crole, the lawyer, said it wasn't possible! To be sure!—kid-napped! I knew it—felt it!"

"By whom were you kidnapped. Miss Merchison?" asked May-thorne quietly.

Sheila unconsciously lowered her voice as she bent forward to answer.

"Alison Murdoch!" she replied.

"And where is Alison Murdoch?" continued Maythorne. "But —I suppose you don't know!"

"No!" answered Sheila. "I don't know!"

Maythorne nodded at the door of the bedroom.

"Does Mrs Elphinstone know?"

"No!—no more than I do! Disappeared, of course."

Corkerdale cleared his throat—the sound suggested that he thought it was high time he came in.

"What I'd wish, Mr Maythorne," he said—"that is. Sergeant Manners and myself—would be if the young lady would just tell us what happened after she and her mother and this woman left the hotel three nights ago. Seems to me we want a consecutive narrative, as it were. Then——"

"I'm going to tell you," interrupted Sheila. "But I shall have to begin before that. I must begin where Mr Maythorne and Mr Holt came to Miss Apperley's flat that evening—the even-ing that my mother arrived here. After you two had gone," she continued, turning to Maythorne and me, "I thought a lot—a tremendous lot—about the whole business. I was very uneasy about everything—the will—the general situation. To tell you the truth, I felt that if things were going to remain where they were I should come perilously near to suspicion of my own mother. So——"

Mr Elphinstone smote his knees with his open palms and groaned audibly. But Sheila gave him a glance and went on.

"So, eventually, I said to Miss Apperley that I was going to Short's, to have it out with my mother if I could. I came here—I saw my mother in that bedroom."

"Alone?" asked Maythorne.

"Alone! We had a sort of row at first—she was naturally furious with me; first, for taking the will out of her possession; second, for running away to London with it and giving it to Mr Holt. But in the end she calmed down, and eventually, when we had restored amicable relations between ourselves, she told me that I need not have been so hasty, for it was her full intention to send the will, either to Mr Postlethwaite, who had prepared it, or to Mr Crole, the very next day, with an account of how it had come into her possession."

"I told you—I told you!" exclaimed Mr Elphinstone triumphantly. "I knew there would be a proper and full explanation!"

"How had the will come into Mrs Elphinstone's possession?" asked Maythorne.

"In this way," replied Sheila. "I told you and Mr Holt that my mother was out late in the evening for two evenings in succession, and that on the second evening I stole downstairs on hearing her come in, and unperceived by her, saw her examining a document which I afterwards discovered to be the will. Her explanation is that on coming in that night she found one of the French windows in the library open, and on the carpet, just within, an envelope containing the will! She had just picked this up and was examining it when I saw her."

"To be sure—to be sure!" muttered Mr Elphinstone. "Perfectly clear!—perfectly!"

But the three listeners said nothing. Nor did their faces express anything. They exchanged glances—but the glances might have come—if such a thing were possible—from marble statues.

"Proceed, if you please," said Maythorne quietly.

"Well," continued Sheila. "I then began to talk to my mother about various possibilities as to how the will had come there. I pointed out that the possession of it, and her refusal to account for it and to reply to questions (all of which is due to her natural pride and obstinacy and dislike of being coerced by anyone) would make people—like you, for instance—suspicious about her. She cared very little about that, but we began to discuss the question of the identity of the murderer. For it seemed to me that whoever had stolen the will had previously murdered its maker! And eventually, and I think, accidentally, I told her about that cairngorm brooch which you showed me the other night."

"Ah!" exclaimed Maythorne, with a subdued betrayal of his keen interest. "You did? Good—good! And——"

"She immediately became excited. She jumped to the conclusion that you had picked it up at the scene of the murder——"

"I did!" remarked Maythorne.

"So she suspected—and said that that of course was why you were taking care of it. Then she told me that—from my description—the brooch was one of two which Mr Elphinstone had bought, years ago, in Scotland, and given to her. She had never worn either, as they were cumbrous and heavy: she still had one, but she had given the other away, some time before."

"Aye, and to whom?" asked Maythorne eagerly.

"To Alison Murdoch!" replied Sheila, giving us all a swift, enveloping glance. "And, of course, as soon as I heard that, I saw through the whole sordid business. Alison Murdoch was the guilty person! She had murdered and robbed Mazaroff; she had dropped that brooch at Reiver's Den: she had thrown the will into the library at the Tower—the one fatal mistake she made for her own chances!—and . . . there she was, calmly eating her supper in the next room to that in which we were talking! I saw it all . . . I told my mother my conclusions. And then I fetched Alison Murdoch in, and accused her—point-blank!"

CHAPTER 28 THE SCEPTICAL DETECTIVE

There was a murmur that seemed to denote a mixture of interest and of admiration from the two policemen; Corkerdale, who sat twiddling his thumbs and watching Sheila intently, smiled broadly.

"You plumped her with it, miss!—straight out!" he exclaimed. "Yes—yes?"

"Straight out!—there and then," assented Sheila. "But let me tell you why—in addition to what I've already told. During the last few minutes of my talk with my mother I'd been thinking, harder and quicker than I'd ever thought in my life. Now, I remembered something about Alison Murdoch and about her family. Although my mother rarely mentioned such matters to me, I knew more about Marrasdale and my father's connection with it than she had any idea of—I had picked up a lot of knowledge and gossip from the old people round about us. And I knew that my father, Andrew Merchison, was well known in those parts before his marriage, and that his people had been folk of some consequence there. I knew, too, that Alison Murdoch's family had been there a long time, too, and that between it and my father's people there was a deadly enmity, arising out of——"

"Land!" interrupted Mr Elphinstone. "Land! The Merchison lot did the Murdochs out of a bit of land—some years ago. Piece of oppression and chicanery—but it was done. Unforgivable, of course, in the minds of these Border people. Feud! Land feud! Such things are remembered for ever."

"They rankle," said Sheila. "There was blood shed over it at the time—a Merchison shot a Murdoch; though not fatally. All that's well known—Mr Elphinstone knows all about it——"

"Countryside gossip to this day," agreed Mr Elphinstone. "There are men and women there in Marrasdale who remember it."

"Well," continued Sheila, "it struck me that Alison Murdoch, who is a silent, grim, reserved, determined woman, probably not only remembered it, but was the very sort of person who, if she got the chance of revenge, would take it without hesitation. I figured it all out this way. Alison Murdoch, when Mr Mazaroff—who, of course, was really Andrew Merchison—came to the Woodcock was helping there: helping with the cooking and so on. She saw him, and recognised him. She no doubt got acquainted with his habits and knew that he strolled out on the moors, after dark. Now she didn't live at the Woodcock— she lives at a cottage of her own, on the way to Birnside. I came to the conclusion that having made up her mind to revenge the old feud on Andrew Merchison, she watched for her opportunity. On the night of the murder she saw him go out and take the path towards Reiver's Den. She abstracted Musgrave's gun from the parlour and followed him—and shot him. And——"

"A moment!" interrupted Maythorne. He glanced at the two policemen. "Corkerdale and Manners will understand the meaning of a question I want to put to you," he continued. "It's this— does this woman, Alison Murdoch, at all resemble your mother, Mrs Elphinstone?"

"Very closely!" answered Sheila. "They're of the same height and build, anyway—very similar in figure and not at all unlike in general appearance."

"Supposing they were dressed alike——?" suggested Maythorne.

"They're very often dressed alike," replied Sheila. "For the simple reason that for years, to my knowledge, Alison Murdoch has never worn anything but my mother's discarded clothes!"

"One could easily be mistaken for the other in the dark, eh?" asked Maythorne.

"I should say, very easily," asserted Sheila. "In fact, I have so mistaken them myself."

Maythorne turned to the policemen.

"That accounts for what Eccleshare and Parslave saw—or believed they saw," he remarked in an undertone. "Eh?"

"Seems so—to me," answered Manners. "Yes—I should say it did."

Corkerdale, however, said nothing: he was still watching Sheila.

"You were saying, miss——?" he suggested.

"Well—I was going to say that that seemed to me a good ground for suspecting her, taking other things into consideration," continued Sheila. "But I had another ground. It was well known that the gentleman at the Woodcock was a very wealthy man—it had already got talked about. He was careless about displaying his wealth—I myself heard, as people do hear things in villages, that he left large sums of money and even diamonds lying about on his dining-table. Now I knew that Alison Murdoch is a covetous, avaricious, grasping woman; miserly to the last degree. If she murdered Andrew Merchison out of revenge, she was just the sort of woman to rob his dead body of everything on it out of sheer greed! She is, I say, that sort——"

"A hoarder!" muttered Mr Elphinstone. "A saver of farthings! I think you're quite right, Sheila. But murder?—dear me!"

"Well, that's the conclusion I came to," said Sheila, "and these were my reasons. In the few minutes in which I thought all this out, I came to the absolutely definite conclusion that Alison Murdoch had shot Andrew Merchison, had robbed him of his money, valuables, and papers, and that it was she who had thrown his will into the open window of Mr Elphinstone's library, where my mother had picked it up. And, as I said at the beginning, as soon as I'd arrived at that conclusion, I called her into my mother's room—that room!—and accused her of the murder!"

Mr Elphinstone treated us to one of his groans. But Corkerdale, unconsciously, edged his chair nearer to Sheila.

"Now this is where the really interesting part comes in, miss!" he said. "You charged her! What might she reply, now?"

"She denied it, of course—indignantly," answered Sheila. "She was for flouncing out of the room, to complain to Mr Elphinstone. Then she changed her mind, and said she'd go to her own room, pack her things, and leave the hotel. I soon settled her, though!"

"Aye?—and how, miss?" asked Corkerdale, still more interested.

"I told her that if she attempted to leave that room until I'd finished with her, I'd ring the bell, send for the police, and give her in charge!" said Sheila. "And I should have done so—nothing would have stopped me. That calmed her down—she knew me! Then I talked to her. I pieced things together—finally. I told her that her cairngorm brooch had been found on the scene of the murder——"

"How did she take that?" interrupted Maythorne.

"She turned very pale," replied Sheila. "But almost instantly she retorted that my mother had an exactly similar brooch— why wasn't she suspected? I replied that my mother never wore the other brooch, evidently she, Alison, did. Then I went on to rub it into her, frightening her all I could. My mother, on her part, begged her to tell of anything she knew. Finally, on my telling her that unless I got some explanation, I should give her in charge there and then, she admitted that she knew—something!"

"Ah!" said Maythorne. "Something!"

"Something!" repeated Sheila. "And having admitted that she made a strange offer—though I'm bound to say that it didn't seem so very strange at the time. She pointed out that she was alone there in London, that she was, in a degree, at my mercy. Then she reminded us that she had a brother here in London, a man who left Marrasdale years ago, and who had, she said, a business in the Harrow Road——"

"Aye, to be sure!" muttered Corkerdale. "The Harrow Road!"

"And she made us an offer," continued Sheila. "She said that if we would go with her, there and then, to her brother's house, and allow her to consult with him first, she'd tell us the absolute truth about all that she actually knew. We were fools enough to go—and we set off at once, without telling anybody. We expected, of course, to be back in a very short time."

"What happened, miss?" enquired Corkerdale.

"We left the hotel and got a taxi-cab round the corner of the next street," continued Sheila. "Alison Murdoch told the driver where to go. I know where the Harrow Road opens into Edgware Road at Paddington Green; we went a long, long way beyond that. At last we got out——"

"A minute, miss," interrupted Manners. "When you got out, did you happen to notice if you were being followed? By another taxi-cab, now?"

"I did see a taxi-cab pull up on the other side of the street, lower down," replied Sheila. "I noticed that while my mother was paying our man."

Manners sniffed, and whispered to his colleague—an audible whisper.

"That 'ud be—him!" he said. "Tracked 'em! Beg pardon, miss, for interrupting you."

"We walked up the road a little way," continued Sheila. "Then we turned into a side-street, and into a still smaller street that ran off that—a dark, gloomy street. Outside one of the houses, Alison Murdoch asked us to wait a few minutes while she went in. We did. She was away perhaps five minutes. Then she came out and fetched us in. It was a dark, gloomy house—as gloomy as the street outside. She took us into what seemed to be a back bedroom, on the ground floor, where there was a dim light from a gas-bracket, and asked us to wait a few minutes longer. Then she went out—and that was the last we saw of her."

Corkerdale, still twiddling his thumbs, took his eyes off Sheila for the first time. He cast them up to the ceiling, and stared at whatever he saw there, thoughtfully. Manners, however, let out one word, sharply.

"Trapped!"

"Of course we were trapped," asserted Sheila. "We deserved to be!—anyhow, I did. We hadn't been in that room five minutes before we knew it. We heard the door locked from outside, and what seemed to be a bar put across it, too. I immediately flew to the window and tore the blind and the curtains away. Then I saw that there were heavy shutters across the window—on the outside—and I found that the sashes of the window itself were nailed down. We were trapped, indeed! Horrible!"

"What happened?" asked Maythorne softly. "In brief."

"In brief—yes," said Sheila. "I'm not going into details of that horror for anything—now, at any rate. I beat on the door, but there was no reply—everything was quiet enough. After about an hour, a panel that I'd noticed in one of the walls—the sort of thing, a hatch, you know, that communicates between a kitchen and a dining-room, was suddenly slipped open, and a hand and arm thrust in a big basket and dropped it on the bed. Then the panel was banged to again, and I heard it secured. There was food—plenty of it, and good—in the basket, and a couple of bottles of wine—good claret—and glasses and a corkscrew. So we weren't starved. But there we were, trapped!—until this evening—two nights and two days. We never saw anybody. Each evening another basket was dropped in, so suddenly that we'd no chance to seize the hand that dropped it, or to get a glimpse of the adjoining room. We neither saw nor heard anything, all the time."

"And you got out, how?" asked Maythorne.

"This evening, when we were about done up, for lack of fresh air—though, to tell the truth, I'd long since broken the window!" replied Sheila, "we suddenly heard sounds outside the door. Then we heard the bolt withdrawn, and the key turned, and somebody outside ran away—the hall-door banged. We immediately went out—the place was all in darkness and silence. We left the house and hurried off to find a cab——"

"And I'll be bound, miss," interrupted Corkerdale, with something of a chuckle, "I'll be bound that you didn't look at the number of the house, nor the name of the street, nor yet the name of the other street that it turned into—what?"

"We didn't!" retorted Sheila. "We were too jolly glad to get away from the whole vile neighbourhood! But now——"

The door of Mrs Elphinstone's bedroom opened and the nurse looked in on us.

"Mrs Elphinstone wishes to see Mr Elphinstone and Miss Merchison," she said.

A moment later, Maythorne, I, and the two policemen were alone. Maythorne rose from his chair, put his hands in his pockets, and looked enquiringly at Corkerdale.

"Well?" he said.

Corkerdale smiled—inscrutably—and nodded at the door through which Mr Elphinstone and Sheila had just vanished.

"Don't believe that yarn!" he said, almost contemptuously. "Romance!"

I was on my legs at that—I dare say I turned on the detective in a fury.

"What the devil do you mean!" I demanded. "Are you questioning Miss Merchison's word?"

The detective looked at me as a man of fifty might look at a cheeky schoolboy: his sardonic contempt for me was obvious—and stinging.

"Steady, Holt!" said Maythorne. "Corkerdale means——"

"I mean that however true the young lady's story may be—and I ain't questioning it," said Corkerdale, "I don't believe that the old lady, in there, isn't in this! She and the woman Murdoch —put-up job between 'em! The kidnapping! a piece of bluff— to enable the other woman to get away. Of course, the other woman—Bownas came across her, and she tricked him into that alley, and did him in! Obvious! But—Mrs Elphinstone's in it, and I'm not going out of this hotel, nor Manners, either, till we've done a bit of questioning. That's that!—as they say now-a-days."

I was still boiling with rage, but I looked at Maythorne, inwardly wondering that he was so calm. He had kept on nodding his head while Corkerdale spoke, and he was evidently about to give him some meditated reply when a knock came at the outer door and a waiter looked in.

"Mr Maythorne?" he enquired, glancing round the room. Then as Maythorne moved towards him, he added, "Will you come to the telephone, sir?—name of Cottingley asking for you."

CHAPTER 29 THE BOAT TRAIN

Maythorne hurried out of the room, leaving me, still indignant and glowering, alone with the policemen. Presently Corkerdale, who had been whispering to Manners, turned to me.

"It's all very well, and I've no doubt very natural, for you to be a bit huffish, Mr Holt," he said, half protestingly, half apologetically. "You're sweet on the young lady, as anybody with half an eye can see, and——"

"Leave the young lady's name out of the question, if you please!" I exclaimed. "And mine, too!"

"Bit difficult to leave her out, isn't it?" he retorted, smiling. "After what we've just heard! I don't disbelieve her tale—not I!—though I'm more than a bit surprised that a young woman of her type—clever girl!—should let herself be trapped in that fashion. Trapped she was, no doubt!—but I don't believe her mother was trapped!"

"What!" I exclaimed. "Why, you've just heard——"

"I've just heard what we've all just heard," he interrupted. "My opinion is that it was all a put-up job between Mrs Elphinstone and this woman Murdoch, and that Miss Merchison's been taken in by both. I think that Mrs Elphinstone went willingly to that house and stood the detention there—she wanted for nothing—you heard!—so that her daughter, who was beginning to know too much and to get dangerous, should be kept safe and quiet while the Murdoch woman got right away! And I'll lay all I'm worth to a penny piece that Murdoch knocked that chap Bownas on the head in that back alley, and that by now she's—somewhere!"

"You don't think that Mrs Elphinstone knew anything about Bownas!" I said. "Good Lord, according to you——"

"According to me, sir, Murdoch murdered Mazaroff, and Mrs Elphinstone's well aware of it," he said determinedly. "There's what the lawyers call *prima facie* evidence of that, anyhow, and Manners here agrees with me! And we're not going out of this hotel until that doctor comes back, and then we're going to see if Mrs Elphinstone isn't fit to be questioned. And if she isn't—just yet—then we're going to stay on the premises till she is! So there!"

Before I could say anything the outer door opened and Maythorne stuck half his face inside the room.

"Holt!" he said.

I went to him; he drew me into the corridor and closed the door.

"Message from Cottingley," he said in a whisper. "He's been carrying on a close investigation of steamship offices this last forty-eight hours, working like a nigger. And at last he's hit on something! This afternoon a woman, closely answering to the description I gave him of Alison Murdoch, booked two passages for New Zealand at the New Zealand Shipping Company's offices in Cockspur Street, by their ship the *Rimertaka*, which leaves Southampton early tomorrow morning. The boat train is the ten o'clock tonight from Waterloo. Cottingley's down there—he's got a couple of detectives with him from the Yard: to save time he went there and told what he'd discovered. We'll get down there at once—the immediate question is—shall we tell those fellows inside? What do you think?"

"Corkerdale's just declared that he won't leave this hotel till he's questioned Mrs Elphinstone," I replied. "He's going to wait for the doctor's return."

"Then come on!" he said. "It's now about nine-twenty—we shall be at Waterloo in plenty of time. Gad!—I shouldn't wonder if Cottingley's struck the trail at last!—I told you what a sharp chap he is."

We ran down to the entrance hall; outside there were two or three taxi-cabs standing about: Maythorne made for the first.

"We'd better pull up a little short of Waterloo," he remarked as we got in. "Stop in York Road—by the hotel there," he added to the driver. "You see, Holt," he went on as we moved off southward, "if this woman is Murdoch, she'll know you, from having seen you at the Woodcock: she may know me, though I don't remember her. So we must move warily: if she's attempting a total clear-out, the least thing will put her off. But—she booked two passages, this woman of whom Cottingley's heard! Now, for whom can the other be?"

"Can she have had an accomplice?—if this woman really is Murdoch?" I suggested.

"She's had accomplices here in London, in that Harrow Road affair, without doubt," he answered. "May be the brother she spoke of to Mrs Elphinstone and Miss Merchison. But as to an accomplice in the Mazaroff business—now! If she had——"

He paused there and remained silent so long that at last I asked him what he was thinking about.

"I was thinking this," he answered slowly. "This!—that if this woman Murdoch really murdered Mazaroff and had an accomplice, and if Murdoch is the woman who booked two passages for New Zealand this afternoon, and if—it's all if, you see!—if the second passage is for the accomplice, why, then, we're probably going to have a very astounding surprise and revelation! But as I say, it's all ifs."

We got out of the cab at the corner of York Road and walked quickly towards the big station. Before we were half-way up the incline we met Cottingley. He was lounging along with his hands in his trousers pockets and a cigarette hanging loosely from the corner of his queer mouth, and he looked as phlegmatic and unconcerned as ever.

"Thought you'd come this way," he said as we paused. "You're in good time—twenty-five minutes yet. I should say she—they, I mean—'ll not turn up till the last thing. And all's ready. The only thing is, if this woman is the woman we think—Murdoch—who can recognise her, positively?"

"Mr Holt can," answered Maythorne.

Cottingley regarded me with speculative eyes—I fear I was not of any great account in his opinion.

"Knows her?" he asked.

"I know her!" I answered.

Without another word he turned on his heel towards the front of the station.

"What'll be done is this," he said, walking between us. "The Southampton train leaves number four platform ten o'clock precisely. I've got two thoroughly dependable men from the Yard—had to go there and tell 'em everything, of course, if I meant to do any good—and they and I'll be on the platform. She'll not know us. Now then, is there any fear of her knowing either of you?"

"The strong presumption," replied Maythorne, "is that she'll know us both."

"Very well," said Cottingley. "Then, this is what we do. I've already, with the detectives, given the tip to the railway authorities—that there may be an important arrest, d'ye see? Now, I'm going to post you two just within the barrier, where you can't be seen. You'll keep there till the passengers begin coming through for the train. I shall be close by—the detectives'll be a yard or two further on, in touch with me: there'll also be two or three railway police about, in case there's any bother. Now if Mr Holt there recognises this Murdoch woman, he'll signal to me by lifting his hat the instant she passes him—and you can leave the rest. The only other thing is that if we make the arrest, I've arranged with the station people that the detectives are to hurry her off to a little office on the platform—you follow."

"All clear!" said Maythorne. "We've got you, Cottingley."

Cottingley threw away his cigarette.

"Come on, then," he commanded with a glance at the great clock. "They'll be opening the barriers in a minute. After me."

We passed into the big brilliantly lighted station. Even at that late hour of the evening it was crowded. Cottingley moved swiftly ahead of us through the groups, passed us through a barrier with a whispered word to the man in charge, and suddenly twisting to his left, ushered us behind a high wooden partition, a few yards away from the gate whereat tickets were punched. There was a dark cavernous recess there; he signed to us to step in.

"Remember!" he said. "If it's the woman we want—up with your hat! But—be sure!"

He swung on his heel, moved off into the light of the big lamps above the platform, and pulling out his cigarette-case began to smoke, loafing idly about. A few yards away two solidly-built men, who, from their outward appearance might have been highly respectable citizens going home late to their suburban residences after a day's business in the City, stood; loafing, too. But as they chatted together, I saw that their eyes were not long away from Cottingley, nor from the barrier, nor from the gloomy recess in which Maythorne and I waited.

That waiting was about as big a trial of my nerves as I had gone through—since I heard the last shots fired in Flanders. Folk came streaming in upon the platform; porters went by with piles of luggage; there were all the scenes and sounds, hurryings and bustlings, incidental to the departure of a big express bound for a great shipping centre. But what we waited for—I with straining eyes and throbbing nerves—was long in coming. Across the broad expanse of station, above some far-distant platform, hung a clock—I could not avoid an occasional glance at it. Never, surely, had the hands of a clock moved more slowly! Twenty minutes to ten. Fifteen minutes to ten. Ten minutes to ten. Five—four—three . . .

"Holt!" whispered Maythorne. "Sharp, now! Is this she?"

A woman was just coming through the barrier—a tall, slim woman, of erect, easy carriage. By her side was another woman, slighter in height, of fuller figure, and heavily veiled. I could not see her face, but the face of the taller woman was that which I had seen two or three times in the big kitchen at the Woodcock. A second later she and her companion, each carrying a substantial-sized valise, had passed the ticket-puncher and come full into the light. I had no doubt then, and my hand went up to the brim of my hat as if a machine had moved it.

"Come on!" said Maythorne. "Now for it! But—who's the other?"

The two women were being hurried into a third-class compartment by an already impatient guard as the two detectives, some railway policemen, Cottingley, and Maythorne and I closed round them. One of the detectives laid a hand on the taller woman's arm . . .

It was the first time in my life that I had ever seen an arrest, and I was amazed at the quickness, the dexterity, the absence of fuss, in it. We had the two women into the little office close by, and the door locked, and the blinds drawn, before I had realised what was happening—as the key turned in the door I heard the whistle of the guard and the shriek of the engine as the ten o'clock sped out to time. And then I turned . . . to answer a question.

"That's Alison Murdoch—yes!" I said. "Yes—without doubt."

The senior detective turned on the other woman. She was leaning against a table; her breath was coming in short, sharp gasps; her whole frame trembled

"Take off that veil!" snapped the detective. "Come on, now!"

We stood staring intently as the woman lifted a hand and divested herself of the thick veiling that had completely obscured her features. It fell aside—and it was from Maythorne, usually so cool and collected, that the first excited exclamation broke.

"Good God! *Mrs Musgrave!*"

Mrs Musgrave burst into tears and turned on Alison Murdoch, who stood close by, grim and defiant.

"You said it would be all right!" she wailed reproachfully. "You swore to me that we were safe, this way! You said and said again that there wasn't the least chance of 'em catching us——"

"Hold your tongue, you fool!" snapped Alison Murdoch.

I stood by, sick, wondering, while Cottingley, under the detectives' supervision, unlocked the women's valises and turned out their contents. There was money there in a surprising quantity—banknotes that had been Mazaroff's, of course—and there were diamonds, and Mazaroff's personal properties. And in Alison Murdoch's valise there was a gold hunter watch, within which was an inscription to the effect that it was a present to James Bownas from his colleagues...

"There's always something that these people forget," remarked Maythorne, when, a quarter of an hour later, he and I were driving back to Short's Hotel. "Or, rather, always some absolutely idiotic mistake they make. If Alison Murdoch hadn't thrown that will into the Elphinstones' library, it would have been hard to get at the real truth about Mazaroff, and if she hadn't been so covetous and grasping that she couldn't refrain from carrying off that poor chap Bownas' presentation watch, we should probably never have convicted her of murdering him. However—there they both are! But ... Mrs Musgrave!"

"Which of them shot Mazaroff?" I asked.

"Ah!" he replied knowingly. "That's a stiff 'un, Holt! But—Mrs Musgrave knows, and—Mrs Musgrave will tell! She'll not face it out like the other."

We hurried upstairs as soon as we reached Short's Hotel—to find Corkerdale and Manners talking to the doctor and Sheila in an alcove that opened off the corridor. Corkerdale was evidently still indiscreet; the doctor looked somewhat annoyed and Sheila was obviously angry.

"—you must see, doctor, that it's a question of duty," Corkerdale was saying as we came upon them. "I want some explanation from Mrs Elphinstone——"

"There's no need now, Corkerdale," interrupted Maythorne, laying his hand on the detective's shoulder. "It's all over! We've got 'em!—they're safe under lock and key."

Sheila uttered a sharp cry of surprise, and Corkerdale turned quickly on Maythorne.

"Got 'em?" he exclaimed. "Who's got 'em?"

"Well, if you want to know, my clerk, Cottingley—smartest man in Europe at your game!—he got 'em. With the help of some of your own people, to be sure. But the kudos is Cottingley's," replied Maythorne. "Top-hole capture!"

"And who's he captured?" demanded Corkerdale, almost incredulously. "Who?"

Maythorne glanced at Sheila.

"Well," he replied, "there's no secret about it now. Two women! Alison Murdoch and Mrs Musgrave. And there's no doubt about it, either—they had property belonging to Mazaroff and property belonging to Bownas on them—actually on them!"

Corkerdale turned to Manners, who at the mention of Mrs Musgrave's name, had opened his mouth and his eyes to their widest extent.

"Oh, well!" said Corkerdale. "In that case, of course, I think we needn't wait to see Mrs Elphinstone!"

It was some days before I myself saw Mrs Elphinstone. At last I was admitted to see her. We exchanged a few conventional remarks about her state of health. Then she sat for some time in silence, steadily staring at me—staring so steadily that I began to feel desperately uncomfortable. Suddenly she spoke.

"I suppose," she said, "I suppose that you and Sheila will become engaged—eventually?"

I thought, then, that I had better speak.

"The fact is, ma'am," I replied, "the fact—er——is—that Sheila and I are engaged already!"

Printed in Great Britain
by Amazon